A Girl in the Head

J. G. FARRELL was born in Liverpool in 1935 but spent a good deal of his life abroad, including periods in France and Ireland, where he spent much of his childhood, and some time in the Far East to research the background of earlier novels. His novels include *The Lung*, *Troubles*, which won the Faber Memorial Prize in 1970, *The Siege of Krishnapur*, which won the Booker Prize in 1973, and *The Singapore Grip*. He went to live in County Cork in April 1979 where only four months later he was drowned in a fishing accident. *The Hill Station*, an unfinished novel, is published posthumously.

D0620569

J. G. FARRELL

A Girl in the Head

FONTANA PAPERBACKS

First published by Jonathan Cape Ltd 1967
First issued in Fontana Paperbacks 1981
Second impression June 1982

© 1967 by J. G. Farrell

Made and printed in Great Britain by
William Collins Sons & Co. Ltd, Glasgow

For my brothers
Robert and Richard

'Women are caught as
you take tortoises,
she must be turn'd on her back'
JOHN WEBSTER (1580–1625)

At the beginning of August a band in scarlet uniforms began to play in the municipal gardens. To Boris, watching them through binoculars from the top of a tree, they appeared like bloodstained weevils that were shortly to bring about the collapse of summer.

Inez should have come to the sea in June but there had been no sign of her. He had thought that perhaps she would come with the holiday crowds that first began to flood into the town at Whit. But then July came and there was still no sign of her . . . although a second letter arrived from her parents (who were busy getting divorced in Stockholm) asking if their daughter could possibly spend the summer in Maidenhair Bay. And this second letter was exactly identical to the first . . . which made it all most peculiar. Boris could not help wondering if the child (whom he had never met) might not have been lost in transit. But then it was none of his business.

At about the time when Inez was originally expected to arrive Boris suffered a mild heart attack while carrying a parcel of potatoes up a long flight of stone steps. He dropped the parcel and sat down abruptly. He saw the potatoes bouncing and rolling away down the steps, their skins gleaming in the sunlight. Then he became unconscious for a moment or two. Subsequently he was discovered, a stretcher was summoned and he was conveyed to a nearby hospital. Meanwhile someone had collected up the potatoes and arranged them on the stretcher around his recumbent body, rather as if he had been a side of beef on its way to the oven. At the hospital he was encouraged to get off the stretcher (he had been reluctant to move a muscle in case he should die instantly) and sit down. After examination the doctor told him that it was nothing to worry about but that he should take things easy, avoid alcohol and overwork, get plenty of rest, and so on. Pondering this from his perch in the gently stirring treetop, Boris formed the impression that the doctor had taken a rather sanguine view of his heart attack.

For a few days afterwards he had stalked about the house doing things 'for the last time' and taking a melancholy view of his affairs that was not, he discovered, altogether disagreeable. But this soon wore off. It left behind it, however, a certain notion of the transience of life. And the fact that his heart attack had coincided with the non-arrival of Inez slowly assumed a strange significance. This girl whom he had never met, the transience of life, the passing of summer without her, the sudden collapse of his own health – all these things gradually melted into each other and fused in his mind as if they had some direct though concealed link. And now the band in scarlet uniforms.

'Boris.'

'Yes?'

'What are you doing up there?'

'What does it look like?'

'Well, be careful you don't fall.'

Flower was standing at the kitchen door and looking up at him anxiously.

'I hope you can get down all right,' she added before disappearing into the house.

Boris ignored her, staring back at the past weeks through the grey oblivion of his unfocused binoculars. July passed slowly. With the passing days he noticed that the sea was warmer when he went for his daily swim. He no longer had to tense himself against the shock as he first waded through the shallow surf. While drying himself afterwards he no longer shivered so violently. More and more people appeared on the beach as the month progressed.

8

'Wouldn't you like to come down for some tea, Boris?' asked Flower, appearing again at the kitchen door.

Now he sometimes blundered into cricket matches as he left the sea and crossed the hard, wet sand to where he had left his clothes. Walking towards the broken cement steps that led up to the promenade he now found himself having to step over oiled bodies and thread his way between sandcastles. The summer was in full swing and the girl still had not arrived.

Throughout July he travelled back and forth between Maidenhair and Boscobel, plodding over the beach and sand-dunes, following a serpentine path up and down the crests where the sand was firmest. One day, while careering down a particularly steep slope, he only just avoided (by springing like a deer at the last moment) treading on a boy and a girl who were busy coupling in a sheltered hollow. Mere children, he had thought wearily. He was exhausted. His shoulders hung forward as he trudged on through the hot days. His mind travelled blankly over the shingle like a vacuum cleaner, collecting random and meaningless objects – seaweed, dry and tattered, a piece of glass polished smooth by the sea, an empty cigarette packet crushed into the shape of a flying seagull, a clear patch of sand with hoofmarks.

'It doesn't look terribly safe to me,' said Maurice, who had now appeared, no doubt summoned by Flower, and was staring up at him with his mouth open. 'What I can't understand is how he got up there in the first place.'

And the girl still had not arrived. In the meantime his shoes were slowly filling with sand. On another day, while passing The Groaning Board, he overheard Jean Arthur giving orders (mixed with snatches of one-way conversation) to the Spanish girl. The dining-room windows were open. As he came level with the restaurant there was a bang from the back door and she came out on to the veranda with a pair of secateurs. Before turning away he caught a glimpse of her short grey hair, of the cigarette dangling from her brilliant lips. He pretended to be absorbed in a smudge of black smoke on the horizon. She must have seen him but she didn't say anything. And then he had passed the restaurant and moved out of her line of vision on to the rocks, his feet clattering now down the staircase of days that led into August.

'That branch may not look very strong,' declared old Dongeon who had now joined Flower and Maurice, 'but you'd be surprised. There's strength in branches like that.'

And yesterday, yet another disturbing experience. Instead of going round by the garden gate on his way back from the beach he bent double and with his eyes tightly shut as a precaution against sharp twigs and brambles crawled through a hole in the hedge. On the other side, still crouching, he opened his eyes. He was face to face with a magnificent, dazzling sunflower. It stood there as if guarding the hole in the hedge, its beautiful golden face and bulging brown eye lifted to stare arrogantly at Boris. A bumble-bee droned past it, hesitated, moved on. As he knelt there he was suddenly appalled by its fragility. Death, he thought. Death before winter. It was very quiet in the garden. He was exhausted. His shoulders drooped so much that he wobbled violently and almost lost his balance. A gasp went up from the group standing at the kitchen door.

'Careful there, old chap,' shouted Maurice. 'Better hold on to another branch.'

Boris scowled but said nothing.

'D'you think the altitude might be bad for his heart?' wondered Flower anxiously.

'I think the main problem is how we're going to get him down,' said Maurice in a sombre tone.

'I'm perfectly capable of getting down by myself,' said Boris peevishly. Picking up the binoculars which he had let fall against his chest he focused them determinedly on the beach where he had glimpsed a flash of white and scarlet. That must be Alessandro.

'All right then,' said Maurice. 'Let's leave him to it.' He turned and went into the house.

'Come down soon though, dear,' said Flower. 'It's getting late.' With that she also vanished. Trailing blue smoke from his pipe old Dongeon wandered off down the garden to inspect his flowers.

Left alone, Boris wondered for the first time how in fact he *was* going to get down. Convenient branches stopped a long way from the ground. Too far to jump. He would be sure to break a leg or fracture his spine. Getting into the tree had been easy. He had merely swung himself nonchalantly from the window-sill of his room on to a branch that grew out towards the side of the house. But to get back the same way was out of the question.

Uneasily he swept the dunes with his binoculars. He could see the houses now. He could see, at least, their wooden roofs and stone chimneys breaking the surface of the dunes as if they were floating objects on the vast, solidified storm-waves of sand. They were beach-houses, used during the summer only, with no other connection to the hinterland than a sandy track disappearing inland between two fields and around a farmhouse. The horses. Where Alessandro kept his infernal horses. Nearer stood the restaurant, a couple of other houses and (so close that it appeared merely as a mist of pink brick) the Victorian mansion called Boscobel in which he himself lived. These more solid houses were directly connected to the coast road, which at this point made an erratic swerve seawards, by a paved lane lined with stunted trees permanently deformed into flinching away from the sea wind.

Time passed. There was no sign of Alessandro although he continually swept the countryside with his binoculars. Instead he saw himself poised on the window-sill, humming absentmindedly as he prepared to launch himself into space. One graceful swoop and here he was.

The minutes ticked by. Old Dongeon returned from his stroll round the garden, stared up into the tree, shielding his eyes with a blue-veined hand, and then shuffled into the house. Half an hour later Maurice put his head round the kitchen door, glanced up to see if he was still there and withdrew again promptly. Boris pretended not to notice him. By this time the sun was beginning to go down.

He was cramped from sitting so long in the same position.

11

Hugging the tree-trunk for safety he stood up shakily. From this position he had a better view of the countryside. Just as he was focusing on the beach once more a splendid white horse appeared at full gallop from behind the obliquely slanting shoulder of a sand-dune. It was Alessandro. The boy was crouched so low that his dark hair was almost buried in the horse's flowing white mane, while his scarlet riding-cloak (a present from Boris who had originally bought it for himself but had never had the nerve to wear it) floated beautifully in the air like the rapids of a bloodstained river. A hundred yards along the beach he slackened the horse's speed to a canter and turned it in a wide circle through the shallow surf and back up the beach with its hooves spitting sand. Then he disappeared into the dunes again.

A strange boy, thought Boris, scratching himself cautiously. He had been sent to stay with them in Maidenhair to learn English before going to a private school (although he already spoke English perfectly). Boris liked him. He was so shy and sensitive. They were friends. They understood each other.

'We speak the same language,' Boris said aloud. He sat down gingerly, wondering whether he might be able to catch Alessandro on his way home and persuade him to find a ladder without letting the others know. But the dusk slowly gathered. In the distance the street lights in Maidenhair were switched on.

'If you don't come down soon, Boris, you'll be late. Shall I get Maurice to help you?'

Silence. After a few moments he heard the kitchen door close again. It seemed to him that he was floating in the night sky far above the earth. And he was now stuck there for ever. He would never again be able to descend. He lifted his head to drink the light of the stars that glittered above him.

An hour later Maurice appeared round the side of the house dragging a ladder. Flower followed him holding a flashlight. Muttering curses he succeeded in propping the ladder against the tree-trunk.

'The damn thing's too short,' he said. 'What the hell are we going to do?'

Boris looked down at them with remote eyes, not listening to what they were saying. After a while they went back into the house leaving the ladder against the tree.

I have no idea why I got off the train. In retrospect it appears to have been a mammoth mistake. There was, however, no way I could have known that at the time.

I remember that I was standing in the corridor. A girl with a sweaty, olive countenance had been throwing inviting glances in my direction, but as soon as I left my seat she disappeared.

Telephone poles vanished rhythmically before my eyes. A grove of silver birches glinting like fish. Then a boy balancing on a bicycle at a level crossing. Some pines. A cluster of houses and a church steeple. More pines and a broken wall One thing after another fled past the window in the deep silence of a dream.

The train began to slow down. I sighed and rested my elbows on a dirty steel rod in front of the window. Now the houses above my sleeve were thickening and between them I occasionally glimpsed the sea in a bright glint of steel. Now we were cutting into the heart of the town. Amputated ends of cobbled streets. Plane trees. The sea again. Slate roofs bulging and gleaming in the sun. We crept past a signal box. MAIDENHAIR BAY. With a prolonged creaking and a slight shudder the train stopped. The silence came down like a heavy mist. I was bored stiff and I had run out of cigarettes. In fact, perhaps that was why I got off the train.

It was merely a reconnaissance at first. I clambered cautiously down to the platform to stretch my legs. Nothing happened. I ventured a few yards along the platform keeping an anxious eye on the train in case it should decide to bolt with my suitcase. The air was fresh with the smell of the sea. I inhaled deeply.

My eye rested for a moment on a diminutive shrub dying slowly in the sunlight at the end of the platform; on some twittering parcels of day-old chicks piled on an abandoned wagon; on a brace of bicycles with their skeletons wrapped in brown paper; on a teenage girl looking at me lasciviously and scratching her upper thigh through the pocket of her shorts; on the dirty cement platform at my feet, littered with bent crown corks and, yes . . . a couple of flattened fags. But the paper was torn and they were unsmokable.

The girl with the sweaty olive countenance still had not reappeared in the corridor but in any case I had to be getting back. I inhaled deeply once more. MAIDENHAIR BAY, I read on a poster featuring the habitual sunburned girl with snowy teeth, 'Seaside Attractions. Golf and Hydro'. A man with a fat, unshaven face gingerly put his head out of the window and revolved it to see what was going on. Between his lips was fixed the stub of a cigarette, charred and extinct. He probably didn't even know it was there. He muttered something. His head disappeared.

The train gave a nervous jolt. I regained the carriage door with an unnecessary turn of speed. The train remained where it was. I inhaled deeply. There was still no sign of the olive girl with garlic on her breath (I imagine).

Why not? I thought. Why not? You can do as you like You're as free as the wind. You have to answer to nobody You're your own man, Boris.

It took me ten minutes to decide that I wanted to get off the train. When I finally clattered down to the platform with my suitcase a man in a dark-blue uniform was standing with his back to the train. He turned to stare at me curiously. Regaining my composure I stared back. He lifted a hand to his peaked cap in a gesture I at first mistook for a salute. Instead of saluting, however, he removed his cap and smoothed his thinning hair. He was clearly perplexed by the fact that I had waited ten minutes before descending from the train.

As I prepared to move off towards the exit he averted his gaze from my face and, studying his fingernails, called in a loud, official voice: 'Maidenhair Central! Maidenhair Central!' He then glanced at me covertly to see what effect his words had had on me. I paid no attention. On my way out I passed the teenage girl. She seemed no less interested in my behaviour than her father. For all that, she did not stop scratching her upper thigh through the pocket of her shorts. As a matter of fact, I was later to learn . . .

By the station clock the time was one fifty. The train still had not moved. I showed my ticket to the station-master, who had somehow or other doubled round the back and now reappeared breathing hard at the exit. He looked at me suspiciously. I told him that I had decided to break my journey. With increased suspicion he looked at my ticket while I waited with one eyebrow ironically raised. He pursed his lips and furrowed his brow in a vain physical effort to marshal some abstract thoughts, tapping the ticket against his thumbnail. Then his concentration burst slowly like a bubble of treacle and subsided into apathy. I had arrived.

On leaving the station I embarked on a diagonally-pointed zebra crossing and exchanged a few words with an old gentleman sitting in the sun on a grass island. He had no collar and . . .

Sorry. I then moved on through the sunlit afternoon silence accompanied only by my shadow and by a stray dog that had appeared from somewhere. Remember that I had come from another world . . . a world of summit discussions and top-level talks. I was naturally ill-prepared for finding myself suddenly landed in Maidenhair Bay, the cemetery of all initiative and endeavour. There wasn't a living creature (apart from the stray dog) to be seen in the streets. The ring of my crocodile shoes lingered strangely on the hot, still air as I advanced slowly in the direction indicated by a 'town centre' sign, passed through a small square with a feeble fountain and a few shops, along another cobbled street with a few more primitive shops and . . . yes, came upon another 'town centre' sign pointing back in the direction from which I had just come. Poor Boris. Needless to say, I was hardly accustomed to finding myself in such an insignificant little tropolis.

So there it is. That's how I arrived here all those years ago. A pure and unfortunate chance. Yes, there he is, Count Boris

Slattery. There he is . . . that lonely, rather distinguished figure making his way slowly, nobody there to greet him, through the silent, sunlit Albert Gardens, followed (I regret to say) at a respectful distance by a stray dog with blue eyes. There he goes. He's turning the corner now into Jubilee Road. Yes, all those years ago. He's crossing the street (no need to look right and left here, Boris, unless you're afraid you'll be run over by a bicycle!), he's crossing the street into the shade. There he goes. In the shade now. *That's* better! There he is.

Sorry.

I have reason to believe that my arrival in Maidenhair didn't go quite as unnoticed as I had at first supposed . . . at least, let us say, among those Maidenhairians who belonged to the fair sex. From a window here, from a doorway there, interested eyes followed me. It is, of course, not the first time in my life that I have been desired from doorways and wanted from windows. Far from it.

At midnight a fire-engine arrived with a blue light revolving on its cabin roof. There was a great deal of shouting as it was manoeuvred into position on the strip of concrete between the old barn and the kitchen door. Floodlights were directed at the tree in which Boris sat, blinding him so that he could no longer see clearly what was going on below. After a few minutes a ladder reared slowly up towards him out of the dazzling brightness. He clambered down it stiffly and without a word to anyone stalked into the house and up the stairs to his room. As he was closing the window from which he had earlier taken his graceful, disastrous swoop into the tree he was just in time to see old Dongeon press half-a-crown into the palm of an astonished fireman. To another helmeted figure Flower was explaining that her husband had climbed up into the tree to rescue a cat and then had got stuck himself. With a sigh Boris closed the window and went to bed.

'It's always harder on the children,' Flower was saying.

The dining-room was panelled with imitation oak and at the far end a french window gave access to the garden. It was a sombre and depressing room only redeemed, it seemed to Boris, by two magnificent paintings facing each other on the lateral walls. One of these, 'The Rewards of Luxury', represented Salome being offered John the Baptist's head on a platter by Herod. Salome, dressed in some diaphanous material, was showing a good deal of thigh and bosom to the interested Herod, while from his plate John the Baptist looked on with a faint air of disapproval tinged with resignation. On the opposite wall was a smaller painting entitled 'A Maiden's Honour', which depicted an evil, wrinkled gentleman emptying a purse of gold coins on to a table (laden with colourful fruit and underdone beef) in front of a concupiscent old lady with heavily rouged cheeks. Meanwhile her daughter, a wan but determined girl dressed in white, had snatched up the carving-knife and was about to plunge it into her already somewhat dishevelled bodice (Boris assumed that the wrinkled man had insisted on a preliminary look at the merchandise).

'It's always harder on the children,' Flower repeated with a sigh.

What is? Boris asked himself automatically. Divorce, of course. Whose divorce? As he went to the sideboard for his private jar of marmalade he listened expectantly but the conversation seemed to have petered out.

'What is?' he allowed himself to ask.

'How time does fly,' murmured Granny Dongeon, seated at the far end of the table and eating cornflakes in a world of her own. 'Worms'll have eaten him up by now.'

'Please, Granny,' Maurice said sharply. 'Not at breakfast. Not while we're eating.'

Boris wondered uneasily if Flower was ignoring his question on account of last night's episode with the fire-engine. However, she continued placidly:

'They say she's half Portuguese. So that would explain it.'

'Explain *what*?'

'All these years under the grass,' added Granny Dongeon gloomily, possibly referring to her dead husband, Antoine. 'How time does fly, my word.'

'Her name not being Swedish. Inez.'

'Why? Is she coming or something?' Boris, consumed with impatience, couldn't help asking.

'Well, they *said* she was.'

Overcome with nervous frustration Boris snatched up a piece of dry toast, tore it into three jagged pieces and buttered it.

'Snow in winter,' Granny Dongeon said. 'Apples in the autumn, year in, year out.'

'Have they sent another letter?'

'I don't know,' Flower said mildly, stirring her tea. 'If they have it hasn't arrived here yet. For the child's sake why couldn't they have waited until she was older?'

'Hot pants, I expect,' murmured Maurice sotto voce to Boris.

'They spend all their time getting divorced and committing suicide, those Scandinavians,' said old Dongeon, pushing aside his plate and fumbling for his tobacco pouch. 'They say it's the cold winters.'

It's perfectly obvious, thought Boris as he opened the marmalade jar, that if she were coming she'd have been here by now. There's no point in discussing it There's nothing to be said. Yet outside the window he noticed that the leaves of the apple trees were still green and gleaming with health. 'The orchard walls are high and hard to climb,' Inez said to Boris, 'and the place death, considering who thou art, if any of my kinsmen find thee here.'

'Do stop it, Boris,' Flower said.

'Stop what?'

'You groaned.'

'Groaned.'

'Groaned? I was just clearing my throat.'

'He groaned,' Maurice said with authority. 'But then he's always groaning. Could someone pass me the sugar?'

Beyond the apple trees and the thick hedge of hawthorn and bramble Boris could see glorious white clouds mounting into the blue sky. Below them the glittering sea.

'Anyway,' he said more calmly, 'if she's Portuguese I think you'll find she pronounces her name *i'neige* . . . like the French for "it is snowing".'

Nobody paid any attention. Granny Dongeon muttered something about corn ripening in the fields while old Dongeon launched into an explanation of why Irish girls made the best maids. Boris, staring at 'A Maiden's Honour' while he munched his toast, noticed for the first time an alarming resemblance between his own features and those of the wrinkled gentleman emptying gold coins on to the table. The girl, however, seemed rather anaemic for his taste, and the amount of gold coins was out of all proportion to the satisfaction she would be likely to afford. But then, he thought indulgently, people do get obsessed about things.

'Going riding today?' he asked, catching Alessandro's eye

Alessandro nodded shyly and dropped his dark eyes to his plate on which lay an untouched heap of scrambled egg.

'Eat up, Sandro, there's a good boy,' Flower told him patiently.

'Don't make him eat if he doesn't want to,' said Boris sharply. 'He's old enough to look after himself.'

'You'll never get into the first fifteen if you don't eat up your meals,' old Dongeon said with a twinkle, puffing out a dense cloud of smoke.

'First fifteen?' asked Alessandro with a touch of alarm. 'What's that?'

Boris shook his head sadly to indicate to the boy that it was nothing he should worry about.

'Never mind. We'll put a bit of muscle on you before we send you back to Italy,' Maurice said cheerfully. 'After a term or two you'll be so tough that all those signorinas won't be able to keep their hands off you.'

Alessandro looked painfully embarrassed. He said nothing.

'Autumn one day, spring the next,' declared Granny Dongeon.

'It's time for your newspaper, Granny,' announced Flower in a penetrating tone as if the old lady were deaf. 'Time for Maurice to read to you.'

'You can train them up, you see, Boris. You can train them up,' old Dongeon said. 'D'ye get my meaning?'

'You're coming through loud and clear,' Boris murmured sardonically and received two glares, one from his wife and one from Maurice, who was busy sifting the newspaper for items of interest. Boris looked to Alessando for support but he wasn't listening. His dark eyes were resting once more on his plate, glowing in passionate abstraction beneath their long lashes. The black cardigan he wore over his snowy cotton shirt enhanced the startling pallor of his face. How extraordinarily good-looking the boy was!

'You can train them up like dogs, you see. And why? Because they're willing, that's why.'

'Listen to this, Granny. "Sky diver dies . . . Parachute fails to open".'

'What d'you say, child?' asked Granny Dongeon with a touch of lucidity.

'"Parachute fails to open",' Maurice repeated more loudly. 'He dropped from ten thousand feet or something, Granny. D'you understand? With nothing to stop him.'

'Oh Lord,' said Boris. 'Must we thrash all this out?'

'I don't know,' Granny Dongeon said. 'Don't ask *me.*'

'She doesn't know what a parachute is,' Flower said in an urgent undertone. 'Try something else.'

'Granny,' insisted Maurice. 'Do you know what a parachute is?'

Granny Dongeon's face puckered as if she were about to burst into tears. 'It's not my fault. Don't ask me.'

Old Dongeon who was sitting beside Boris touched his arm and confided: 'They're all called Mary, these girls. Beats me how they tell them apart back there in the stone cottages they live in. Of course, they don't have our habits but they can be trained. Train them up, man. That's what they need. They're crying out for it.'

'Of course it's not your fault, Granny. Don't you worry about the parachute. Here's something that will interest you. "Driver of radio taxi disappears" . . . what d'you think of that? Now let's see . . . "same firm over forty years" and so on and so on . . . Now here's the interesting bit: . . . "called HQ to report passenger with axe. Then the radio went dead and later the taxi was found abandoned on waste ground. Police do not suspect foul play." There you are. What d'you think of that?'

'Think of that?' repeated Granny Dongeon.

'Foul play,' Maurice explained patiently. 'Police do not suspect it.'

'I suggest we give it a rest,' Boris said acidly. 'She hasn't any idea what you're talking about.'

Flower said nothing, but cast an anxious glance in the direction of Boris as if afraid that he was on the point of starting another argument, as if she could already see the lethal words flashing over the teacups like tracer bullets. But Boris was thinking: take away all the objects that surround Maurice and he would cease to exist. Take away his beard, and his striped pseudo-sailor jersey, and his Volkswagen, and his jeans, and his tape-recorder, and his rope-soled shoes, and his dark glasses and he would vanish completely. There's nothing inside them. And yet he's always surrounded by girls . . . the plump, experienced kind who like sex and always remember to send people birthday cards. How does he do it? What do they see in him?

'"Forty-year-old Italian forbidden to see ward of court. Unhealthy influence. A manufacturer of artificial limbs, described by neighbours as a quiet and respectable . . ."'

'Funny people, those Italians,' old Dongeon said so close to his right ear that Boris jumped.

'Artificial limbs, Granny . . . he makes them. He's an unhealthy influence.'

'I ran into a few of them in the war, you know,' old Dongeon went on. 'Funny chaps . . . That was the First War, of course, and they were on our side in those days. Can't think why. In the Mess we always used to call them "the enemy". Used to pinch anything left lying around . . .'

Boris left the table suddenly.

The kitchen terrified him. Everything in it was painted pale blue or acid yellow with the exception of the floor which was tiled in black and white squares (and gave you a headache if you looked at it for too long). All this was the work of Maurice. When approached for his advice before re-decoration Boris had given the matter a great deal of thought. His final recommendation had been that the entire kitchen should be painted black except for a blood-red table, sink, and cooker, with one fierce spotlight over each of these essential areas. Since this advice had not been taken he had decided to remain aloof in future from all matters of family interest. Boris took a deep breath and penetrated this blue-and-yellow iceberg in order to make himself a cup of coffee.

On the kitchen table (pale-blue Formica) he found a biology textbook, abandoned there by Alessandro who was preparing himself without enthusiasm for his new school at the end of September. There was also an exercise book with an elaborate inscription 'Biology' inked on the cover. The word was repeated on the first page of the book together with three lines of an unfinished sentence about osmosis and the drawing of a dagger dripping spots of blood down the page. Boris rather liked the dagger.

As the electric kettle began to growl Boris opened the textbook at random. 'Living creatures', he read, 'ultimately consist entirely of chemicals. Basically, the story of life is a story of chemicals.'

The growling of the kettle quietened and a great feather boa of steam rose into the dazzling kitchen.

'The universe is made up of 92 different basic kinds of materials.'

Though it was still early the sun had already travelled far enough to shine obliquely into the kitchen. Boris read on grimly as the morning glare mounted inexorably around him.

'Death is a built-in characteristic of all living things!'

Let us at least go through the motions. After all, that is what life is all about . . . if it is about anything, which it probably isn't. I won't bother you with further speculation on this subject. Perhaps I should mention that I habitually respond to life's ups and downs with no greater sign of concern than a raised eyebrow and bitten fingernails. I don't pretend to have remained uaffected by all the shattering events of my life. They have clearly left their marks on me, like footprints in wet concrete. But in the last few years the concrete has dried and hardened. So now at last, though covered in footprints, I am able to meditate impassively on my life.

The motions. Let me pick up this photograph album. It is one of the heavy, indestructible kind. Each corner is sheathed in a sort of triangular metal cache-sexe and it has a rusty iron lock on which I have just cut my finger. Never mind. It was with this indestructible album that our ancestors hoped to preserve their immortality. And so they have, for the moment. But I am the last survivor of a distinguished line.

They say she is merely a schoolgirl and in my opinion she almost certainly has dirty fingernails and a bad attack of spots. Yes.

This is my grandmother. She is quite young, quite beautiful. There is a high wind blowing from one misty edge of the picture to the other. With one hand she is holding a cloth helmet to her beautiful head while she anchors her long skirt with the other. She is smiling in the direction of some young men in boaters. These young men are obviously (I deduce from their tense smiles and the downslant of their eyes) wondering whether my grandmother is good for a roll in the hay. She *was*, as it happens, according to the testimony of a decayed great-uncle who made some remarkable confessions to me on his death-bed under the mistaken impression that I was a priest.

The picture isn't very clear, of course. Her skin may not have been as tight and soft in reality as it appears in the photograph. Still, take away the fashionably shapeless dress (as the young men in boaters are already doing in their immobilized imaginations) and one could reasonably expect to find beneath it an india-rubber-breasted, desirable body. I might even have fancied her myself and, God knows, I've always had my pick of beautiful women. I've had my share, as they say.

The point is that there could be no possible connection between the attractive girl in the picture and that stooped, baggy-skinned creature with a sweet tooth who used to decorate my childhood with despair. The looseness of her skin. Did some essence of Grandmother shrink inside it to leave all that unoccupied space? But let us move on. Heaven knows, there are grandmothers enough in this story without her.

Take a look at this cruising uncle playing deck-tennis against a background of palm-fringed coastline. He looks like one of those sozzled commercial travellers who soldier on valiantly week after week doing their best to sell things to imbecile grocers. Will that slight discoloration of the photograph that I take to be the imprint of the flying quoit ... will its trajectory continue up and over the sagging curve of net to furnish my drunken uncle with a surprise victory fifty years too late? His poor bloodshot eyes are uplifted to the discoloration, following its flight with indifference, with equanimity, with weariness, desperation, anguish, utter despair and . . . but indifference will do. How very, very dead my uncle and his friends are.

Here too is a male baby, a blurred little fellow on a rug in an English garden. A water-spaniel is sniffing him cautiously. How strange to think of him later, to think of him as a grown man riveted to some perspiring, naked female (this one, say, a distant cousin on the opposite page, already on her back and already naked except for her nappy). Well, I expect he's rotting underground by now, poor devil, 'his journey over', as my wife would say.

On the whole there's no denying that the dogs come out of these old photographs better than the humans, I suppose because they are less ambitious about themselves. And then, one dog looks very much like another. Though if it comes to that . . .

Get down, sir!

Sorry about that. Where was I? Have you ever ridden a bicycle that has a tendency to slip out of gear from time to time? That's how I feel sometimes. My mind is pedalling peacefully down the same street of thoughts and then . . . whizz! It has jumped out of gear and there's no resistance to my spinning feet. But one thing is clear. We've had enough of these photographs. Enough!

Yet just as I lift the album to snap it shut with an air of finality a loose photograph comes cartwheeling out from between two pages and slithers on to the floor. I stoop and pick it up.

Here we are. Written across the back in fog-coloured ink are the words: 'Baby Boris. Hyères, Summer 1920. Taken by his loving mother.' Yes. But I have a bitter disappointment to communicate. The picture is merely an aerial view of my fat little limbs and diminutive buttocks. Seen from behind (or, indeed, in front) all babies look identical. There is, however, just one interesting thing about this photograph: the position of the limbs. Boris is sprawled face down on the carpet as if arrested in the act of crawling. I need hardly add that this is the classic posture of castaways thrown exhausted on to the sandy beaches of desert islands. And let's not forget that the Boris in the picture is a baby who has only just been dropped into the world. I hope I have made my point.

The trouble about looking at these old photographs is that history leaks into the present through insignificant details. Here we see a pair of trousers at half-mast, there some bearded bloke in the background is consulting a turnip watch or a tram is drawn along by nodding horses. It's the details that are so distressing. When I look at myself now in the light of these old pictures I get a most disagreeable sensation of being nothing but a detail myself. It's like looking at your face painted on one of those vast historical canvases. I look at myself. In close-up my face is commanding, terrible, awe-inspiring. Here I am . . . a great politician unrolling a map, or a general on a horse, or a renowned lover of the bluest blood surrounded by his mistresses. Look at those stern cedillas that cling to the corners of my mouth, at the piercing stare of my steel-grey eyes, at the granite jaw on whose determined lines everything depends. But then, as I step back from the canvas, other parts of the picture creep into view with equal importance. Who the hell is that oafish character grinning vacantly as he scratches his armpit? He should be holding my prancing horse. And why is that dog allowed to chew a bone so near to me? It dilutes my importance. And who gave orders for that soldier to rape a milkmaid in a haystack when I'm so obviously about to give the signal for attack? It's all rather disturbing if you want to know the truth. Of course, I realize that it's nonsense to think of one's life as a meaningless detail rapidly receding into a mass of other meaningless details. But I confess that the thought has occurred to me from time to time. On the other hand, I haven't been feeling too well recently. I had a bad attack not long ago and that may have something to do with it.

Well, there it is. Things haven't been easy for me. I'm not complaining. Nevertheless, things haven't been easy. I'm covered in footprints. And now I'm afraid it rather looks as if I'm coming to the end of the . . .

They were walking through the municipal gardens where a band in scarlet uniforms played away industriously, clashing and thundering, shooting brass arrows of sound away into the misty blue sky. The band had been engaged for thirty-one days. It was the same every year. These splashes of scarlet represented the climax of summer. It would soon be over. Inez had been sent to some other beach to stay with some other family. In France, perhaps, or in Italy. There were so many other beaches.

His companion, Dr Cohen, was laughing for some reason. Boris looked around but failed to find anything amusing. However, he laughed too and squared his shoulders to resist the weariness he felt, the result of a lunchtime spent drinking with the doctor instead of eating.

The doctor laughed again, more bitterly, and stopped to survey a group of elderly ladies seated in deck-chairs listening to the music. Beside them sat men in shirtsleeves and sandals. Here and there a small captive child twisted and turned between somebody's feet or tried to balance on the edge of a seat.

'Who'll come a-waltzing Matilda with me?' sang out a grey-haired lady near by, although it had seemed to Boris that the band was playing 'Home on the Range'. The lady's arms and a triangle of her breastbone had been stained to a painful shade of pink. 'Where the deer and the antelope,' he hummed, trying to get in the mood.

'Too many people,' muttered the doctor fiercely. 'Let's go, for God's sake.'

Crossing Marine Road a youth with a grimy, sunburned face tried to sell Boris a paper hat inscribed with the words I LOVE MYSELF. A whiff of vinegar and frying fish from the open door of a nearby café at this moment became involved in his mind with the sunburned youth and the idea of loving himself. At his side the small, plump figure of Dr Cohen had for some time been lurching along rather unsteadily at his side, leaning heavily on a walking-stick. He now stopped and sat down suddenly on the kerb outside the Winter Gardens Theatre, telling Boris that he needed a rest.

'September Attractions!'

Boris looked down at the old man dubiously, wondering whether he should sit down too. Instead, he wandered over to inspect a brightly coloured poster plastered on the wall of the theatre.

'By special arrangement for one week only!'

'Too many people!' cried the doctor from a few paces away, addressing nobody in particular.

'Lady Jane, England's only debutante lion-tamer. Savage Fangs!' That's more my speed, thought Boris, reading on with interest. 'King of the Jungle. Lovely young model will face naked jaws . . .' A vivid picture showed Lady Jane clad in white trousers and shirt tapping her black boots with an enormous whip. Beside her a lion sat on a stool and gazed with interest at her bulging breasts. The trouble was that the girl and the lion would be together for a mere five or ten minutes. For the rest of the evening he would be obliged to watch dogs jumping through hoops and men riding bicycles backwards.

'Lash! The horse that can almost talk!'

Strangers on the promenade. Everyone was grinning for some reason. They were on holiday, of course.

'The Flying Urbino Sisters. They flirt with death!'

Boris surprised himself by abruptly hammering his clenched fist against his forehead. September attractions. The summer was ebbing rapidly. The girl. The summer. A young girl

28

wearing thin denim trousers neatly corrugated by her under-wear sauntered past him, idly swinging a net containing two white and hairy tennis balls. She looked at me, her eyes bright with devotion. I patted her head and groped her avuncu-larly.

'The Mysterious X. He can read your mind!'

Boris wandered back to the doctor, dubious about the advantages of having his mind read. Still, he regretted the thought of missing the girl and the lion.

The doctor struggled to his feet and they walked on, passing a man who stood beside an ice-cream van staring out to sea with eyes that were a very pale and watery blue, as if faded by continual exposure to the glare from the sea.

'He's a strange man,' Boris said. 'He's always standing there . . . even in winter. I can't help thinking that for years he must have been scanning the horizon for a white sail to appear, his lover returning . . . *Yseult des Blanches Mains* and all that sort of thing.'

'Nonsense,' said the doctor sharply. 'The man is simply standing there in a bovine reverie waiting for someone to buy his ice-creams.'

Glancing at the doctor Boris noticed an expression of irritation pass over the old man's wrinkled features. It was an interesting face. Traces of a vanished nobility still remained in the deep lines about his eyes, but it was as if the face had been made of wax and subsequently melted by the hot sun of Africa where the doctor had spent most of his life, the features sagging slightly as they melted. Actually, the truth of the matter was more simple. The doctor, as everyone in Maidenhair knew, drank. Boris could see that the old man was tired. He stopped and suggested that they should rest in deck-chairs.

The doctor shook his head. 'Too many people. Let's go to the Turkish Baths.'

'I think it would be bad for my heart,' protested Boris weakly. He had spent most of the morning encouraging the doctor in his professional capacity to tell him the worst about his heart attack. But the doctor had remained firmly optimistic and had insisted, moreover, on treating Boris's health as of no importance whatsoever.

'Rubbish!' the doctor was saying now. 'Do you a world of good. Besides, you can't live in cotton-wool.'

With deep misgivings Boris agreed to accompany him.

Opposite the post-office an illuminated sign for the Turkish Baths competed feebly with the heavy battery of sunlight that flooded the street. Bad for the heart, he thought as he paid and followed Dr Cohen into the vast, marbled foyer. An attendant handed him a towel and snatched back the heavy red-velvet curtain of a cubicle for him to enter. He undressed and then went downstairs to the vapour room with the thin towel around his waist. Opening the door he plunged into dense clouds of hot steam.

A moment later the plump grey silhouette of the doctor appeared at his elbow. He sat down on the bench beside Boris. The moist heat seemed to have revived his spirits.

'Can't stand crowds, you know. The bastards are everywhere. And when I think that I spent most of my life trying to stop them dying . . . well, it makes me sick. They should make Russian roulette a school sport.'

'I'm sweating,' Boris said uneasily. 'I don't think this is good for me.'

'Does it surprise you that I gave up my practice?' demanded Cohen. 'People will tell you that the practice gave *me* up, but don't you believe it. I'd had enough of it. I'd had it up to here.' He lifted his chin and poked his Adam's apple with a long, bony finger. 'I couldn't stand another minute of it and that's the truth. In Africa, you know, between the wars . . . that endless line of ailing black men. Millions of them. Just like machines. Day in day out. And I was a sort of mechanic who was trying to repair them.' He chuckled as if the memory amused him, and suddenly reaching out into the thick grey steam astonished Boris by producing from it a half-bottle of Johnnie Walker, as if it had somehow been hanging suspended there in the surrounding fog. He took a gulp of whisky, wiped the neck of the bottle with his palm and handed it to Boris.

'You know, Boris, I used to think it was because their skins were black that I couldn't see them as people any more . . but not a bit of it. When I came back here I was merely mending white machines instead of black ones. Alcohol on my breath? They were damn right I had alcohol on my breath!'

'It's too hot in here,' Boris said uncomfortably. 'I'll have to go in one of the other rooms.' He wondered what the doctor would do if he had another heart attack in the middle of the conversation. It seemed likely that he would just shake his head wearily and go on drinking.

'Machines,' the doctor pursued, still chuckling. 'Alcohol on the breath.' You'd die laughing. Let me tell you something. There's only one decent pastime on the whole planet . . . and that is chess'

'Oh, chess,' Boris said indifferently. He had been expecting something more dashing.

'You remind me of a friend I once had. An alcoholic. He was ruining himself. I did everything I could to stop him drinking but it was no good because he had just one single idea about life and nothing else interested him. One single idea in his head . . .'

The doctor wasn't listening. 'Chess,' he repeated firmly, taking another gulp from the bottle.

'But there are other things surely? Women and so on.'

'Women? You can't be serious. The act of sex? Nothing but the automatic coupling of two machines, take my word for it.'

'There's more to it than that. I mean, the heart has its reasons and so on . . .'

'The heart's a muscle,' retorted the doctor sharply. 'That's all I know about the heart.'

Boris could think of nothing to say in reply. Instead he sat listening to the painful thudding of his own heart. The thick grey steam seemed to close in around him.

Later in the afternoon Boris found himself once more adrift in the crowded streets. He walked slowly, staring into shop-windows intently as if in search of some revelation. But what could possibly be revealed in Maidenhair Bay? Tinned groceries. Shirts and ties. A man operating a dry-cleaning machine. A row of brilliant yellow jam tarts beside a mound of bulging sugary doughnuts. Motorcycle accessories. He trudged on under a heavy snowfall of banality. At the very end of the street a butcher was standing in his shop surrounded by the mangled, bloody remains of some once-living animals. Boris remembered a barracks in Madrid where an accidentally exploded grenade had brought about just such a selection of steaks and ribs, livers and lights, brains and sweetbreads. And at this very moment, while he was standing in the nauseating unreality of Maidenhair Bay, people all over the world were dying grotesque deaths in unromantic wars. Only in Maidenhair Bay could one ignore reality in such a way. And it was surely a crime.

On the promenade once more. Boris was abruptly ambushed by a patrol of violent anger that leaped out of nowhere, out of the importunate evidence of summer that strolled and laughed around him through the littered streets. Further on a young man with a camera stopped him and told him that he had taken his photograph.

'That's very kind of you,' murmured Boris politely, at a loss to know why the man should want to photograph him. He felt that something was expected of him. There was a silence. The man was looking at him as if he too were at a loss. He began to twist a knob on his camera while Boris passed a hand in front of his face in the confused manner of someone who has just walked into a bead curtain and finds himself ensnared. Invisible lines of beads were dripping from his head and shoulders.

Lovely model will face naked jaws!

The man launched into an explosion. His chin and part of his neck were studded with angry purple spots. He wanted money. After a few moments he produced a photograph and handed it to Boris. If Boris didn't want to be photographed he should watch where he was walking. These things came out expensive. Boris looked at the picture which was of someone else.

'This isn't *me*!' he cried suddenly in a very loud voice. There was a distant rattle of applause from the municipal gardens. Somewhere a woman shrieked. Her shriek slowly modulated into a hysterical laugh.

The man looked apprehensively at Boris and then at the picture. 'Yes it is. Look at the clothes.'

Boris looked dubiously at his shirt and trousers. The man was right. Stunned, he paid him and walked on.

A hundred yards away he paused and took another look at the photograph. It showed a gaunt man with receding hair who was wearing one of his own shirts. Two deep, descending wrinkles were cut into the cheeks, compressing them into a wild grimace that might have denoted either pain or a kind of insane amusement. Moreover, the man's shoulders were stooped and his neck twisted. All that, of course, might have been nothing but a momentary lapse caught, as ill luck would have it, by the camera. It was the face that worried him.

The wild look. The wisps of receding hair. The mouth twisted into a demoniac grimace at some uncontrolled thought or impulse bubbling behind the wrinkled forehead. He groaned.

Mopping his brow with an orange silk handkerchief he leant heavily against the promenade railing. A few bodies wreathed in fat. A saturnine young man paddling a rubber dinghy loaded with a fleshy woman in a bikini. The sky was beginning to haze over. His shadow on the pavement had become very faint. He no longer had to screw up his eyes when he looked at the sea. Here and there sunbathers were sitting up to stare anxiously at the vanishing sun. She still might come, he thought without hope.

On his return to Boscobel he noticed a handbag on the hall table and a strange perfume on the stairs. Just for a moment he thought that it might be Inez, arrived unannounced from Stockholm because her parents were too busy getting divorced to think of sending telegrams. Then he remembered that

Maurice had invited one of his plump, sexy girls to look at his paintings.

With weary steps Boris climbed the stairs past 'The Letter' (depicting a husky girl in a crinoline holding an unfolded letter to her bosom while tears sparkled in her eyes and a soldier with bowed head proffered in the background a crimson tunic and silver sword), past a 'Head of Christ' (signed 'Dongeon '61'), past 'A Son's Devotion' (a young man giving his last few groats to his tattered mother, general emotion), reached the head of the stairs with his heart unpleasantly thumping and, after a pause, shambled down the corridor past 'Study in Motion' (Maurice's only incursion into the twentieth century and an attempt to imitate in chicken-wire a beautiful sculpture in steel by Robertson-Swann) to his room. As he opened the door he was welcomed with furious excitement by Bonzo, who left his basket and advanced cringing and wagging not only his tail but his entire hindquarters. Boris aimed a kick at the animal because it had a weak bladder (which it tended to relax when shown affection).

He undressed slowly. Even more slowly he put on the white shirt, white tie and tails that Flower (although he had on numerous occasions forbidden her to enter his room) had laid out neatly over the back of the sofa. Bonzo retired to his basket and followed Boris's movements with eyes full of reproach and devotion, uttering an occasional groan.

Impeccably dressed Boris moved to the window. At an angle on the floor above he could see the window of Maurice's studio, formerly the billiard-room. As ne glanced at it he saw a horizontally sliced girl. Then the white plastic venetian blinds abruptly opened, pulled apart like the lips of a huge mouth. Inside the mouth was the girl's head. Naked model will face lovely jaws!

After a moment a powerful, hairy forearm with the rolled-up sleeve of a pseudo-sailor jersey gathered around the elbow made its appearance around the girl's neck. The slats of the blind blinked down suddenly, leaving a ribbed shield of impenetrable white plastic. Boris and Bonzo groaned in unison.

Boris sank down on to a chair. In his pocket the gaunt man was still printed in black and white, grinning or grimacing at the thoughts bolting hither and thither like wild horses across the desert of his mind.

What am I doing here? It's quite obvious that I'm not the sort of primitive individual who is suited to living in a place like Maidenhair, 'the cemetery of all initiative' as a local genius once described it. The truth is simply that my past life had become too heavy to carry any further. The weight of one's memories becomes altogether paralysing. You try to live on as if nothing had ever happened. But it's useless. It's like trying to swim the Hellespont in an overcoat.

I'd forgotten her completely until I saw the chairs. That's to say, I was passing through Madrid . . . it must have been about a week before I first arrived in this place. I was merely changing trains, you see. Going from somewhere to somewhere else. I just forget. And then the chairs.

Get down! You're moulting, you filthy beast!

Yes, they were brightly coloured and empty but grouped in a friendly way under enormous yellow-ochre parasols. More or less the colour of sunflowers, as it happens. I thought: But those seem familiar. I must have been here before, some other time. And then, quite suddenly, I remembered Ylva's navy-blue pullover and her white skirt. I remembered them as if she had just been sitting there for a moment before. I remembered her presence so vividly that it was as if she had just gone round the corner to buy a newspaper, say, or a packet of cigarettes. I half expected to see her handbag lying there on one of the circular metal tables beside a glass of lemonade in which tiny columns of bubbles were still rising around a mangled straw (she had a bad habit of masticating straws with her sweet lips and sharp little teeth). Frankly, it all came as quite a shock to me.

And she was saying: We'll write, of course, Boris. Nothing can stop us from meeting again. After all, we're free. We'll write to each other. Nothing can stop us. We can do what we like. I'll write to you on the train this evening. Yes. I'll post it when we change trains at the frontier. There's always a place to post letters at the frontier.

Half an hour sitting under those yellow-ochre parasols in the café outside Atocha. It was almost too much for me. Mind you, I'm well aware that life isn't all roses and it's true that I was somewhat inexperienced then. But all the same.

Better just go away and leave the station. There's no point in waiting.

How can I *not* wait when I know you're still in Madrid?

Only ten minutes . . . We'd better be thinking . . .

So there you are.

I'll never forget that afternoon. It unreeled itself so slowly, so hopelessly. Mind you, I was very young in those days. In those days I was just a young lad, of course. But after she had gone the city became like an open wound in which every familiar street was throbbing unbearably. I sat here and there in different parts of the city, waiting as the afternoon dragged by. I remember, for example, sitting in some municipal gardens where a scarlet-uniformed band was playing. And there were fifteen men in the band. Fourteen of them appeared to be almost identical, with plump, bluish cheeks and rimless spectacles that flashed in the sun. They played mechanically, their heavy, expressionless faces beaded with sweat. But there was another man standing slightly to one side with a pair of cymbals which he clashed from time to time. He was so thin that his scarlet uniform hung in great empty folds from his shoulders, and every time he came to clash his cymbals his gaunt, exhausted face decomposed into a look of utter desperation. And then, after a while, his hands hung loosely at his sides as if he no longer had the strength to bring those two gleaming brass plates together. But nobody paid any attention to him. The music pounded on. He merely stood there looking out blankly over the heads of the cool nannies, and children, and sweating tourists.

And all the time I sat there with one eye on the afternoon and the other on the spool of time as it whirred and creaked through its ponderous revolutions, liberating one inter-minable second after another. Yes. But then we're all put through the grinder sooner or later. That's the way things are.

The surprising thing is that I'd forgotten all about Ylva until I saw those chairs and realized that I'd seen them before somewhere. Until that moment I was merely changing trains in Madrid as if I'd never been there before (though I remembered the place, of course, and trivial things I'd done there once upon a time). And it hurt me, this memory of Ylva, even though I hadn't given her a thought in almost twenty years. Well, not so much 'hurt' as made me feel atrociously tired all of a sudden. She later married a bacon-exporter.

I was walking into Atocha when I saw the chairs. Abruptly my suitcase was filled with concrete. I felt a hundred years old. You know, I couldn't even collect myself sufficiently to do something about a young Spanish girl not far away who seemed to fancy a piece of Boris. She kept glancing at me hotly and hopefully from behind a large ice-cream cone she was licking with an experienced pink tongue. I shook my head sadly. The girl pouted and gave her ice-cream a disappointed lick. It was a pity but there it was. They wear you out, these memories. You feel so discouraged. That may even be the reason why I was washed up at Maidenhair Bay a few days later. I felt so discouraged.

Ylva was rather a nice girl, I think. She had the regulation golden hair and spoke a number of languages (the way these people always do). Back home in Copenhagen I believe she was some sort of secretary of a superior kind. What else was there about her? She was scrupulously clean in her habits (something that can't be said of a lot of young girls, particularly these days). And she always appeared gratifyingly interested in what Boris had to say. I was a rather impassioned speaker in those days and hadn't yet acquired my present habit of greeting life's vagaries with an ironic smile and perfect indifference. She also had an attractively shaped bottom, rose-pink in colour and thus making a surprising and agreeable contrast to the golden-brown of her legs. As I recall, she had been sunbathing somewhere in Portugal immediately prior to our love-affair. To tell the truth, that's about all I can remember about her. Apart from the fact that we were deeply in love, of course.

But I still find the memory, poorly documented though it may be, discouraging. And if the girl herself has disappeared, well, the pain remains, the loving remains, as hard and real as a stone in my kidneys.

It was Sunday. Boris sat with his bristly chin cupped in his hands for a long time before he summoned up enough energy to shave it. As he finally plugged in his electric razor it occurred to him that if Ylva were still alive she must be a middle-aged dumpling of a lady by this time, eating cream cakes under a flowered hat in Copenhagen. The real Ylva had disappeared in a puff of steam with the train taking her out of Atocha. If I'd known that at the time, of course, I'd have committed suicide without further ado. It would have been the least I could have done in the circumstances.

And what difference, he wondered as he watched the reflection of the razor travelling busily here and there over his blue-black cheeks, would that have made? Boris cut off in his prime. Boris spreadeagled on the double bed of that small pension room with polished wooden floors, an empty vial of poison clutched in his nerveless fingers. Outside in the Plaza Santa Barbara the horseless carriages chug past in the sunlight, heedless of the waxen pallor of young Boris's cheeks.

It was Sunday. How he detested holidays! From his window he could see a line of cars crawling along the coast road. He hated to think of the people crowding into Maidenhair intent on enjoying themselves. He hated to see it in their faces, this fugitive belief that life was, against the evidence, to be enjoyed. You blind imbeciles! he wanted to shout at them from his window. What use is one day of escape in your rotten little lives?

Escape to nothing! Can't you see it's only a joke? One day at the sea isn't going to make any difference.

The cars inched their way relentlessly into the town. A line of cars moving as slowly as lava towards the beach. Yes, they seemed to say, yes, even one day in a year, makes all the difference. In a lifetime, if you like. Go there just once and everything is changed.

It rained later in the day. Black clouds raced by like puffs of gunsmoke and the rain volleyed against the flaking wooden door of the old barn (now used as a garage for Maurice's Volkswagen). The bedraggled sycamore towering over the tangled mass of brambles and hawthorn in the garden had taken on a deeply neurotic appearance, tensing and shivering and baring its teeth at each fresh gust of rain. It depressed him just to look at that tree. At any moment, he thought, the damn thing will start having hysterics and screaming that it can't stand this any longer, this rain and time and being rooted in Maidenhair.

Sunday. From the beginning of the afternoon he was nagged by a dull headache. He had smoked too many cigarettes, perhaps. He had stared too often at his reflection in the mirror over the washbasin. Moreover, thanks to these frequent inspections of himself in the mirror, he had convinced himself beyond any possible doubt that his hair was receding, had receded a matter of inches since . . . well, since hardly any time at all, since Christmas. Two deep inroads, he was perfectly sure, had been made towards the crown of his head. Now there merely remained a slender promontory of hair that ran out into the raging sea of wrinkles on his forehead. What earthly use was that? Such a derisory strip of hair could not possibly interest a young girl accustomed, no doubt, to admiring excessively hairy pop-singers. He grasped one or two of the fringe hairs and pulled them experimentally to see if they were secure. They came away without argument.

In the course of the afternoon he decided to stop sleeping with Flower. This idea came while he was pacing up and down his room, a tiny seed blown into his mind on a random gust of thoughts. It lodged there and grew rapidly. He spent the rest of the afternoon trying to summon Flower to his room to inform her of his decision. But she kept on saying she was too busy. Oh, so you're too busy, are you? he said to himself grimly (she appeared to be peeling something in the kitchen). Well, if that's the way you want it, all right. That's fine by me. But don't say I didn't try to talk it over with you. Don't say I didn't try to warn you.

I have a confession to make (*Boris admitted to the tape-recorder*). It concerns the photograph of myself as a baby that I mentioned earlier. I'm afraid I invented that bit about 'taken by his loving mother' although I'm perfectly sure in my own mind that she did take it. You see, some time in the autumn of (shall we say) 1922, while we were staying in some awful rustic inn near Regensburg (tr. 'raintown'), my mother's beautiful, sad face appeared out of the oaken darkness and thrust itself into the hollow orange pumpkin of light provided by the candle at my bedside. A single ruby glowed at her throat and two diamonds sparkled in her lovely eyes. Then the diamonds fell flashing from her eyes and vanished into the counterpane while two more formed in their place. And as she leant forward to kiss me one sparkling candle-diamond after another splashed on to my tiny face. With the result that when little Boris awoke the following morning his diminutive features were rimed with white tidemarks from the evaporation of his mother's tears. In fact, he looked like a small piece of salt cod.

Well, there it is. My mother went off with her Moroccan carpet salesman or whatever he was and left me to do the best I could by myself. I don't blame her. I can't deny that almost any carpet salesman would have been more entertaining than my father. Curiously enough, I never discovered whether the man himself was Moroccan or merely his carpets.

But don't think I'm bitter. The only reason I mention this business at all is that some explanation is required to account for the absence of pictures of my mother from an otherwise well-stocked family album. The album was, in fact, censored of all traces of my mother's existence in what was, I'm sure, the only passionate gesture of my father's life (with the possible exception of that act which generated Boris himself . . . if this was not, as I'm inclined to suspect, the work of the Moroccan carpet salesman or of some other interested bystander).

And so it was that I witnessed, clad in my sailor-suit with my eyes barely above the level of the table, this dry-cleaning of the spots left by my mother on the fabric of my father's life. With round eyes I watched him (he was a portly man in tweeds with a drooping moustache who used to move silently round the house emptying miniature slag-heaps of charred tobacco from his pipe into various ashtrays) as he removed all the photographs of their life together.

I watched him (somehow it seemed as if his tweeds had become shaggier since my mother's departure) as he poured all his life through a sieve. There I stood with my little mouth open in astonishment as everything vanished through the sieve: uncles and aunts, camels and pyramids, ancient Rolls-Royce and gaitered chauffeurs, ladies with tennis racquets, gentlemen with tropical helmets, school groups, cricket teams, men holding up fish . . . yes, they all slipped through the sieve. Yes, even the shipboard transvestites, even the water-spaniels with permissive pheasants in their jaws. But not my diamond-eyed mother. She remained in the sieve. She was torn up and, to make doubly sure, incinerated.

Boris has been through the mill, I'm telling you. He certainly has. That's life, of course, correct me if I'm wrong. That's the way it goes . . .

(Oh my
mother!
I saw her
face once in
the doorway of
a beer-cellar in
Munich as I was being

42

dragged past with aching
arm-socket by a French governess
and she didn't see me and I was
too surprised to call out to her
and there was a man's arm on her
shoulder and her face was half
turned towards his in that
square of gloom that I was
trying to penetrate with my
astonished eyes . . . The man
must have been looking in
my direction and he must
have seen the child
dragged by in the
stream of passing
people but he
didn't know
me of course
and merely
went on
chatting
calmly to
my mother or
listening calmly
to what she was
saying about the
excellence of the
Weisswurst and mustard
or the beauty of his carpets
and all that without knowing
that a small lump of agony in
short trousers was being hauled
along outside and though I
should have looked at the
man's face to see whether
my mother was with someone
who looked kind and what

sort of person could he
have been anyway?
Though I should
have I didn't . . .
and I looked
at the hand
on my
mother's
shoulder and
by that time it
was too late too late
to look at the face but
it seemed to me that the
hand was very brown for an
ordinary white man or possibly
even that it was the hand of a
definitely black man but the
wretched thing, the hand, had
already changed colour fifteen
times in the first fifty metres
of surprised pavement and when
the acid-faced, heartless French
girl had realized that there
was something the matter with
the weeping object on the other
end of the hand she was holding
and had underground what information I was managing to cram in between hiccups to my surprise, why,
she suddenly burst into tears herself
and bought me an ice-cream and said
it was better not to go back to
the cellar and better merely to
try to forget her . . . *et ton père
aussi* she muttered under her breath
. . . and when all those years later I
ran away from a lycée in Strasbourg

and somehow or other stealing carrots
from fields and apples from trees
along the side of the road and
begging lifts and freezing
in ditches managed to get
back to Munich one night
in November and find
the same beer-cellar,
why, she wasn't
there any
more.)

The sofa turned out to be harder than Boris had expected. He tried to avoid the idea that he was acting like one of those pathetic elderly gentlemen who suddenly take to sleeping in a tent in the garden wearing full battledress in an attempt to relive their youth.

'Darling, please tell me what's the matter.'

'Nothing's the matter.'

'Well, come back to bed and stop being silly.'

'I'm sleeping here in future. I've been trying to tell you that all day but you couldn't find the time to listen.'

'All right then. Do as you please.'

'I intend to.'

'Well, you just do as you please,' Flower repeated, at a loss for an argument. She lingered at the door.

'Good night then.'

'Good night.'

And there he was. Alone at last, without a great mass of rhythmically heaving flesh beside him. He had left the window open. A perfume of pine trees and of the sea crept into the room. A soft glow of starlight made the polished wood of the floor glisten in the darkness. As he twisted and turned in search of a comfortable position it was somehow as if he were easing his way out of the scaly dead membrane of years that clung to him.

'Living creatures ultimately consist entirely of chemicals.'

The weather remained warm but in the mornings and evenings Boris could scent a melancholy dampness in the air. He had been right all the time. Before anyone else he had detected the deadly gold creeping into the green of the leaves; the sharpness of his eyes had been able to distinguish the skeletons of butterflies in the fluttering streaks of colour.

'The Earth will soon be going to sleep, Antoine,' Granny Dongeon had said the other day to her dead husband while munching a water biscuit. 'Soon be going to sleep. Not long now.' (As it happened, Boris didn't fancy very strongly the chances of the old lady herself of surviving the winter.)

There were still some people on the beach, however, laughing and playing as if it were the first day of June. At the sight of them Boris's heart lifted for a moment. Nevertheless, he could not help comparing their number with the dense crowds of July and August. Of the dozen hotels on the sea-front there now remained only a couple that still displayed 'No Vacancy' signs. In the others, vacant rooms. Silent and still, counterpanes unruffled, towels starched as stiff as cardboard on the towel-rails, ashtrays collecting nothing but fine dust, no sand in the sheets or on the carpets, no sunburned limbs reflected in the long mirrors, nothing now but the long ranks of empty days that lined up like soldiers, slowly diminishing in size as the nights lengthened towards Christmas. He pondered this thought as he ploughed through a drift of hammered copper leaves, rolled like brandy snaps, swept up into a pile by some invisible roadman and then abandoned.

The leaves were dead because death is a built-in characteristic of all living things, and they had been swept up by a roadman who ultimately consisted entirely of chemicals.

Boris moved on, trying to see into the windows of the houses he was passing, hoping as usual for some revelation. But he could see nothing of interest. Some anonymous people drinking tea. A child twisting the arm of another child. A row of savage purple flowers. 'Will the person who has been interfering with my flowers kindly refrain from doing so', written in an offensively large and extrovert hand. Nibbled by a sensation of

46

vicarious guilt Boris left the notice to expend its urbane menace on the empty pavement air. A basement kitchen in which a woman with short grey hair (who bore a disturbing resemblance to Jean Arthur) was washing dishes while cigarette smoke curled around her ears.

'No hawkers,' said a hostile gatepost.

In front of Maidenhair Central in Victoria Road there was a grass island roughly the shape and size of a canal barge, with twin zebra crossings sweeping diagonally back from its prow like mathematical bow-waves. As he stepped on to the crossing Boris glimpsed the stout, uniformed figure of Mr R. Furlough, the station-master, who always gave him (or so it seemed) an oddly hostile look as if he somehow suspected that . . . But no. That was out of the question. Nevertheless, he decided not to linger in the vicinity of the station.

La Coiffure de Madame. A lady attached to the window with dirty Sellotape was smiling bravely from beneath a hair-dryer and holding out her bloodstained fingernails to be kissed by passers-by. Beside her was fixed a poster announcing that the circus was soon to begin its long-awaited visit to Maidenhair. This one depicted neither the lion nor Lady Jane, though the lovely model and the naked jaws were mentioned (with curious equanimity) in the list of attractions. Here it was The Mysterious X, clad in evening dress and mask, who was staring piercingly across from the top right-hand corner at the horse, Lash, whose head occupied the top left. Lash, the horse who could almost talk, was looking understandably uneasy. Boris took two deep gulps from a silver flask he carried in his pocket and stood with his feet planted wide apart, gasping as if he had just emerged from an icy shower.

He had been aware for some time of music, perhaps coming from a radio playing full volume beside an open window a couple of streets away. Someone was playing a violin. The strains of 'September Song' echoed in the empty street with agonizing sweetness. But as he turned the corner the sound died abruptly. The street was empty.

He thought it was empty. A cat emerged from a dustbin and

streaked away from him, up and over a wall. Somebody slammed a door somewhere. Then he saw that there was a ragged figure sitting on the pavement with his back against a partly demolished yard wall. Boris stopped when he saw him, hesitated, and then took a few paces forward. The man was pitifully thin. There was desperation in the gaunt face that looked up at Boris. Boris nodded with an artificial smile. He was walking past. In an instant he would be out of range. He was almost . . . His hand, he realized, had dipped into his pocket, seized a coin, and dropped it into the upturned cap on the pavement.

'God bless you, sir, and keep you,' the man said in a surprisingly cultured tone, struggling to his feet. 'You want me to play something for you.'

'Play something?' said Boris thickly. The music. He could see no instrument. He began to walk on quickly. But the man was hurrying after him, tearing with exasperation at a parcel wrapped with dirty newspapers. He seized Boris by the arm and he was obliged to stop.

'Listen,' Boris said. 'Please don't trouble. I really don't . . .'

The man was still tearing away the newspaper, his gaunt face working with excitement.

'My music . . . I insist. That's all I have in the world. The only way I can repay your kindness . . . I absolutely insist . . . won't take no for an answer . . .'

A battered violin had now emerged from the parcel of dirty newspapers. The man crammed it against his bony, un-shaven cheek, and withdrew a bow from beneath his ragged overcoat.

'Now listen,' Boris said firmly.

'You appreciate music,' the man cut in, poised to begin playing. 'I can see that, see it in your face. It's obvious. Music . . . all I have in the world . . . no roof over my head . . . always on the move and nowhere to rest and bathe my wounds. NOWHERE!' he ended with a shout. A fleck of foam had appeared on his thin, bluish lips.

The man is quite insane, Boris thought, looking around

desperately for a way to escape. Ignore him. That's the best thing. He withdrew his eyes from the man's painfully agitated face, turned and began to stride away. But the man hurried after him.

'Sucker!' the man said suddenly. 'No, sorry, I didn't mean that, really I didn't. I meant . . . *beauty* . . . *art* . . .'

There were tears in his eyes. He clipped the bow under his left armpit and held out a grimy hand in front of Boris. Boris stopped.

'Robertson,' the man said. 'Pleased to make your acquaintance.'

Boris gripped the cold, bony fingers but the man snatched them away again, grasped the bow and began to play 'Come Back to Sorrento' with piercing sweetness.

'Stop it,' Boris said wildly. 'For God's sake stop it, man. Here, I'll give you some more money. Here you are.' He dropped a handful of loose change on to the cobbled street and walked away as fast as he could, his ears full of the aching sadness of the man's violin.

'Wait!' Robertson shouted without ceasing to play. 'Don't go . . . music . . .'

Boris hurried on without looking back. In the next street he could still hear the violin. Now he was playing 'September Song' again. Boris was almost running. He looked over his shoulder but the street was empty once more.

Where am I? Boris wondered. He could hear music again but this time it was not the violin. He was near the Municipal Gardens. He kept walking as fast as he could. What was he doing? Yes, he remembered, he had arranged to meet Alessandro in front of the cinema. He still had a few minutes to spare.

I knew all along that she wouldn't come. I knew perfectly well. So why did I waste so much energy? In any case, she's probably a spotty child with dirty fingernails so it doesn't matter very much.

He drank from his flask and paused to stare at a long and intensely boring list of bye-laws governing the operation of the

Municipal Gardens. Dogs are only allowed entry provided that they are kept on leashes.

Inez floated away into an aching void. The heart's a muscle. That's all I know about the heart.

A number of dogs, bounding unattached through the shrubbery, were sneering openly at the notice about dogs on leashes. He looked at his watch. Ten to six on the last day of August. A spaniel colliding with a young tree as it turned to attack a companion dislodged a shower of javelin-shaped yellow leaves.

As Boris approached the bandstand the music died out with a ponderous flourish that squeezed a few claps from the handful of spectators. The bandleader, a man with rimless glasses, turned to the audience and told them in a thin, flute-like voice how much he and his lads had enjoyed playing for the wonderful people of Maidenhair Bay and how much they looked forward to coming back again next year. And so that was that. The summer had finally collapsed.

Alessandro, dressed in a dark-grey jacket with silver buttons, was already waiting outside the cinema. For some reason he was looking both tense and gloomy.

'Hello there,' Boris greeted him breezily. 'Been waiting long? I'm afraid I had one or two things to attend to.'

'Hello, Boris. I only just got here myself. I don't think it's started yet.'

'Let's have a look at the programme times.'

Thanks to the fact that he had stopped in the doorway of a shop round the corner for a final sip of brandy from his flask Boris felt himself to be well in control of the situation. 'We still have a few minutes. Let's take a walk round the block while we're waiting.'

Boris put a paternal arm over Alessandro's shoulder and steered him away from the cinema. Alessandro put one hand in his pocket, removed it and then put it back again. The sun, which had disappeared behind a large cloud of ominously vaporous appearance, now suddenly came out and cut two shadows along the pavement with heads bent back against the walls and shop-fronts they were passing. The shadows were very long considering that it was only six o'clock and still the month of August.

'These provincial towns are all the same, Sandro,' Boris declared with cheerful vigour. 'They're all as dead as the grave.'

Alessandro, with his eyes flickering restlessly into each shop-window, nodded his agreement.

'And yet people here think they're living at the centre of the universe. Extraordinary!'

Passing a bakery Boris caught the aroma of freshly baked bread and was filled with a sudden elation. It was strange to find a boy with such sensitivity when for years he had seen nothing but the sort of depraved morons that June Furlough hung around with.

'You can say what you like against me but at least I know what life's all about. I've knocked around the world.'

Alessandro nodded quickly and said with warmth: 'Of course, Boris.'

Even the fish shop, though closed and fishless, increased Boris's elation, as with his hand still on Alessandro's shoulder they crossed the glistening wet pavement in front of it and inhaled the salty air.

'Of course, I've had certain advantages . . . being born into a noble family and so on. I don't deny it for a moment. But what initiative have these people here ever shown?'

Alessandro cleared his throat as if to reply but said nothing.

'None at all!'

Without turning his head Alessandro followed with his eyes two passing girls who were bubbling with amusement, apparently at some private joke. Receding laughter. He kept walking with his head stiffly to the front.

'What have they ever done for themselves? Not a thing!'

'I see,' Alessandro said soothingly.

'Not a thing!' repeated Boris so loudly that a woman waiting at a bus stop turned her head.

'Of course not, Boris.'

'People like Maurice and old Dongeon are nice enough in their way but they don't see things in the same light as you and I do . . .'

Alessandro was looking at his watch.

'Yes, of course. We'd better be getting back.'

Deserted traffic lights turning green for them alone. A good sign, Boris thought. Alessandro had quickened his pace, obliging him to remove his arm from the boy's shoulder. Turning to look at his reflection Boris found himself staring into a shop-window which displayed nothing but an ornate marble vase from which protruded half a dozen red-hot pokers. Behind the vase hung a dusty curtain of white muslin. How odd, he thought, half checking his stride. They can't only be selling red-hot pokers. And then he read the sign over the window. 'Maidenhair Cremation Service.' Death before winter!

Alessandro hadn't noticed his hesitation. Boris plodded on beside him. The boy was walking much too fast. 'All arrangements taken care of by our organization. Day and night service.' Boris stopped in his tracks and pulled the handkerchief from his top pocket. It exploded before his eyes like a burst of orange flame. He mopped his brow. Day and night service. That was very reassuring anyway. Someone waiting at the telephone day after day, night after night, in the perfect certainty that . . .

'Are you all right, Boris?'

'Yes, thanks. You walk a bit fast, that's all.' All things considered those red-hot pokers were rather appropriate. 'I'm afraid I talk a lot of nonsense, Sandro,' Boris said in a low voice as a television repair van rattled past over the cobbles. With the noise he was uncertain whether Alessandro had heard him.

'We'd better be getting on,' Alessandro said.

Will anything be left, even the merest trace? All the white skeletons of dead emotions, are they visible to someone? Do they somehow continue to exist once they are over and done with? Can these delicate white skeletons of emotions be picked out against the black velvet of eternity? Is anything left at all afterwards? A melancholy calm descended on Boris. All the people who were alive at the same time as Shakespeare, for example. While they were alive they too must have been slowly grilled by love and lust, fear and anguish . . . does anything now remain of all that boiling emotion?

As the universe was made up of ninety-two different basic kinds of materials it seemed unlikely that much would remain of emotions.

'No, no. I insist,' he said with authority, edging in front of Alessandro at the box-office. If this were true then it would be better to be someone like Maurice. At least Maurice had some fun. Boris sighed wearily as he followed Alessandro into the sweet and smoky darkness.

The lights went up. A girl with a tray moved up the aisle selling refreshments. Boris, wedged between Alessandro and a fat lady with an umbrella and what seemed to be a suitcase, was assailed by mild claustrophobia. He kept twisting his head and trying to shift his position. From time to time the lady cleared her throat loudly. Alessandro said nothing. At last the lights dimmed. Advertisements.

Dark enough now. Boris lowered his head and took a furtive gulp from his flask. He was strolling through a leafy forest dappled with sunlight, hand in hand with a beautiful, laughing girl whose white skirt swung like a lantern as she stepped down towards a waterfall. Turning towards him the sunlight flashed on her golden hair and smiling face. He took another gulp of brandy.

'I deprecate advertising cigarettes on the screen,' he said loudly.

Alessandro didn't reply. Boris became bored with the advertisements and let his mind wander. Time passing. How quickly it fled. Winter now. It would be winter when they left the cinema. The long winter in Boscobel. Granny Dongeon would be sure to die this time. She had only just made it through the last one. That would mean tears and long faces and everyone dressed in black. They would say he was heartless if he went out for a drink or showed any sign of enjoying himself. The winter. Cold rain and high winds. Snowbound in Boscobel with Granny Dongeon's corpse. Incarcerated with the Dongeon family. And for God's sake don't think of Christmas with all the little messages of love tied to things.

'Are you all right, Boris?' whispered Alessandro urgently.

'Fine,' he whispered back. Perhaps Alessandro was merely wondering whether he could see the screen all right. Fine, he repeated to himself. Unless, he though uneasily, unless it were true that he sometimes groaned without realizing it.

The film began. At last. It was in colour. He could do with some colour in his drab life. Oh, the time! he thought. And the people!

No credit titles. It started straight away with a shot of a man on horseback with a gaunt, sweaty face and a stubble of beard, riding slowly over a bluish plain.

And the seasons! He was living alone inside an enormous clock. Beside him the cogs and wheels clicked over and over relentlessly, round and round in the same cruel circles. The same revolutions endlessly ending, endlessly beginning again, repeating, ending, beginning. He was alone in the clock.

He was riding alone over an ocean of yellowish-blue desert. He was a tiny moving speck on the earth. He had been travelling all his life, since he had been a young child. He could go only a certain distance and no farther. There was a limit to everything. He was tired and thirsty and by the shadows he could tell that it was past midday. An old miner with a beard and a shotgun told him the way to the mearest town when he stopped at a water-hole to drink and it was so hot that he couldn't even dismount. On the horizon there was no town. Nothing but a bluish haze of impenetrable despair.

'No roof over my head,' Boris said.

Then it was twilight and he was riding very slowly into the town. There was nobody there. Time passes and ends and begins again. Time passes. And Ylva. Alessandro still had to go through all that, of course. The trouble.

The saloon. A weakling was beaten up by a man with a moustache and black tights. Then the music changed and the credit titles came up.

'I deprecate violence on the screen,' Boris may have said. A man in front turned his head sharply. The film continued. Aware that his flask was almost empty Boris took a circumspect sip of brandy. The cinema was enormous. A vast cave of darkness with row after row of silent people waiting it out, a sort of cosmic air-raid shelter.

'I exaggerate, of course,' he said with an urbane laugh, somewhat disgusted with this histrionic Boris.

Somebody clicked his tongue in the darkness. Boris merely uttered a low, derisive laugh, merely stood in the doorway giving the man in black tights a steely look that brought a sudden hush on the cinema.

'Here we go,' said Boris, gritting his teeth. A chair scraped. At a table covered with money and playing cards a man with a black beard stealthily got to his feet.

'It's a long time since we . . .'

On the contrary. It was a short time. A short time endlessly repeated. And this was the very thing that nobody appeared to understand: that everything went in circles and not in straight lines. This was the torture of the thing!

'I thought I told you not to come back.'

I should never have gone back. Boris drooped in the darkness. The yellow-ochre parasols wilted slowly like dying sunflowers in the glare outside Atocha. It was all so futile. But of course it was an accident. The sort of thing you can't do anything about.

'Not so loud, Boris,' whispered Alessandro nervously.

They were like fireworks exploding in the darkness. Each generation had a brief flash of glorious hope and after that . . . yes, the separate sparks filtered rapidly through the layers of night to become extinguished long before they hit the ground.

'Look out, man!' roared Boris. The bearded man had dropped his hand but Boris was too quick for him.

'He won't try that again.'

'It's all right,' Alessandro was saying. 'He's just a bit tired.'

A light flashed in Boris's face, blinding him. He felt Alessandro tugging at his sleeve. As he blinked back owlishly into the painful beam of light he wondered whether he should get up and punch the man who was holding it. But he felt too tired. Really, he thought, I feel abominably tired.

'Let's go, Boris,' Alessandro said desperately. 'The film's no good.'

Boris stared at the boy in surprise but he could see nothing except the fierce eye of the flashlight engraved on his mind.

'But I thought you wanted to see it.'

'I made a mistake. I thought this film was another one I heard about . . . Come on, please, Boris.'

'All right then.' Reluctantly he heaved himself out of the seat. The eye of the flashlight dropped to the sloping carpet of the aisle. Will the person who has been interfering with my flowers.

'My soul, like to a ship in a black storm, is driven, I know not whither.'

'D'you think we should ask for our money back?' Boris had somehow imagined that the foyer outside would be as black as ravens' feathers. He was astonished to be greeted by pallid daylight. Alessandro was looking at him unhappily.

'Oh, let's not bother. Let's just go.'

The commissionaire was a giant with pock-marked cheeks and small eyes which had a steely look, reminiscent of one of the characters in the film (or possibly all of them, he now had difficulty remembering).

'He's had a few. Take him away and don't bring him back.'

Perhaps I should punch him after all, thought Boris. He hesitated with one hand gripping the varnished edge of the chocolate counter. Perhaps I should thrash this little matter out.

Alessandro took his arm and steered him into the street. It was still the month of August. The last few hours. The winter had not yet begun.

'What d'you want to do?'

Though the daylight was beginning to open small chinks in the wall of his mind through which a bitter reality was already leaking, he couldn't help feeling slightly aggrieved that he had taken Alessandro to the cinema and the boy hadn't wanted to see the film to the end.

'I think I'd better go home and do some biology,' Alessandro said, avoiding his eye. 'Won't you come too?'

Standing with one foot on the kerb and the other in the gutter

Boris cupped his nose and eyes in the fingers of both hands. He could still see the grim eye of the flashlight.

'I think I'll stay in town a little.'

Alessandro watched him uncertainly. 'Will you be all right, Boris?'

Boris nodded and said with an effort: 'I'm so sorry. I really don't know quite what came over me.'

'That's all right,' Alessandro said with forced cheerfulness. 'See you later then.'

However, he made no attempt to move. He was staring across the street at something. Following the direction of his gaze Boris saw that a very large, red-faced man had just emerged from the lounge bar of The Emerald Isle about thirty yards away and was staring fixedly at him.

'Holy Virgin, I'd swear it was Mick Slattery from Limerick!' the man muttered with an expression of wonder on his flushed features. He stood there swaying uncertainly while Boris looked at him with astonishment.

'He seems to know you,' Alessandro said.

'The man's drunk,' cried Boris loudly. 'I never saw him before in my life.' He turned and began to walk away with violent steps, no particular direction. The sun was now standing on the horizon. His shadow was immensely long. After a while he entered a coffee bar and sat by the window.

'A white coffee,' he said to the waitress. Well, there you are, you see. What d'you expect? The waitress placed the coffee in front of him. He didn't touch it. That's what you get, he added senselessly, if you go on like that.

Boris sits there, motionless in the dying light. On the other side of the street stands the Church of Our Lady Queen of Heaven, a mock gothic building incongruously sandwiched between a Chinese restaurant and the office of an estate agent. On its façade one can see a mosaic of bright tiles which represents a man wearing a red cloak and white undergarment. On his head a golden crown studded with large blue stones. One hand is clasping his cloak around his neck while the other places a crown without stones on the head of a girl dressed in blue with both hands crossed at the wrist over her breasts, head slightly inclined, eyes downcast. On each side of the mosaic a disembodied head with white wings sprouting from under the chin is hovering. One of the heads is blonde and the other brunette. Both of them are hovering at a slight angle from the vertical, a feeling familiar to Boris.

Next door the restaurant features a red dragon with golden scales painted on a white panel. The dragon is arranged vertically and from its mouth a forked tongue floats back over its head. What look like incipient antlers are erupting from its forehead.

The last few hours of August, the last few minutes, are slowly ticking away.

It's true that when I first arrived here I had very little money. My wife's claim that she 'picked me out of the gutter' is an exaggeration, however. I was clean. I was suitably dressed. At great personal risk I had somehow or other managed to shave myself that morning in the swaying *toilette* of that sweaty train. Mind you, I have a strong beard and we didn't arrive in Maidenhair Bay until the afternoon. Nevertheless, my suit was impeccably cut and my shoes, though dusty and slightly worn, were of the finest crocodile skin. Moreover, the fact that my wife only uses this accusation in periods of emotional stress (or periods *tout court*) is sufficient proof, I think, that it is not to be taken literally.

Unfortunately, it was overlooked on some occasion (presumably through a keyhole) by her brother, Maurice, who then let it fester in his immature imagination for a while. The next thing I heard was Maurice describing with a smile to some friends of his how Boris had got off the train wearing a dirty corduroy jacket and concertina trousers and how as he alighted there was 'a veritable blizzard of dandruff'. With an ironic and rather pitying smile that I'm sure wasn't lost on his interlocutors I asked him mildly what evidence he had for making that statement. Naturally, he lost control of himself and began to bluster, calling me an 'adventurer' and saying that I had only married Flower for her money. *(What* money?

you are wondering. It's a good question!) I'm fairly sure that at this point the witnesses to his regettable tirade began to nudge each other and roll their eyes to heaven.

But not content with this *soi-disant* blizzard of dandruff Maurice also had some wildly improbable story according to which I'm supposed to have emerged from the railway station (Maidenhair Central) and started molesting an old gentleman sitting on a bench in the sun for a loan of ten shillings.

What in fact happened was this. I emerged from the station carrying my suitcase and on my way over the zebra crossing I came upon this collarless old codger (who, as ill luck would have it, later turned out to be the mayor's father), playfully sighted him along my malacca cane as if about to shoot him, and asked him if he wouldn't like to earn ten shillings (he looked as if he could do with a square meal) by carrying my bag.

Now let me be very clear about this. My wife, Maurice and I were not acquainted at the time of my arrival so their story rests entirely upon 'evidence' furnished by a third party. Interesting. Very interesting. And who *was* this third party? You may well ask. Maurice's evidence is the diary of the station-master's daughter, an odious teenager of secret habits whose advances I've had occasion to reject (I regret to say) more than once.

I've seen this document (the sorry coincidence by which it fell into Maurice's hands need not detain us here) and I can assure you that it makes unrewarding reading. It consists almost entirely (apart from inane observations of the genre: 'It's raining today.' 'We had frankfurters for lunch.' 'Can't be bothered to do my homework.') of lewd speculation about what is going on behind the drawn blinds of the sleeping-cars she sees from her bedroom window . . . and these lewd word-villages are isolated in forests of exclamation marks in case her readers should have missed the point.

But enough of this. I need hardly enter into this sort of controversy. I have often noted during my life that mediocre people find the mere company of genius an insupportable

61

criticism of themselves. And I have never in all these years of my life in Maidenhair Bay once lifted my voice in rebuke. Never.

I've already explained how I came to arrive in this wilderness. On that afternoon I walked the streets (still followed by the stray dog) for hours trying to find a hotel for the night. None of them, however, were to my satisfaction. Poor Boris! The night was closing in fast. He had no roof over his head. Even in the month of May (as it was when I first got here) these Northern nights are likely to be too sharp for the unnaturally bright-eyed, near-tubercular, deliriously brilliant Boris.

As the light faded I found myself back at the zebra crossing at Maidenhair Central. The collarless old ruffian had disappeared by this time so I sat down on the wooden bench he had vacated and rested my head in my hands. The stray dog sat down at my feet and looked at me with anxious eyes of a disturbing blue that gave it the appearance of a transmogrified spirit. It was an ugly animal with a square, bulging body roughly the shape and colour of a sandbag. Its tail had been crudely amputated (no doubt bitten off by another dog) to a length of about six centimetres. From a metal plate on its collar I learned that it had been named 'Bonzo', thanks, I suppose, to some grotesque collapse of the imagination as regards animal nomenclature (incidentally, my guess is that Bonzo had belonged to some short-sighted elderly lady with a defective sense of smell).

When I had rested a while I got to my feet to investigate the only road I had not yet tried. There were no hotels in sight. After five minutes' fruitless walk I lost heart and sat down in the dust at the side of the road. The dog Bonzo stood beside me and inspected me gloomily for a while, then went to lift a leg against a gatepost. While Bonzo urinated in a succession of short squirts my eye came to rest on a sign fixed to the gatepost above him. It said . . . Yes, it said 'Room to Let'.

The room in question turned out to be more of a greenhouse. It was made entirely of glass and stood in an overgrown garden, a fact which encouraged the landlady to describe it as 'self-contained'. The landlady, an eccentric old widow who looked at my cheque for the first month's rent as if she'd never seen a cheque before (she hadn't as it later transpired), told me that there had once been beautiful flowers in the greenhouse and that now there was me. I smiled at her politely as if she were talking sense. Encouraged she went on to tell me that her husband had been a railway worker and that every time a train passed she remembered him and said a prayer for the repose of his soul. Ah, so trains passed? Yes, of course. Hadn't I noticed those four long, shining pieces of steel at the bottom of the garden? They formed part of the main railway line between Maidenhair Central and Maidenhair West. You could set your watch by the trains.

I studied my fingernails while Mrs Gray heaved a rapid sigh and said that things weren't the same as they used to be when her poor husband was alive and what were things coming to when people gave you pieces of paper instead of money ('But money is only paper,' I tried to cut in), but she could see that I was respectable and that I was probably even a business or professional gentleman and that the way prices were going up every day how could a poor old widow without a person left in the world except for her daughter married to a lazy mechanic in Edinburgh who did nothing but make children who had to be fed hope to survive when she had to pay the rates and the electricity and the doctor had told her not to drink coffee because it over-stimulated her heart and she had been over twenty years in the same neighbourhood and all the neighbours said that they only wished that some of the younger folk today were as honest as Mrs Gray because she would rather die than cheat anyone the way so many people were doing these days. And anyway, she concluded with a touch of resignation, it was perfectly clear that anyone with such a sweet little dog could be relied upon because animals had souls too as was clearly demonstrated by the pigeon she kept in her kitchen.

Bonzo and I looked at each other in consternation.

However, it seemed the wrong moment to disown him so I knelt to tickle him behind his anxious ears. Hardly had I touched him than he began to yelp and groan languorously and scratch the ground with his back paws, leaking a small dark pool on to the dusty path where we were standing. Satisfied, Mrs Gray gave me the key to the greenhouse and disappeared into her own quarters.

There was a slight misunderstanding then between Bonzo and I over where he was going to sleep. When I had clubbed him off the bed with a stale Viennese loaf that I found in my suitcase and he had retired to sleep on some yellowed copies of the *Maidenhair Courier* in one corner, I threw myself fully clothed on to the bed and fell into a deep sleep of total exhaustion.

I was woken up about an hour later by a cataclysm I at first mistook for an earthquake. The express for Maidenhair West. The glass walls of my lodgings rattled alarmingly. Bonzo vanished under the bed. A half-bottle of whisky (fortunately I'd taken the precaution of emptying it before retiring) danced for a few moments on the table and then smashed on the floor.

There was another train (this time for Maidenhair Central) at two in the morning and another at six (for Maidenhair West). It was a haggard and unnerved Boris who looked at himself in the mirror the next morning and tried to shave himself with a trembling hand. It was hopeless. I gave up threatening my grey face with the razor and went to sit down shakily on the bed. Even the dog was looking pale.

During the dark days spent in that glaring greenhouse my morale was so low that it was all I could do to struggle out of bed in the morning. More often than not I couldn't even bring myself to do that . . . not because I was tired but because I could see no reason to get up. I would lie on the bed (the bed, Mrs Gray informed me, in which her husband had expired – I shuddered to think of the poor bastard banished to the greenhouse for his last days on earth – and in which her daughter had lain until her marriage . . . pure as driven snow

until her *dépucelage* by the mechanic, Mrs Gray insisted, though I had never offered any suggestion to the contrary)..
I would lie there day after day, wearing my dark glasses against the glare. Bonzo, from his corner of the room, would watch me anxiously and at intervals of about ten minutes would heave a deep sigh and scratch himself.

The problem of nourishment solved itself in a curious way. While treading on a column of red ants that were making their way down one glass wall, across the tiled floor and into a home-made wardrobe (the work of the late Mr Gray) I came upon a vast stock of baby-food. Mrs Gray had made no reference to it so I concluded that either she didn't know it was there or had decided to ignore its existence. This was not, of course, a matter of great importance to me, engaged as I was on an inner spiritual battle with the waves of darkness that threatened to engulf me. Nevertheless, I did manage to tempt my listless palate with an occasional diminutive tin of meat extract or apple purée. As for Bonzo, although reluctant at first to touch the sickening powdered-milk gruel I offered him, he shrewdly came to recognize it as his only chance of survival and took to lapping it up with a will.

Since the first (and only) time that I had tickled his ear he had become utterly devoted to me. Though I detest dogs it was virtually impossible to get rid of him. I made one or two vain attempts, it is true. I made him sit down and tried to run away from him. Without success. I even tried making him sit still in the middle of the road whenever I heard a car coming. On one occasion, huddled nervously on the crown of the road and under strict orders not to move, he even vanished beneath the thundering wheels of a passing lorry. I emerged from the bushes to which I'd withdrawn, wondering whether in the heat of the moment I mightn't be able to surprise a few shillings out of the driver for running over my dog. Bonzo, however, was still huddled in the middle of the road, terrified but unscathed. I recall that one of my old Sladerewski aunts (the Polish side of the family refused to change their name for some reason) who lived with a million cats in a gloomy flat in

Warsaw had over her mantelpiece an embroidered sampler imploring God to help her accept the things she couldn't change (which must have been just about everything). Rather sad, really. I've often wondered what happened to that fatalistic old crone. I remember that she used to give me a peppermint every time I went to see her. But that's neither here nor there. In any event, I reached the conclusion that I couldn't change Bonzo (the only acceptable change would have been the rather fundamental one I'd already failed to achieve) so I had to accept him.

One other thought, by the way, has just occurred to me, though oddly enough I never considered it at the time. Could there have been some connection between Mrs Gray's somewhat obsessive insistence on her daughter's pre-mechanical chastity and that bountiful stock of baby-food that saved my life? I just mention this in passing, as it were, for this is a problem I must leave to future scholars. I won't attempt to disguise my pleasure, however, at the thought that Count Boris Slattery should owe his life to this unfortunate girl's disgrace.

September the third. Boris moved to the open window and stood there, immobilized by the autumnal smell of burning leaves. Somewhere out of sight on the other side of the barn Maurice had swept up some dry leaves and started a bonfire. That was just the sort of normal, ritual thing that Maurice always did after an afternoon's sex behind the white plastic venetian blinds with one or other of his plump girls. The thought depressed him but he continued to stand there tethered to the window by the melancholy perfume drifting up from the garden.

'Boris!' Flower called up to him from the foot of the stairs. 'Are you ready? You're going to be late.'

He moved at last, changed rapidly into a white shirt, white tie and tails and then went downstairs.

'You look tired,' Flower said. She was standing at the kitchen table kneading dough made from wholemeal flour (because old Dongeon had a theory that ordinary white flour was poisoned with chemicals). 'I'm sure that sofa can't be very comfortable,' she added in a carefully neutral tone.

'I'm all right,' Boris said. Even at seven o'clock in the evening he found the kitchen intolerably bright and hostile. 'Don't bother to wait up for me. See you tomorrow.'

He was surprised to catch a hurt look on Flower's face, melting promptly, however, into the impassive expression she normally wore.

'I'll probably be awake,' she said, kneading again. 'I could make you a cup of chocolate or something.'

'I can do that myself,' Boris said. He turned to go.

'By the way, there was a letter,' Flower said to his disappearing back. 'From those people in Sweden. The girl will be coming to us for a few days before going to a school in Norfolk. I think it was Norfolk . . . somewhere like that.'

'Oh?' Boris said blankly, returning a few paces. 'A school?'

'A finishing school. She'll be here for the week-end I should think.' Flower rubbed her cheek wearily, leaving a white mark on it. 'I don't know where she's going to sleep, but I suppose we can find a bed somewhere.'

Now that it had happened he felt completely indifferent. As he walked down to the beach he rummaged in the grey ashes of his memory, trying to find one or two bright embers of elation with which he could re-kindle enthusiasm for the girl's arrival. But it was useless. Everything was dead and cold. If she had come earlier. But she hadn't come earlier. The summer was over. There was nothing more to say.

The sky was clear except for some haze on the sea horizon, bronzed by the declining sun. Above his head the void, greyish-blue and darkening imperceptibly. In it the remains of a vapour trail, swelling, ready to collapse, grotesque, losing its identity slowly but surely. The plane itself had already long disappeared on its journey to wherever it was going. Infinity made his eyes water. Returning to the earth he saw fresh hoofmarks on a patch of sand. Alessandro was somewhere in the vicinity. Presumably he had ridden in among the dunes towards Maidenhair.

Boris took a deep breath, plodded through a strip of dry sand in front of The Groaning Board, climbed two steps cemented on to the rock, and rounded the boiler house towards the back door in the hope that he might manage to slip in without being seen by Jean Arthur. She was there, however, in the kitchen arranging flowers with the eternal cigarette dangling from her lurid lips. Before he had a chance to speak she said briskly:

'You're late, Boris, but it doesn't matter if you start in straight away and put the menus on the tables and when you've done that check the cutlery and bring some more table wine up from the cellar.'

Without a word he went through to the dining-room, took a pile of menus from the drawer beneath the cash-desk and wandered around the room distributing them.

'And put a "Reserved" card on six and twelve.'

'Yes, yes, yes,' muttered Boris, not loud enough for her to hear.

Maria, the Spanish girl, came bustling downstairs carrying a pile of white linen.

'Hello, Boris. You here at last. We thought you must have be drown.'

Boris grunted.

'Miss Arthur almost telephone you up.'

'Yes? That was almost nice of her. Who's reserved for tonight, d'you know?'

With her bony hip Jean Arthur pushed through the swing door from the kitchen and said with an air of quiet authority: 'No time for chattering, Maria. Please go and get the cheeses out of the fridge and arrange them on the cheese-board.' She deposited the flowers on a table by the window and began to straighten the cutlery.

'It would be a help if you could get here in time, Boris.'

The place is crammed with customers hammering on the tables, Boris nearly said.

'What's all this?' Frowning she picked up a menu. 'Really, Boris, you must be more careful. You've got the wrong cards again. You know very well we don't have goulash and sweetbreads on Thursdays. You'll just have to go round and change them again.'

'All right.'

'But first go down and get the table wine.'

Departing once more she raised a veined wrist to her short, straight hair in a gesture to indicate exhaustion with the incompetence of those around her. Boris, detached, watched the gullet of the swing door gulp down her bony bottom (the seat of her slacks was so loose and empty that twin creases ran converging right up to the small of her back). God help us all. He looked around the room in a daze.

When the first customers (a man, his wife and his secretary) arrived soon after eight, Jean Arthur greeted them, swept the room with her falcon eyes for the last time and then retired to her apartment upstairs in order, Boris surmised, not to be confused with the servants. He advanced on the trio with the stony expression he liked to maintain during working-hours, handing menus to the women and a wine-card to the man. He waited impassively with pencil poised.

'Well now. We'll have three dry martinis to start with. All right? And make sure they're dry.'

'Very good, sir.'

A restaurant fascist, thought Boris as he retired to mix the drinks. In front of the women he has to flex his muscles.

When he returned with the martinis the heavily powdered wife was puffing at a tipped cigarette and musing aloud that she didn't think she could eat anything. Boris, pencil poised once more, waited while she continued to study the menu with a disabused air. When he had given their order (rump steaks and spaghetti) to Maria he took refuge in a little alcove near the window, partially shielded from the restaurant by a brace of potted palms. Maria took care of the service. The minutes slowly ticked by. At a quarter to nine he heard Jean Arthur's tread on the stairs. He emerged from behind the palms and hovered around the rump steaks. She walked through to the kitchen and back again, nodding to Boris. When the coast was clear he bolted behind the palms once more.

Outside it was very dark and a mist was coming in off the sea. Not yet nine o'clock. He re-lit the cigarette he had extinguished when he heard Jean Arthur coming downstairs. Time passed. From his nest of potted palms he idly watched tendrils of spaghetti writhing up into moist and fleshy lips. Beside him the window. The bottle-green sea was swelling gently under a curtain of fog. The sea window was darkening quickly. The green sea was swelling under a grey mist. The sea was moving its gentle muscles under a grey skin. The grey sea and the grey fog.

Green and grey. Grey as mist. As life. The grey. Grey. Grey.
Grey. Grey. Grey. Grey. Blood scarlet. And grey. Grey. Grey.
Grey.

That must have been Alessandro going home, he thought.
What does the boy think about while he's riding alone in the
dunes all day? He thinks of mortality. And he thinks of the death
of love.

By eleven o'clock the restaurant was empty. After a half-
hearted attempt to persuade Maria to feel his muscles he retired
to the kitchen with a bottle of Château Margaux to swig the
couple of inches remaining in it. At eleven thirty, when the
restaurant had already been idle for an hour and a half, Jean
Arthur came downstairs and said that she didn't think there
would be any more customers and that he might as well go home
when he had seen to the cutlery and the menus and scraped the
candle-grease off the tablecloths

'I don't think we'll be needing the rest of the chicken in the
fridge, Boris,' Jean Arthur said as he was leaving. 'You can take
it home.'

'No thanks.'

'I'm sure Flower would like it,' she insisted.

'If Flower wants a chicken she can buy it herself,' Boris said
curtly. 'Thanks all the same.'

He left by the kitchen door without meeting anybody's eye
and climbed carefully down to the beach in the black and total
darkness. The air was cold, damp with mist. He plodded over
the beach towards the invisible mass of Boscobel. He could see
nothing. An intense silence over the planet. Alone in salty
darkness. Now there was a slight gurgle close at hand, a
receding wave. His foot scattered a pile of invisible pebbles.
Magic bells. Alone in blackness. He stopped to urinate at
random into the night. It was as if he were the last living person,
alone in emptiness and chaos. From further down the coast a
foghorn sounded wearily.

Before he dozed off the foghorn sounded again, a long sigh,
muffled, filtered through the dense mist and drifted to him over
the black water which gradually became his sleep. Shortly

before dawn he woke abruptly, thinking that there was something he must do that he had forgotten. He had wanted to speak to someone, but who the person was or what exactly he had wanted to say he could no longer remember. In spite of the deep sleep from which he had surfaced he still felt desperately tired. Without switching on the light he crawled off the sofa and made his way unsteadily to the washbasin, where he cupped his hand under the tap and drank some water. After that he lay on his back motionless with fatigue while the room slowly lightened. Just before sunrise, however, he fell asleep again and dreamed of Ylva.

She was calling to him from the foot of a long flight of stone stairs. She appeared young, a mere child. Her voice was very faint, scarcely more than a sigh.

'I'm coming,' he called to her. 'Wait for me.' Racing down the stairs towards her he found himself going too fast. He was unable to stop himself. Faster and faster until his impetus became too great and he fell forward. Hurled forward by his speed, bouncing and cartwheeling over those sharp stone teeth. When he finally came to rest at the foot of the stairs his body was shattered. He saw his skull with a dark crack running across it. And as he watched, the crack began to bulge. It bulged until a white liquid oozed out of it. And then the white liquid forced the crack open and collected in a white pool and the pool became a white bird, a dove, which flew away into the sky with a glitter of white wings.

At breakfast, while ruminating toast and marmalade, it occurred to Boris that there was something dated about his dream. Certainly its symbolism had a faded Pre-Raphaelite flavour, a faint perfume of peacock feathers and antimacassars. Did this then mean . . . ? Was he merely . . . ? His jaws slowly ground to a halt though his mouth was still full of toast and marmalade. A pathetic old chap whose mind was geared to one world while trying to operate in another? A dated Boris, corpulent with years, puffing over the sands of time only to be caught in the end by the returning tide of years. Nonsense, he told himself firmly. His jaws began to rotate again.

She had arrived!

Shuddering with emotion, his hands clasped tightly between his knees, Boris sat at his desk and listened to the approaching growl of Maurice's car, the swish of gravel as it turned off the road and into the drive.

A spotty schoolgirl with dirty fingernails, he told himself in an attempt to arrest the clockwork muscles working in his cheeks. I have other things to think about.

The car had come to a stop in front of the barn door immediately below the window. As Boris peered out cautiously a door opened and Maurice got out and walked briskly round the front of the car. The other door opened hesitantly, a mere few inches, and Boris caught a glimpse of white. But the door still remained almost closed. The girl was waiting for Maurice to open the door for her. A sign of sophistication. His heart pounded. The girl could hardly have dirty fingernails

Maurice, grinning pleasantly, had now rounded the car and was opening the door. Boris braced himself for the shock.

The door was open. A slim, white-trousered leg was lowered tentatively from the car, an arm in a snowy white pullover appeared and placed a small sunburned hand in the hairy fist which Maurice was gallantly proffering. And then she was standing there beside the car with a half-smile on her lips, looking around. Maurice had dropped her hand and was leaning over the front seat of the car to wrestle with a suitcase.

Boris stared down with painful intensity at the molten gold that drenched the girl's shoulders. She stood there with arms serenely folded looking casually up at the white plastic slats of Maurice's venetian blinds, at the closed back door, at the relaxed and smiling sycamore tree and then (Maurice was still struggling to get her large suitcase off the back seat and, no doubt, making one or two gay little jokes against himself for being so slow), so suddenly that Boris had no time to move, she turned and gazed straight up at his window with her clear blue eyes. The raised finger with which he had been about to erase a tremor of one of his eyelids was abruptly arrested in front of his face as if in benediction. He remained frozen in this odd position until the girl, still half smiling, unfolded her arms and made a vague and friendly gesture in acknowledgment of his blessing.

Bonzo, for no apparent reason, suddenly uttered a sharp bark.

The girl had turned away to follow Maurice who was walking with short, rapid steps, heavily laden with her suitcase, towards the back door. They vanished. The door closed behind them. Bonzo barked again. Boris, unnerved, scratched Bonzo's ear and patted his bulging sides. Everything was suddenly out of control.

She was in the house. He crossed to the mirror and examined his appearance. An unnatural flush had stained his cheeks a dull red. She would be brought up to his room to be introduced at any moment now.

He jerked open a drawer, hesitated, rummaged for a moment and selected a pair of dark glasses. He dusted them and put them on. The room appeared intolerably grey and gloomy. A scratch on one of the lenses followed his gaze like an irritating insect, settling on whatever object he happened to be looking at.

There was a light knock and the door creaked slightly as it was opened. It was Flower. She said: 'Have you a headache, dear?'

'Headache?'

'The dark glasses.'

'A headache,' he said peevishly. 'I wish you wouldn't always interrogate me.'

'All right then,' Flower said in a resigned tone. 'Aren't you coming down for some tea? Inez has arrived.'

'I'll be down presently.'

His excitement had evaporated. On his way downstairs it occurred to him that there was something distinctly grotesque about the scene depicted in 'The Letter'. The very idea of offering someone an empty uniform and saying: Sorry but this is all that's left of your deceased lover! Of course, if the dead man had been a sort of Maurice – that's to say, a mere collection of external material objects – then perhaps it would make no difference. The poor girl might not even realize that the uniform was empty.

There was something odd about the scene that met his gaze as he opened the door. There was dead silence, for one thing. Not even the clink of a spoon. For another, there seemed to be not the slightest movement. The members of the family were grouped like statues, sitting or standing, staring with frozen features at each other, at the walls, at the carpet. It was odd. It was most disturbing. It was as if . . .

However, sound and movement returned instantly. An arrested head continued its revolution from one object to another, a cup and saucer chimed, the cloud of smoke that old Dongeon had been holding like a blue feather gripped between his teeth rapidly began to swell and ascend, a plate of scones continued gliding from one person to another. Boris uttered a sigh of relief and strode into the room.

Inez was sitting on the arm of a chair, serene and composed, her head (Boris had never seen such delicate features) tilted slightly towards old Dongeon's white-whiskered lips to catch what he was saying about the two workmen who were going to mend the leak in the barn roof. She was perfectly relaxed and though, yes, she was certainly very young, almost a child, her assurance made her age of no importance. Boris advanced, smiling enigmatically and holding out his hand.

'Hi, I'm Boris,' he said.

'And I'm Ineige,' Inez said, parting her lips in a thrilling smile. 'I'm pleased to meet you.'

'Would you like an aspirin with your tea, dear?' asked Flower with her hand on the teapot.

'No thanks And I don't want any tea either, thanks. Or rather – yes, I might have some if it's going.'

He had turned away from Inez, but he could feel, nevertheless, her ultra-violet eyes warming the skin of his back.

'But it doesn't really matter,' he added senselessly.

'Crab-apple jelly,' declared Granny Dongeon from the depths of the sofa. 'Crab-apples in October. Into the boiling pot they go. Grow again next year.'

'That's right, Granny,' Flower said soothingly.

'Every year the same. He used to love them. Can't eat them now though.'

'Your father . . . I told him straight, man to man . . . your father used to mend our roofs, and his father before him . . .'

'Don't do it like that, Antoine, or you'll bruise them. The worms will get them. Get you too, I shouldn't be surprised.'

'Unions, I said. I don't want to hear the word. It's a dirty word. You won't find it in *my* dictionary . . .'

'Isn't it time for Granny's rest?' demanded Boris loudly to make it perfectly clear where he stood.

'They may have done good for the workers. That I don't dispute. But what have they done for the country? Eh? Answer me that if you can.'

'Well, I think . . .' Inez said politely, under the impression that she was expected to reply.

'Ah yes!' declared old Dongeon, tapping the girl's beautifully creased white thigh (How does he dare? wondered Boris) and blowing a thick cloud of blue smoke towards her shining hair, causing her to wrinkle her little nose just a fraction. 'But it's all right for you Scandinavians. And why? Because you're all workers, that's why. I told them to their faces, man to man, I told them . . . You scratch my back and I'll scratch yours.'

'Please,' Inez said with a trace of surprise, 'scratching the back?'

Boris winked at her to indicate that she shouldn't take old

Dongeon too seriously. However, Inez failed to notice, possibly because he was wearing dark glasses.

'Poor Antoine. Crab-apples will come again next year . . but will he? Oh no, he won't.'

'I wonder could someone possibly dislodge Granny from her crab-apple fixation,' suggested Boris. 'She's beginning to get on my nerves.'

'I warned him. Worms will get you. And now where is he?' A small tear appeared in one of Granny Dongeon's rheumy eyes and lost itself to irrigate the deep wrinkles of her sagging cheeks

'There, there, Granny. Have another nice hot cup of tea You'll get yourself in a state.'

'What's this, Granny? You're in a state?' demanded Maurice cheerfully, ushering Alessandro into the room before him. 'Look what I found. Another member of the family skulking outside. Too shy to come in and meet our beautiful guest.'

Alessandro halted awkwardly in the middle of the room with his eyes on the carpet.

'And who are you?' Inez asked, with a smile of such charm that no trace of condescension remained in her words.

'Alessandro.'

'Then you must be the boy who rides horses all the time Maurice was telling me. Will you teach me to ride?'

Alessandro brushed a lock of charcoal hair from his forehead and for an instant raised his shining black eyes to hers.

'All right,' he said at last. A fierce blush stole over his pale cheeks, and in the silence that followed the two words he had spoken he shot a glance of distress towards Boris. And yet it seemed to Boris that Inez's smile had become quite tender as her magnificent blue eyes played over Alessandro's face like twin rays of sunlight.

'Come on, Sandro,' said Maurice jovially. 'You're letting the side down. We all thought you Italian chaps were supposed to be terribly gallant with the ladies. You might at least shake hands with Inez.'

Inez shifted her gaze to Maurice and her lips parted once more, revealing her milky teeth. She held out her small sunburned hand to Alessandro, who took it stiffly and sketched an awkward bow over it. He dropped it again hurriedly.

'I'm very glad to meet you, Sandro.'

Alessandro murmured a reply and stepped back, jarring the table and rattling the cups.

'Today's grapes, tomorrow's wine,' Granny Dongeon murmured with resignation.

'What I want to know,' old Dongeon wondered aloud, 'is how you can hope to build a house when all the bricks want to be equal. That's what I asked them. You chappies know about building houses, I told them. You know as well as I do that some bricks must be on top and some underneath. It's a law of Nature . . .'

'You can't make omelettes without breaking eggs,' declared Granny Dongeon.

'Oh Lord,' muttered Boris, swiping viciously at a mosquito hovering in front of his face. He missed, swiped again, missed again.

Flower got to her feet and came to collect a cup on the table beside him, whispering fiercely: 'Stop that, Boris.'

'Stop what?' he demanded, grinding his teeth and swiping so viciously at the mosquito that the springs of the sofa wheezed like a mouth-organ. The mosquito remained where it was. The others, with the exception of Inez who was studying her fingernails, were all looking at him oddly. An awful thought crossed his mind. He lifted his dark glasses. The mosquito vanished.

'Good Heavens!' he laughed. 'You know, I thought there was a . . .'

'Did you have a good journey, dear?' Flower was asking Inez.

Boris got up and made for the door.

Ignoring Inez's reply Flower called after him: 'Don't go, Boris. We're going to have a game of Monopoly before supper.'

Boris looked at his watch and furrowed his brow.

'All right then. A quick game.' The thought of thrashing the Dongeon family before Inez was infinitely attractive.

They began to play. After a few minutes a bitter argument

broke out. Boris insisted that as he held all the railway-stations he could build hotels on them if he wanted.

'Have you never heard of a railway-hotel?' he demanded with heavy sarcasm.

'It's against the rules of the game,' Maurice replied calmly.

The rule book was produced. It stated categorically that Boris was not allowed to build hotels on his railway-stations. For the rest of the game he maintained a sullen silence.

As it turned out, Granny Dongeon (helped by Maurice) quickly gained a stranglehold on the game. Boris retired to his room, speechless with rage, planning to compose an angry letter to the makers.

After breakfast Boris opened the french windows and stepped out into the misty sunshine. The garden lay about him, calm and glorious. He lingered for a moment in front of the house and then headed diagonally across the tennis-court, avoiding the broken net that straggled over the dewy grass like a deflated black snake. On the far side of the lawn he ploughed through a bed of roses in order to avoid a detour by the garden path whose artificial crazy-paving offended him. Turning furtively he noticed that old Dongeon, who had followed him to the french windows, had noticed this act of sacrilege. Boris bowed his head and moved on towards his destination, the sunflower.

It had lost its magnificence. The face that stared up at him was haggard and tense, no longer the gleaming, golden eye of the sun. The blades of its petals were bent inwards, dulled, as if clutching despairingly for the vanished beauty. The green leaves that alternated on its stem were paralysed and withered. I'm not dead, of course, the sunflower told Boris, but I'm dying. I know that much. I'm dying. Slowly but surely as the season advances. Who will help me now?

'Uh! Sorry. You startled me,' Boris said to old Dongeon who had forged silently over the grass behind him.

'Lovely day,' old Dongeon said, emitting the words with a trail of royal-blue smoke. He took Boris by the arm and steered him back over the grass towards the crazy-paving. Boris realized with alarm that old Dongeon had decided to have a serious word with him.

'You like flowers. So do I. Why do we like flowers? Because they're a part of Nature, that's why. I'm an old chap now but I still get pleasure from a nice bit of garden.'

'Of course,' murmured Boris, staring with fascination at old Dongeon's clipped moustache. His habit of breathing out blue smoke every time he spoke gave him the appearance of some minor pagan deity. The white moustache had been slightly yellowed by nicotine over his right lip.

'I'm an old chap now though,' old Dongeon pursued. 'I won't live for ever . . . No, no, don't contradict me,' he added, though Boris had made no attempt to do so. 'I know what's what. I won't live for ever. One of these days, Boris, you and Flower and Maurice will inherit all this' (he waved expansively at a roller half submerged in grass, at a broken cloche against the wall of the barn beneath which two lettuces were rotting peacefully). 'One of these days. Nobody lives for ever.'

Boris said nothing, made uncomfortable by the old man's refutation of his immortality. His elbow was still firmly gripped by an elaborately veined hand. Coming to a fork in the garden path he was steered to the left around a bed of rhubarb.

'But you must play the game,' old Dongeon went on with a little sigh. 'We all must.'

Boris felt a slight twinge of guilt, thinking by some coincidence of the refused chicken of the other night. Oh Lord, he thought. How long is this going to go on?

' "Housewife and mother of three goes berserk with husband's harpoon-gun",' came Maurice's voice drifting out to them as they turned in front of the french windows. 'No, Granny. Just *one* person. Housewife and mother at the same time. D'you understand? With her husband's harpoon-gun . . .'

'That's the boy,' old Dongeon said. 'The game's the thing.'

'I see what you mean,' Boris said.

'I'm keeping my eyes open. A little restaurant of your own one of these days, who knows? I'm an old chap now but I don't miss much and I'm keeping my eyes open. No promises, but we'll see what we shall see.'

'Well,' said Boris. 'I mean, don't do anything specially . . .' His voice trailed off feebly as he gave up the attempt to find an adequate reply to whatever old Dongeon had been trying to say.

'But the game has rules and we must abide by them. Not just you or me. Not just Flower. We all must. The rules are the thing. We all must pull together. Abide by them.'

'"Mauled by lion", Granny,' came Maurice's voice very faintly, filtered through a couple of apple trees. Boris wondered unhappily whether it was Lady Jane who had been mauled by the lion. It was unlikely. All the odds were against it. There were lions busy mauling people all over the world. Statistically the chances were slim.

'You know what Renoir said? First of all be a good craftsman. That won't stop you having genius.'

What on earth, Boris wondered, had that got to do with it? Nothing at all. But he knew from experience that old Dongeon liked to back up whatever he said with some hefty, immortal policeman.

'"Immolated in sudden landslide!"'

Old Dongeon had begun a strange purring sound that might have been an attempt to hum 'Onward Christian Soldiers'. By this time Boris was exhausted with the conversation and longing to escape. With a creaking of joints old Dongeon stooped to pluck some groundsel from a flowerbed.

'Flowers,' he said. 'Growing, growing . . . all in their proper place and season.'

'Marching as to war.'

Boris looked at his watch. 'I must go and write a letter if I'm to catch the morning post.'

Old Dongeon was kneeling at another flowerbed so Boris walked off rapidly without waiting for a reply. To avoid hearing Maurice reading to Granny Dongeon he went around to the kitchen door. Flower had her back to him rinsing dishes. As he was passing through she started to turn her head, but Boris was through and halfway up the stairs before she had time to speak.

As he opened the door of his room Bonzo climbed out of his basket, stretched and hurried forward. Boris sidestepped, and when the dog had sped through the door, closed it. Bonzo scratched the door a couple of times hopefully and then groaned.

Boris watched old Dongeon shuffle by under his window with a trowel in his hand. What had the old chap been talking about? He had assumed that all the talk about abiding by the rules had referred to the illicit short cut he had taken across the flowerbed. But old Dongeon would hardly go to the lengths of promising him a restaurant merely to keep him out of the flowerbeds. There was only one other explanation. The old man had been trying to bribe Boris to get back into bed with his fat daughter.

The insolence! I should have given the old buzzard a piece of my mind. Next time I'll say: I should be most grateful if henceforth you will confine your interference to those matters which concern you. Next time . . . But the man has a nerve! Good God!

Later that morning he drove into Maidenhair with Maurice who had some shopping to do. On the way Maurice told him that he thought Inez was a sweet child and that one day she would be very attractive.

'How's the painting going?' Boris demanded abruptly, not wanting to discuss Inez with him and unable to think of any other way to get him off the subject.

'Not bad at all. You haven't seen my latest things yet, have you?'

Boris admitted that he hadn't. But I can imagine, he added to himself.

'I'm trying to get Pat to pose in the nude for me. But I'm not having much success so far. It's easier to get them into bed than to persuade them to pose.'

I can't see why they should think it much of an honour to have you scanning their parts, thought Boris.

'Pat? Is she . . .?'

'No, she's another one. I don't think you've met her. Works in a chemist's.'

Yellowing trees hurried past as Maurice accelerated into Maidenhair. The day had turned soft and damp, bathing the countryside in dull grey light that seeped into Boris and filled him with a muffled melancholy. Not anguish. Merely the ache of weariness that comes from being alive twenty-four hours a day until you die. Who will help me now? the sunflower wanted to know. Nobody will help you because the seasons are remorseless. There's no difference between being magnificently golden and lifelessly withered. The circle chases itself eternally.

'Sorry, what's that?'

'I was saying that I've never understood why *you* never took up painting . . . with your aesthetic sense.'

Boris glanced suspiciously at his brother-in-law but the one eye that was visible was shiny with sincerity.

'Oh, I prefer to leave that to you,' he said cautiously.

Maurice didn't reply until they came to a stop at the traffic lights at the bottom of Marine Road. While waiting he turned to Boris and said:

'It's a shame to waste a talent. One never knows until one's tried.'

Both Maurice's eyes were now visible. Both were misty with friendship. He hammered the wheel absently with the palm of his hand and peered up to see if the lights were changing.

'I might try a canvas or two one of these days,' Boris said carefully. He had a brief and warming vision of a naked girl curled up in Bonzo's basket beside him while he worked. 'I might when I have time.'

Maurice parked the car near the Albert Arcade and put on a pair of dark glasses before getting out of the car. Putting an arm over Boris's shoulder he said:

'Come on, old chap. I'll buy you a quick drink before I do the shopping. Pleasure before business.'

Boris was steered past an ironmongery displaying a sinister armoury of knives and weedkillers, past a seedy bookshop (*Sexual Therapy for Vertebrates* was the only title he managed to glimpse), past The Joyous Years Ltd (displaying tiny boots, cotton dresses with rabbits, mice and other vermin embroidered on them, and a sign saying 'Everything for the tiny guest in your house') and into the pinkly glowing chromium interior of Duke's American Bar, which was empty and still smelled of dead cigarettes from the night before.

Boris cleared his throat and said: 'I'll have a small whisky if I may . . . just a small one,' but Maurice, busy greeting the barman, failed to hear.

'And I don't think you've met my brother-in-law, have you, Jack?'

'No, Mr Dongeon, I don't believe I've had that pleasure,' the barman said, wiping his hands on a dishcloth and stretching over the bar to grip Boris. 'Pleased to meet you, sir.'

'A whisky . . . just a small one,' murmured Boris uneasily.

'The usual for me,' Maurice said. 'What'll it be, Boris? Drinks are on me.'

'A whisky . . . just a small one,' Boris repeated for the third time, feeling a gust of insanity stirring the hair on the back of his head. He was beginning to regret having . . . But turning he noticed that the gust had come from the opening of the door by a man in overalls dragging in a crate of bottles.

Maurice took him by the elbow and guided him to an armchair beside a low table. Boris decided that he was sick to death of being steered to places he didn't want to go by members of the Dongeon family. However, Maurice gave him a friendly wink and smile as they sat down and said something uninteresting about art being the new religion of our materialistic times. Boris gulped his whisky and gradually mellowed.

'How are you, Boris? I mean, *really*.'

'Sorry . . . I don't think I quite . . .?'

'I mean your health and so on.'

'It's all right.'

Maurice said something about over-taxing of resources.

Boris drained his glass. 'I'm fine,' he said guardedly.

'I know it's none of my business really but I've been wondering how things are between you and Flower . . .'

Boris stared at him with his mouth working. 'You're right

when you say it's none of your business,' he cried at last, with a burst of anger of such intensity that it shocked even himself. 'I mean, for God's sake . . .'

Maurice's genial manner had collapsed abruptly. 'I just thought you might want to talk about it. Get things off your . . .'

'Well I don't.'

Boris was on his feet and making for the door with long strides. A chill gust of wind struck him in the face as he pushed through it, bringing water to his eyes.

So that was what it was all about. I might have known.

He found himself miraculously on the promenade, gripping the cold iron tube of the railing and staring out over intoxicating emptiness. The promenade was deserted. Where had everyone gone? There should have been stragglers. Old people in deck-chairs, retired people staying on into September to squeeze the last drops of golden juice from the sun. But there was no one. Only the distant silhouette of the ice-cream vendor at the far end of the promenade, standing there, selling nothing. The man's eyes, however, were slightly elevated to watch gulls rotating over some floating refuse.

Boris felt afraid. The straightness of the promenade rail. Its strength dismayed him. But where could he turn his eyes? The repeated pattern of the paving-stones was equally oppressive. If only he could have telephoned to Alessandro to come and meet him. But that was out of the question. Old Dongeon or Flower would answer the telephone. What else could he do? There were countless bars he could go to and have a few drinks. The only difficulty was that he would have to be Maurice to do so.

A typhoon of jealousy that had been awaiting its opportunity out at sea now raced in and struck him with great force, almost knocking him off balance, flapping his jacket and ballooning his trousers. He had to sit down on the stone kerb. He felt quite faint with jealousy of Maurice. The striped pseudo-sailor jersey (he could buy one himself, of course), the dark glasses, the Volkswagen and the contraceptives and the rope-soled shoes (they were all for sale, no difficulty about that). He could even manage without difficulty, he felt sure, to paint the Heads of

Christ. What he could never do was smile and wink at people and call barmen by their first names, seduce without guilt or passion (but with a pleasant twinkle) these plump girls behind white plastic venetian blinds, act always in the sure knowledge that he had been born in the right place at the right time.

A few minutes later he was standing irresolutely outside Dr Cohen's house. He was still hesitating when the front door opened and the doctor himself appeared, clad in an overcoat as if it were mid-winter.

'Hello, Boris. What are you lurking about for? You look as if you're about to do a smash-and-grab raid.'

'I was just wondering whether I wanted to talk to you or not.'

Cohen laughed wearily. 'I'm sure you don't. But I'm just going to the hospital. You can keep me company on the way, if you like.'

They set off down the street. The old man was looking more tired and haggard than Boris had ever seen him. But he appeared sober. Perhaps that was the reason.

'I haven't had a drink all morning,' the doctor said as if reading his thought. 'And the result is that I feel terrible. The snag is that I'm sure I'd feel even more terrible if I had a few since my liver is packing up. What's to be done? as Lenin used to say. The problem is insoluble.'

'Why are you going to the hospital? I thought you'd retired.'

'I have. I'm on my way to be cured this time.'

They turned into a street of imposing Victorian houses, façades decorated with ornate masonry. What had happened to all the large, solid families who had once lived in these houses? They had been so sure that living in solid houses at the centre of a vast Empire they had a foot wedged in the door of eternity. Boris could find no satisfaction in the thought that they had deluded themselves.

'Not that I want to be cured,' the doctor was saying absently 'That would be worse than the disease. Still, it helps pass the time.'

At the hospital gates Boris stopped to say goodbye.

'Come in for a moment,' the doctor told him. 'I want to show you something.'

With misgiving Boris followed him into the hospital, down a long corridor, across a paved yard and into another building. This was a small gymnasium, furnished with long lines of parallel bars, thick mats, ropes and slings, and a lot of other apparatus that Boris had never seen before. A weak, grey light filtered into the room through a skylight in the roof. But it was the people in the room that held Boris's attention. They were young for the most part, some of them only children. Lying on mats making feeble movements of an arm or a leg, dragging themselves painfully between the parallel bars, taking teetering steps across the wooden floor on legs stiffened by steel calipers, haggard faces strained with effort and concentration, wasted muscles standing out like taut wires . . . some of the people were as thin as skeletons, others unnaturally bloated with limp and lifeless ribbons of fat. Boris looked at the scene, nauseated.

'Why do you show me this?' he demanded angrily. 'Don't you think things aren't bad enough as they are?'

'Things are certainly bad enough as they are,' the doctor replied imperturbably, 'but not for the reasons you think. Just look at these people. What d'you see?'

'It's ghastly,' said Boris. He felt quite ill. He turned to go.

'Look at them again. Look at them as they are. Let me tell you something,' the doctor went on calmly as they crossed the yard and retraced their steps along the corridor. 'When *you* look at those people you don't see *them*, you see great dramas of suffering and pain and heroism and God knows what else . . . But that's all nonsense, perfectly irrelevant. I expect you noticed that most of those patients were young people paralysed in some way or other. Well, it's merely that they have in some respect aged all of a sudden. Part of the machinery has gone out of action. And that's all there is to it. Nothing else.'

Boris said grimly: 'You're quite wrong, Doctor, and you know it.'

The doctor shook his head sadly.

'I'm trying to help you, Boris,' he said casually, almost with indifference. 'You probably have another twenty or thirty years to serve on this planet. I'm just trying to make it easier for you.'

'You'll hardly make it easier by showing me cripples,' Boris replied sombrely.

They were standing once more in the main hall at the hospital entrance. The doctor was tapping the floor with his stick and gazing abstractedly at a receptionist in a white starched overall who was frowning at some papers on her desk.

'I used to be rather like you,' the doctor said vaguely, looking somewhat bored. 'All misery is invented.' After a moment he turned back to Boris and smiled. 'Happiness, too, I daresay.'

Boris was passing the corner where not so long ago a sunburned youth had tried to sell him a paper hat, where a street-photographer had perfidiously snapped him in a moment of decay. Where were they now? Vanished like the sunflowers. For a little while the heat and sunshine made them blossom. Then they vanished. As he walked towards the Capri he realized that Maidenhair was like a giant plant that flowered and withered according to a natural cycle. Maurice and the doctor and the paper-hat vendor and the photographer and he himself were all insignificant petals on this giant flower. For some reason he found this thought relatively soothing after his unpleasant experience in the hospital.

The Capri. They were all there. Nothing had changed. They were all there as if nothing had happened in the interim. As if, for example, he had never had a heart attack. I must be insane, he thought, to start all this again. But where else could I have gone? Not back to Boscobel with all the Dongeons lurking in the bushes to nab me and have words with me.

He sat down at a table near the window. One of the youths was whispering to June Furlough. She looked round. He wished desperately that he had something to read. He felt a fool but he could hardly get up and leave at this stage.

'Well, look who the wind's blown in.'

'On, nello,' he said. 'Didn't notice you sitting there.' The two youths sitting at June's table had hair down to their shoulders.

They were wearing jeans and faded denim jackets. 'A black coffee, please,' he added to the unkempt girl who came to serve him. He aimed what he hoped was a smile in the direction of June's table. The smile went on too long and became a cramped rictus of his lips that he found impossible to dismount and replace by the relaxed and impassive expression the situation called for.

'Well, hello stranger,' June said with an American accent.

There was another girl sitting at the table. Boris had not seen her before. She had false eyelashes and looked as if she couldn't be more than twelve years old. The tension was unbearable. He searched his pockets, hoping for an old letter or a piece of paper that he might pretend to read. All he could find was a screwed-up ball of paper which, when smoothed out on the table, revealed itself to be a printed offer of a sachet of windscreen-wiping fluid in exchange for the tops from three tins of ravioli. Nevertheless, he studied it with intense concentration while he waited for his coffee, trying not to hear a whispered conversation (no doubt an initiation of the depraved child with false eyelashes into certain intimate details of Boris's life) that ended with a loud roar of laughter. Sweating, he was on the point of jumping to his feet and plunging back into the fresh air when the waitress returned with his coffee in a glass cup. She took an interminable time arranging the cup in front of him and turning the teaspoon on the saucer so that the handle was towards him. He kept his eyes at the level of her stomach where there was a jagged triangular stain with greyish edges on her apron, possibly caused by coffee.

'Thanks.'

The stained stomach moved away at last. Thank God. He was afraid that she had been smiling too. He returned to the ravioli. Succulent to the bite of your teeth. A chair scraped at the other table and he took a gulp of scalding coffee. Succulent.

'Long time no see.'

Boris cleared his throbbing throat.

'Yes, it is rather a long time since I've been into . . .'

'You're a bit of a jerk, Boris, hiding away like that,' June said, sitting down opposite him and resting her chin on her hands. She stared at Boris accusingly from eyes that were too close together. Her black hair hung straight down, shrinking her pale face into a narrow blade, piling up untidily on the edge of the table.

'Especially when you know I can't live without you, darling,' she added in a loud and dramatic voice for the benefit of her friends. Her friends laughed. Boris drank some more coffee.

'I've been rather busy,' he said.

'Too busy for me, I suppose.'

'I'm never too busy for you,' Boris said with a ghastly smile. There was a long silence while June stared at him.

'What have you been doing?'

'Just hanging around.'

Boris finished his coffee and dropped a coin on the table, preparing to depart. Beneath the table a hand suddenly gripped the inside of his thigh, long fingernails digging painfully into his flesh through the thin cloth of his trousers. June was still staring at him without apparent emotion. For a moment Boris wondered whether there mightn't be someone else hiding under the table.

'Coming for a walk?' she said softly.

'A walk? Is your father . . .?'

'Not there. I know where.'

Boris was on his feet and moving towards the door.

'See you later, kids,' June said.

Laughter followed Boris into the street. He set off rapidly between the pounding grey houses but June ran after him and caught his arm.

'Not that way,' she said and pulled him in the other direction. She retained her grip on his arm. With jerky steps he walked back up Marine Road towards the sea. The grey pavement seemed to shudder each time his foot fell. Caught by the wind a strand of black hair whipped against his face. He wanted to tell the girl not to hold his arm in case somebody saw them. Maurice, for instance. It was only ten past one. He might still be doing the shopping. Or worse, somebody from the station might see them. Still, he said nothing. Looking down at the pavement he noticed that June was wearing sandals and that a black film of dust had formed between her toes.

'You're in a hurry, aren't you?'

'Someone might see us.'

'So? Who cares?'

You're under age. They could put me in prison. Well, at least he could write in prison without Bonzo staring at him accusingly and old Dongeon telling him to abide by the rules.

They reached the top of Marine Road and crossed on to the promenade. The sea-front was deserted except for the eternal ice-cream man. He appeared to be eating. Perhaps he had sold himself one of his own ice-creams. June led the way down the broken concrete steps. They plodded along the beach in the direction of the harbour. A hundred yards away stood a dilapidated wooden boat-house built against the sea-wall. In front of it an old man was sitting on a wooden chair whose legs had sunk deep into the sand. He looked up as Boris and the girl approached. Greasy strands of grey hair streaked back over the top of his head and foamed out into thick curls over his neck. There was also a greyish fuzz in the hollows of his cheekbones. With bloodshot eyes he stared at Boris and went on chewing into the heart of a square sandwich of which the uneaten crusts approached his ears like the ends of a stethoscope.

'Oh, it's you,' he said to June. 'All right, but be quick about it. The boss gets back at two.'

'Give him five bob,' June told Boris, scratching her ribs and clenching her teeth as if in pain.

The old man held out a leathery hand while Boris fumbled in his pocket for two half-crowns. As he dropped them into the wrinkled palm he noticed that the thumb was smeared with unmelted butter. The old man returned his interest to the sandwich and Boris followed June shakily into the boat-house. He closed the door behind them. The daylight was abruptly eclipsed.

It was a moment before his eyes became accustomed to the gloom. At the far end of the shed there was a small, dirty window, partially obscured by a roll of canvas standing on end. The shed contained two rowing-boats, one of which was upside down on wooden blocks and gleaming with fresh varnish. The other was laid with its keel on the floor and kept upright by concave wooden chocks placed on each side of its spine. What little he could see of the floor was littered with oily rags, spent matches and wood shavings.

'There's no room,' he said feebly.

June had removed her jacket of soft, black leather and thrown it on to a three-legged table that sagged against one wall.

'In the boat.'

'Oh.'

He was watching a corpulent bluebottle struggling weakly to free itself from the tacky lid of a varnish tin that lay open on the work-bench. He scratched the back of his head. All round the walls oars had been propped with their blades almost touching the shadowy roof. The remains of a net hung from one of the crossbeams like a giant cobweb.

He heard a brief buzz. The bluebottle had escaped from the sticky varnish! With a last effort it had . . . But no. It was still there. The buzzing sound had come from the zip of the girl's jeans. With a sort of frenzied determination she was peeling them off her thighs. Boris watched her with a vague notion of impending doom. Her jeans were so tight that she turned them inside out as she dragged them off her legs. While she was unbuttoning her shirt Boris took off his jacket and hung it on a nail. He slowly loosened his tie.

'Help me with my bra.'

Boris advanced gingerly and June turned her back which was covered with angry red spots. He began to wrestle helplessly with the hook fastening.

'Oh, you're so clumsy. Let *me*.'

Boris retired obediently and continued to undress while June freed herself of brassiere and pants. She began to slide the wooden seats out of the boat. When she had finished she arranged some foam-rubber cushions in the boat and lay down on them.

She has nipples, of course, but no breasts to speak of. Perhaps they'll grow when she's a bit older. But she must be almost seventeen. They should have started coming up by now.

'Hurry up, Boris. You're so slow.'

Boris removed his last garment and, shivering, advanced towards the boat. Her pubic hair looked like a wad of steel wool. He stepped into the boat, which creaked violently and listed a few inches to port. He sat down hurriedly for fear it would capsize. Cautiously he eased forward and stretched out.

'What's the matter? Are you sea-sick?' June was wheezing with laughter. Her stomach and diaphragm performed a rapid, irregular contraction and dilation which Boris found exciting. He caressed her awkwardly and the boat uttered a thin crack of protest.

Though the girl's body was soft he was dismayed by its hardness. He was adrift with a statue of sandstone.

She began to gasp and mutter, locking him firmly, digging her nails into his back. The boat creaked rhythmically. Water trapped beneath the planks rinsed from side to side. The girl's gasping and muttering increased. She uttered a sharp cry. Boris, persevering doggedly, hoped that nobody happened to be passing outside. The boat was rocking violently now. Boris was . . . The blades of up-ended oars stared down at them from the walls like silent, faceless spectators. Boris was drowning. He lifted his head and peered blindly over the bows as they pitched and rolled in heavy seas.

'"My soul!"' he cried out suddenly, '"like to a ship in a black storm . . ."'

The girl uttered a high groan like the whine of a circular saw and Boris sank his teeth into her throat. Air rushed out of her body. Her chest collapsed beneath him like a punctured tyre. They cruised on slowly over the dry waves of the boat-house floor. When they finally came to rest the boat had a thirty-degree list to starboard. With glassy eyes Boris looked out over the wood shavings that lay on the gloomy surface like frozen foam. The lateral ribs of the boat's shell were pressing uncomfortably into his flank and shoulder but June still had him securely locked, her legs fastened across the small of his back, his head firmly clamped against her chest. Time passed.

'Get a move on,' came the boatman's querulous voice from outside. 'He'll be back soon.'

Boris wriggled but June still didn't release him. Her thighs were too strong. He was powerless, locked to a girl of sandstone.

'You're so stiff and formal,' June said reflectively. 'It's like it was being done to me in one of those old-fashioned balls you see in films. I feel like you'd just taken off my crinoline and done it.'

'The chap outside,' Boris said desperately. 'The man will be back any minute.'

June unlocked her legs and Boris gratefully slithered off her. He hopped back to his clothes, feeling a sensation of immense relief. June grasped the gunwales and levered herself upright. She scratched herself calmly and inspected her stomach.

'Hurry up.'

'You're all covered in stripes from leaning against the boat,' June said, coming over and nuzzling against him. 'You look like a tiger.'

Boris shrank away from her travelling fingers and pulled on his trousers. He felt more confident. June picked up her white pants and went to sit down on the other boat which lay overturned on wooden blocks. She jumped up again immediately with a cry of annoyance.

'This bloody varnish is still wet.'

Boris rolled his eyes, buttoning his shirt feverishly.

'I can see him on the promenade,' called the boatman from outside. 'Let's have you out of there.'

'Get dressed, for God's sake,' cried Boris.

'But I've got it on my bottom and it's all sticky. Look!'

She pointed at the gleaming back of the boat on which two contiguous oval marks had indeed now appeared. Boris stared at them in consternation. He could visualize a nightmare prosecution in which the boat was shown as evidence against him. 'The marks of the girl's bottom, my Lord, after seduction.

96

They will be seen to fit perfectly the buttocks of the defendant's young victim.'

'How am I going to get it off? I'm all sticky.'

'Get dressed! There's no time. You'll have to get dressed the way you are.'

'But look.' She turned her varnished bottom towards him on the brink of tears. Boris grasped the pants that were still around her ankles and pulled them up firmly, ignoring the varnish.

'Now get into your jeans and shirt.'

The door opened on to the grey concrete of the sea-wall. He couldn't see a thing. He glanced back at June who was struggling with her inside-out jeans. Twin oval patches of her white pants clung transparently to her skin.

He opened the door cautiously and slipped out. There was nobody in sight. He ventured down the beach a few paces and looked up at the promenade. It was deserted. The old man was dozing peacefully now on his sunken chair beside the shed, his chin resting on a bush of grey hair that boiled out of his open shirt.

Boris felt cheated. He kicked at a stone, missed it, and sent up a spurt of sand, part of which descended on the old man's sandwich paper with a sharp hiss. He opened one eye, looked at Boris, then closed it again. Boris stared up at the steam-coloured sky. A moment earlier he had been standing at the door of the shed, gazing fearlessly at the gathering storm of danger. Now he was standing on the beach with his crocodile shoes slowly filling with dirty sand.

His legs turned to water. He sank slowly down on to the sand with his back against the wooden wall of the shed. His stomach felt hollow and deflated. From it tendrils of despair crawled slowly up through the roads of his body like columns of exhausted refugees. I must have been mad, he thought. I should have stayed at home. June appeared at the door, shrugging on her leather jacket. He pulled himself dizzily to his feet and in silence they set off across the sand. Halfway up the broken steps June stopped and patted her bottom.

'What's the matter?' he asked wearily.

'My pants . . . they've dried on me.'

'Well, that's all right.'

'But they've stuck to my skin. I'll never get them off.'

Boris scratched the back of his head helplessly. 'Perhaps you could steam them off?' he suggested. 'Get a kettle and . . .' His voice trailed off.

When they had reached the corner of Marine Road he said: 'I've got to go and see someone now.' He looked at his watch for corroboration.

'All right,' June said indifferently. 'See you.'

'See you.'

Boris walked away hurriedly, feeling a twinge of guilt at the thought that he was leaving her to solve her problem by herself. But what could he do? Nothing. Not even the most exacting rules of chivalry would expect him to go to work on her bottom with a chisel or a blow-lamp. Ha! But his next thought disturbed him. What if the suspicious station-master surprised his daughter in the kitchen aiming a kettle at her bottom? She would tell desperate lies. He would bluster. She would burst into tears. He would bluster more fiercely. She would break down and confess everything.

Boris trudged on gloomily.

On his way home he stopped at The Fox and bought a quarter bottle of whisky to propel himself over the dunes.

The wind that had announced itself earlier by isolated gusts was now blowing steadily, moving the sky. He halted on the crest of a dune to pour the whisky into his empty silver flask. From here he could see wind-shadows careering over the flattened surface of the sea and whipping up a mist of fine sand. As he was trying to connect the neck of the bottle with the neck of the flask the violent flapping of his jacket rocked him back on his heels. Amber drops were snatched by the wind to form solid brown discs on the sloping crescent of sand. With clenched teeth and scowling ferociously he chattered the two vessels together, but only succeeded in soaking his trembling fingers. Flying sand needled his cheeks, sought to penetrate his lowered lashes, made sandpaper of his moist lips. He gave up the attempt and returned the flask to his pocket, greedily gulping from the bottle until he was forced to pause, eyes closed, and inhale deep, shuddering draughts of air. Then he opened his eyes again and staggered off over the rocking dunes towards Boscobel.

It was almost three o'clock and he had eaten nothing since breakfast. Before he had walked a hundred yards the alcohol was roasting his intestines. He felt at the same time as free as the mounting gale, as heavy as death. His crocodile shoes were soled with lead like the boots of a deep-sea diver. His feet dragged laboriously through the sliding sand while his spirit was tossing with the gulls way above in the fleeting sky.

Then he was wading down the last slope and whipping his clumsy limbs into a gallop. And why he was galloping he didn't know, except that the dead weight of his body and the buoyancy of his soul straining away from each other were stretching him so painfully that he could hardly endure it. The whisky had become a rack. To one end his leaden feet had been tied, to the other his dirigible helium soul. But now, perhaps because of his momentum, it seemed that his leaden feet would snap away and free him from the earth. With each pounding stride he became lighter, his spirit more powerful.

As he was flashing past The Groaning Board with his breath growling rhythmically in his throat, his foot caught against a piece of driftwood and he took a headlong dive into a bank of hard grey pebbles. He was more surprised than hurt. He felt as a shot bird might feel, abruptly flapping on the ground.

He felt numb and too short of breath to consider moving. The bottle smashed. The hand holding it drenched in blood. He was aware that an extremely sharp pain, caused by the alcohol coming in contact with the open cuts on his palm and fingers, was electrifying this hand . . . but somehow the current of pain had become unplugged from the main Boris and was short-circuiting round his wrist. He wasn't particularly upset. The only thing that worried him was the fact that he had fallen down in front of The Groaning Board. From behind one of the blank windows Jean Arthur would obviously have been watching and waiting all day for just such an event.

He was still considering the implications of humiliation in front of Jean Arthur when he saw that Alessandro was trotting up swiftly on his magnificent white horse, Starlight. Boris had seen a number of films in which stallions reared up and trampled people to death, usually pregnant ladies. In response to a sudden vision of Starlight's flashing hooves he at last managed to struggle to his feet, breathing hard. Alessandro pulled the horse up a few feet away and slid to the ground. He spoke a couple of sharp words. The horse nodded, sneezed and waltzed back a couple of paces, terrifying Boris.

Alessandro came over with his cloak swinging and billowing in the wind, identical in colour to Boris's streaming fingers. He said nothing but his dark eyes flickered from Boris's face to the hand that was scattering dark drops on the grey stones. Starlight, drooping his head in a bored fashion, had apparently abandoned the idea of trampling him to death.

'I tripped,' Boris said awkwardly. 'Silly. No, it's nothing. Just winded myself a bit . . .'

'Let me see your hand.'

The boy reached forward and grasped Boris's wrist, turning the palm to the sky. Lifting it to his face he began to suck the blood from the palm.

'Careful,' Boris said thickly. 'There might be bits of glass . . .'

'It's all right. It's not deep.' Alessandro produced a handkerchief and bound it tightly round the still-bleeding palm. 'Can you walk or would you like to ride Starlight?'

'No thanks,' Boris said hastily. 'Really, I'm fine. Just happened to trip. Don't worry. Thanks a lot.'

He turned and walked swiftly towards Boscobel.

'See you,' he called, turning to wave.

Alessandro hadn't moved but was staring after him expressionlessly. There was a trace of blood on his lips.

He would have to go through the kitchen because he had forgotten his keys. He braced himself against the pale-blue-and-yellow assault on his eyeballs. Shoving his wounded hand firmly into the pocket of his jacket he opened the door and went in.

She was standing at the kitchen table like some plump insect resting in the heart of an enormous pale-blue-and-yellow flower. She was kneading, as usual, a roll of dough, her wrists and forearms stained with flour. Boris wondered peevishly how she managed to get flour all over herself every time she made bread. The apparent inevitability of it annoyed him. Why does she always stand there in the same position, look up in the same way?

'Boris.'

'Yes?'

'I thought you'd be back for lunch.'

'Well I wasn't, was I?'

'Would you like something to eat now?'

'I'm not hungry.' He turned to go.

'Maurice said you lost your temper with him in town . . Boris,' her voice trembled a little, 'he was only trying to help. I don't know what's happened to you . . .'

'Trying to help! Happened to me!' stammered Boris, with the hand in his pocket aching with fury. 'I'm just tired of the bastards interfering with me, that's all. You don't give a damn about me yourself. You just stand there making that bleeding bread all day . . .'

He glared wildly at the livid lump of dough and at an open carton of six fresh eggs beside it.

'Oh, be reasonable,' Flower said miserably. 'You know very well . . .'

She stopped and looked at Boris in astonishment. He had seized an egg from the carton and thrown it at the ceiling. And then another. Flower was speechless with surprise. One egg after another was plucked from its hollow nest and thrown up at the pale-blue ceiling with a precise jerk of the wrist. One egg after another smashed on the ceiling, hesitated, slowly dropped gleaming tentacles of white and yellow towards the tiled floor. Without looking at his wife Boris turned and strode out of the egg-festooned kitchen.

His head was throbbing painfully as he climbed the stairs. Before he had reached the top, however, his anger had subsided. He felt ashamed of himself, realizing that he would never have dared to indulge in such a fit of rage in front of Maurice or old Dongeon.

At the top he hesitated and then, groaning with exhaustion and despair, went down again. Flower was still standing at the table pressing her knuckles mechanically into the dough, turning it over, folding it, kneading it again, leaving as she did so the imprint of eight small knuckles. Fat, glistening tears were running down her cheeks as she worked and falling on to the white-powdered bread board. Avoiding the gleaming stalactites of egg that hung from the ceiling Boris circled the table and put a hand on her shoulder.

'I'm sorry. I'm not quite myself today.'

Flower sniffed and sighed but said nothing. After a moment she turned her face against the upper arm of her sleeve to dry her eyes.

'Here.' Boris took the orange silk handkerchief from his top pocket and patted Flower's cheeks and red, blurred eyes. Flower sniffed again and made a hollow in the disc of dough, splashing milk into it from a small blue jug. Boris stood indecisively beside her.

'I'll clean this mess up.'

'I'll do it,' Flower said in a neutral tone.

'No, I insist,' Boris said briskly in an attempt to make the situation more normal.

'Leave it. You'll only make a worse mess

There was a long silence. He could think of nothing further to say. Every few seconds, however, the electric clock fixed to the wall above the stove made a faint whirring sound, passing over the silence like the wing beats of a small bird.

I thought I had finished with photographs . . . but no. I find myself picking up the album absentmindedly and flicking through it. None of our actions is ever clearly begun or ended, you see. We half begin . . . half finish, hesitate, begin, finish, begin again . . . The clean, decisive actions we have in our minds slowly collect snowflakes drifting down from other thoughts, other actions, swelling the sharp lines, blurring the shapes . . God! My life has been smothered in cotton-wool!

Sorry.

Well, it's not so very interesting. A human pyramid at a military academy near Jena with young Boris at the top flourishing a cutlass in one hand, in the other the regimental mascot (a white and smelly ram that I subsequently dropped while trying to get down, chipping one of its horns). One of my early ancestors, the fierce General Sladerewski, is reputed to have beheaded two thousand Turks single-handed in the course of one afternoon (my father used to tell this story with great pleasure, perhaps to justify on the grounds that this sort of thing was in his blood, his heartless treatment of my mother) though I have certain reservations about the truth of the legend. For one thing, even if the two thousand Turks had obligingly knelt with bowed heads in front of the General it would surely have taken more than one afternoon of sawing and hacking, with pauses for refreshment and re-sharpening of blades. Two thousand heads is a lot of heads. Moreover, Turks aren't the sort of people to take such punishment philosophically. 'Turks', of course, was rather a loose term for those early Eastern European Christians and might well signify some other nationality ('Irishmen' for example).

Anyway, the General was indirectly responsible for me spending those few miserable months at the military academy, having early established a tradition of inhumanity in the family. The reason I mention the human pyramid, however, is that my position at the top of it seemed to me, as a younger man, to have a certain symbolic rightness about it (though the real reason for my elevation was that I happened to be the youngest and lightest cadet in the place). As a matter of fact, in spite of my youth and lightness I do seem to remember having exercised a certain domination over the lower, sweating echelons of bull-necked cadets, possibly by virtue of my searching intellect (though my rather haunting hazel eyes and beautifully modelled features may also have had something to do with it).

Never mind. The fact remains that during those first days in Maidenhair, as I lay close to death in the greenhouse, I recalled with bitter irony that human pyramid of my youth. I was at a very low ebb indeed. Wearing dark glasses and reclining listlessly on that bed of death and childbirth, bathed in glaring light, I used to say to myself: 'You must do something, Boris. *Il faut réagir, mon vieux.* You must make the best of it.'

In those first days, indeed, I often used to indulge fantasies in which I stumbled on a theatre-owner down on his luck who was obliged to sell up and only too delighted to make me a present of his curtains (only a theatre curtain would have been big enough to cover the vast expanse of glass that surrounded me). But I'm nothing if not a realist. Not for Boris the vicarious relief from suffering that others derive from their daydreams.

Perhaps if things had been different I might have done something . . . rigged up a canopy, perhaps, and broken a few judicious windows for ventilation. As it was, before I had time to recover from my initial exhaustion, a succession of sunny days and cold nights (during which I was roasted and frozen by turns) reduced my normally ferrous will to syrup. Add to this the thrice-nightly cataclysm of the express for Maidenhair West or Central (with extra services at week-ends) and one need hardly wonder at the abject state in which Boris found himself. The only practical idea that occurred to me was suggested by Bonzo, who had abandoned the yellowed pile of *Maidenhair Couriers* in the corner and taken up refuge underneath the bed where there was some shade. I dragged the mattress off the bed and joined him. He didn't smell very good but I was too exhausted to club him away again. Besides, he took to licking my brow from time to time and his tongue, though abrasive, was pleasantly cool to the touch.

But the extremes of temperature were not the only torment I had to undergo at this time. There was also the moral torture, the feeling that I was living in a giant test-tube and taking part in some grotesque, cosmic experiment initiated by God. On the other side of the railway line the ground was banked steeply up to a small copse of brambles and dead trees that formed a vantage point over the greenhouse. One night as I was brushing my teeth prior to retiring at the defunct lawn-sprinkler that provided the only running water *chez Boris*, I happened to look up to see a group of young people from the town watching my movements with interest and derision. The fact that I was stark naked and that the station-master's daughter was prominent among the spectators no doubt accounts, by the way, for her subsequent passion for my person. I assume that she must have noted, on this or some other occasion, the impressive extent of my manhood. In any case, as I had already been surprised naked one evening when the Maidenhair West express was arrested by a technical hitch in the garden it was clear that something had to be done. Henceforth, I took to undressing in the wardrobe with the baby-food and red ants (which had continued their troop movements in spite of my attentions).

And then the weather changed abruptly. I regained consciousness one morning after the usual night of delirium to find myself in a different world. Turning over (with some difficulty because Bonzo had fallen asleep with his bulging body thrown protectively over my neck) I looked out from beneath the bed-frame. The bright knives of sunlight that normally quivered on the tiles were no longer there. The greenhouse was filled with greyish light. I could hardly believe my luck. A cloudy day at last.

'Look! We have come through!' I murmured to the still-dormant dog.

It was only then that I realized that there was a high wind blowing. It was the first day of that strange seasonal wind (a local version of the dreaded mistral) that through some freak of geography assaults Maidenhair Bay for long periods every spring. It did not take me very long to realize that far from 'coming through' I had merely exchanged one torment for another. Hitherto I had been embalmed in listlessness and morbid reverie. Until that morning only once had the external world pierced the armour of apathy that plated me . . . a couple of pigeons mating on the glass roof over my head had roused my interest a little, reminding me for some reason of a hairy-chested swimming instructor I once observed while doing some underwater fishing off Nice 'taking advantage of' (as my wife would say) one of his pupils . . . possibly because there was a certain similarity between the movements of the pigeons and the embraces of the two dark, clumsy creatures up there at the shining surface. Be that as it may, my days of apathy were ended, transformed now by the endless shrieking of the wind into a burning anguish that gave me no rest. Day after day, too restless to stay in his whistling greenhouse, Boris was obliged to lurch out into this sinister gale with his lips curled back in anguish over his perfect teeth. Whichever way I turned the wind seemed to be blowing into my face, making every step an effort, draining me of my last cupful of energy. At my side the dog would claw desperately at the ground with his spindly paws to keep himself from sailing away over the rooftops. And so I toiled bitterly up the descending escalator of my life.

At night, with the waves stampeding like cattle into the small fishing-harbour and thudding against the quays, I would pass along the sea-front, catching sight of a haggard, unshaven stranger in the darkened windows of ships' chandlers, deserted cafés and forlorn postcard shops that all displayed the same 'aerial' view of 'Maidenhair Bay, The Harbour' (taken from one of the topmost branches of the highest tree on Seaview Drive) prominently among the sun-tan lotions and souvenirs. Small wonder that I was well and truly softened up for the next major event in my life. And now we come to . . .

My wife. And my wife's family. This consists of her father, an eccentric old chap but not bad at heart who used to be a quantity surveyor (whatever that is) and once spent as a young man a summer holiday on the country estate of a titled gentleman he met at his tennis club. Hence the esteem that the titled Boris, particularly in the early days, used to enjoy vis-à-vis the old gent.

Also an old granny-figure known by everyone, including the inefficient and infantile postman, as Granny Dongeon.

And, of course, the unspeakable Maurice of whom the less said the better. At that time, though not long out of his teens, he was already showing exceptional aptitude as a poseur and layabout. If my memory serves me correctly he was already, at the time of our first encounter, sporting the wispy growth of beard that provides, in my opinion, his only claim to the title of artist. Four long years have neither improved his credentials in this respect nor thickened his beard. The only thing he has achieved, indeed, is the hanging of his sickening canvases on every wall of every room in the house (not excluding the lavatory) except my own. Some months ago he did make an attempt to defile the monastic simplicity of my room with one of his Heads of Christ or Madonnas and Children (the only two subjects he attempts). I just forget which it was. In any case, he was obliged to retrieve it from the flowerbed underneath my window and since then has not repeated the experiment.

Since the early days there have been one or two additions to and subtractions from the ménage. In particular, at the time of which I speak, there was another old granny-figure, known as Granny Marie-Thé(rèse) to distinguish her from the wirier and more durable Granny Dongeon. This Granny Marie-Thé, incidentally, was the agent for my arrival in this house, a crime for which I shall never forgive her. But she has long since 'gone to a better life' (as my wife would say). As, in a way, has a forbidding but devoted old servant-woman whose name escapes me for the moment (but who was, in fact, merely forbidding). This woman was fondly imagined by the Dongeon family to be the local version of the fierce Scottish nanny with a heart of gold. She subsequently startled everyone (except Boris who had been expecting it) by leaving the employ of the Dongeons for that of a *nouveau-riche* manufacturer of a patent glucose drink who had offered her an increase in wages of a few shillings a week.

For a short time after I took up residence here there was also a sweet little French au pair girl with a lisp. She was called Mélanie and was eventually got rid of, poor girl, because she was such an affectionate creature. Another cause of her departure was the fact that she and I used to have long conversations in French which the Dongeon family, although claiming to their friends that thanks to their Huguenot extraction they spoke the language fluently, were unable to understand (exception being made for Granny Marie-Thé who had been brought up on the Continent but suffered a compensating deafness). Poor Mélanie! I'll never forget her charming lisp and the way she used to call me 'Beau Wheeze'. The last I heard of her she was clicking her fingers and swirling her skirts to amuse the tourist-class passengers of some ocean liner in the company of an Australian 'Spanish-dancer' called Derek (though he normally liked to refer to himself as 'Chamaco'), a nice enough boy though with a slight penchant for his own sex.

Well, at first it seemed nothing more than an accident like all the others. One morning I left the greenhouse in my usual state of nervous desperation and battled my way round the side of the widow's house towards the road. The road was deserted except for a very fat lady attempting to cross it in a succession of inefficacious lurches (rather reminiscent of a zeppelin tugging at its mooring ropes) and a youth erratically descending the slight incline on a *vélomoteur* or some other such embryonic motor-cycle. I ducked out of the wind into the shelter of the gatepost to await the collision which I rightly judged to be inevitable. When they had collided I staggered nobly out to the rescue.

The youth, with impressive skill, had managed to maintain himself in the saddle and had stopped his machine a few yards further on, looking back guiltily. After a moment's hesitation he wisely took to his heels, leaving Boris alone to cope with the floundering Granny Marie-Thé. I just forget how I managed to get her to her feet. She was much too heavy to lift and apparently incapable of aiding herself. I vaguely remember standing over her and looking for a part of her anatomy by which I could grab her without immodesty. The next thing I recall she was on her feet and I was struggling to hold her up while that vicious wind tugged at our clothes and whistled through our hair.

For what seemed hours we swayed there drunkenly in the middle of the road, locked together in an infernal embrace (a portent if I could have read the tripes correctly), and there we might have stayed indefinitely had the postman not appeared and helped me to propel her to the nearest chemist's. There the chemist and the postman clucked around her while she collapsed on to a protesting chair with a trickle of blood running down her porridge-grey face. Boris hung around for a while and then faded back to the greenhouse, a very shaken man.

That might have been the end of it but for the interfering postman who must have disclosed my whereabouts to Granny Marie-Thé. In any case, the following day the widow appeared at the greenhouse door with a letter addressed to 'The Gentleman Who Saved My Life', thanking me for my gallantry, calling down vengeance on the young people of today and inviting me to dinner. The widow (who had just spent an absorbing half-hour steaming open the envelope) was in a high state of excitement. It seemed that I had snatched from the jaws of death a member of one of the most respected families in Maidenhair Bay.

Well, now. Normally speaking Count Boris would have received such an invitation from a family of petits bourgeois with a vaguely ironical smile flickering over his lips. As it happened, however, by one of those distressing circumstances that shape our destinies, my stock of baby-food was running low. The thought of a square meal was not altogether unattractive. After some hesitation I penned a brief missive to the effect that I should be delighted to accept their invitation.

There is no doubt but that the Dongeons were very much awed by my presence. I was shown, with the nervous ceremony beneath which the bourgeois so often attempts to disguise the shortcomings of his upbringing, into a sitting-room furnished opulently but with the most disturbing taste . . . full of polished odds and ends of furniture, hideous chinaware, the walls adorned with those awful Japanese paintings of snow-capped mountains, bridges, swans, deformed willows and all the other *japo-niaiseries* that our little yellow friends depict with such tiresome and obsessive regularity.

Here, standing in the middle of the room, I clicked my heels and bowed slightly as I was introduced to each member of the family in turn. Rustling in their Sunday dresses the ladies went to sit down while old Dongeon, Maurice and I remained standing. I was offered an apéritif, sipped it and pronounced it excellent (the bottle had been specially bought for me). Under the influence of the alcohol and a few urbane compliments I paid to their grotesque sitting-room the ladies became flushed and giggly. As for old Dongeon, he had surrendered to the first click of my heels. Only Maurice maintained a shifty and hostile attitude, though even he was unable to disguise the fact that he was deeply impressed.

'Do tell us, Count Slattery,' Granny Marie-Thé bubbled impulsively. 'We're so silly. We don't know whether to call you "Sir" or "Your Honour" or what.'

'Madame,' I replied gravely, 'I should deem it a great honour if both you and your charming family would call me simply "Boris".'

That routed them completely. Right between the eyes. They didn't know whether they were coming or going. I simply couldn't do anything wrong after that. Each rapier-flash of wit was greeted with girlish enthusiasm by the ladies and with throaty chuckles by the men.

There was just one short moment when my hosts found themselves at a loss. Draining my glass with a flourish I turned and hurled it into the fireplace (in which an extinct electric radiator had been fitted). The Dongeons looked at each other in consternation. There was an embarrassed silence. Then old Dongeon gave me a sheepish smile and lobbed his own glass diffidently after mine. He then nudged Maurice who did the same. The ladies remained frozen in their seats (partly from alarm at the aristocratically destructive turn that events were taking, partly because they were uncertain as to what was expected of them) and regarded us with fixed smiles. However, I pretended not to notice their discomfiture and soon restored their spirits with a banal but amusing little story about a Greek shipping magnate who had recommended the waters of Maidenhair Bay to me. The old man seemed to be on the point of pouring another round of drinks in fresh glasses but at a glance from Granny Dongeon (at that period still in the full possession of her faculties) desisted. The French au pair girl, who had been obliged to dress up as a maid under threat of instant re-export back to France (and to eat in the kitchen because the family had a 'visitor'), appeared at the door and got everybody off the hook by announcing with her sweet lisp that dinner was served.

Is there in these fatal situations a moment when all is irrevocably lost, before which we are free, after which we are enslaved to our destiny? As we moved into the dining-room I still had no other ambition in the Dongeon household than the relatively harmless one of eating myself stupid on their free victuals. Not long ago I overheard Maurice reading to Granny Dongeon the newspaper account of a murder. A young man was being questioned by a policeman in a crowded street at lunchtime. He produced a knife and stabbed the policeman. It happened at five minutes to one. At four minutes to one the young man had become a murderer. One forward thrust of his hand had changed his entire life.

I sometimes think that I should never have given up roaming about the . .

Boris, clad in an immaculate white suit and black boots, armed only with a whip and a wooden stool, advanced recklessly on the lion. A breathless hush in the theatre. The beast's whiskered face split open, exposing enormous yellow teeth and a large pink tongue. As Boris hesitated a woman shrieked and fainted. But the lion was merely yawning. He poked the animal with the wooden stool and waited. Nothing happened. He cracked the whip angrily. And yes, at last the lion stirred, opened its mouth again and gave vent to a shattering crash.

Boris sat up and groped for his watch. The room was still too dark for him to be able to distinguish the figures on the dial. The window, however, was glowing with the first grey light of morning. With vague misgivings he scanned the gloom around his bed. The lion . . . But he didn't see it. The lion had crashed once and vanished. The sound was still drifting round the room, or, if the sound itself had been eclipsed, something it had left in its wake, a vague trembling of the shadows, an agitation of the floorboards. Yes, the floorboards . . . He did his best to retreat once more into the shining, rapidly evaporating mirage of his dream, to see again the lion's jaws open and to hear . . . the sound, possibly, of a dropped stool, the lion, perhaps, mute with surprise, an overturned chair or, it might be, of a bedside table unseen in the dark or a row of bottles on a dressing-table or of a heavy door blown to by the wind though there was no wind, at least he could hear none. The lion, anyway, was fiction. That much was clear. The sound was fact.

It had come through the floorboards from the room below, the room in which Inez was sleeping. Listening intently Boris heard one or two other muffled sounds: a scrape, the click of a door-latch, the faintest of creaks and, just as he was expelling the breath he could hold no longer, the clinking of gravel outside his window. He threw back the blankets and sprang across the room. He was just in time to see the golden hair and white-clad figure of Inez gradually extinguished by the grey morning mist that hung thickly over the yard outside. So thickly, in fact, that even the neurotic sycamore was invisible.

Inez had been carrying a towel, coloured a brilliant orange, draped loosely over her shoulder and dancing slightly with her movement. For a few seconds after the girl herself had melted into the mist this orange flame continued to flicker in the greyness. Then it too vanished. What followed was an appalling silence . . . not, of course, that there had been any sound since the faint clink of gravel that had drawn him to the window.

Boris groaned, scratched his head vigorously and ground his teeth.

In his basket Bonzo stirred, made a heroic attempt to open his eyes and see what was going on, but was promptly gassed once more by the fumes of sleep. He exhaled with the dull whistle of a deflating football bladder. Boris removed his eyes from the window and looked sadly at the dreaming dog. What blurred events, he wondered, were taking place behind the animal's sightless eyeballs? The exhilaration of its youth, perhaps, speeding through the perfumed grass in some meadow. More probably Bonzo was engaged in exploring the central concern of his life (his love for his master, Boris). In any case, the main thing was that he was temporarily out of action. For once Boris was free to leave his room without being followed by a piercing whine capable of rousing the entire household.

Boris pulled on his shirt and trousers. Sockless, shod only in tennis-shoes, he slipped downstairs, through the kitchen and out into the brightening pearly mist. As he crossed the scarcely visible tennis-court he supposed, inspired by his tennis-shoes, that he was treading like a cat. Treading, moreover, with great care on the curving trail of dark prints left on the dewy lawn by Inez's splendid feet. Invisible birds had begun to sing in the garden around him, tentatively at first, then with increasing confidence. Their clear notes sped around his ears like silver bullets as he knelt to crawl through the gap in the hedge. Now the sun was beginning to rise.

There was no sign of Inez. The footprints disappeared on the hard surface of rock, and then as he heard the first whisper of the sea he picked them up again, bitten deep into a bank of grey sand. He hesitated. The mist was beginning to clear. He didn't want to be seen. If he . . . One never knew what might happen. If he went any further Inez might see him.

His stomach rumbled deafeningly. He looked around nervously as the sound rolled over the silent beach like a cannonade. He attempted to belch but without success. He shoved his hands deep into his pockets and peered over the ridge of sand in the direction of the still-invisible sea. Though the morning was mild a chilly emptiness seeped through his body and he wanted to urinate. He knelt on the sand to ease the pressure.

As a sliver of sun appeared over the horizon the grey veil around him was tinged with lemon. Delicate footprints in the sand advanced step by step towards the sea, reached a crumpled pile of empty white clothing, touched off the brilliant orange flame of the girl's towel, and continued into the now golden void. Above him for the first time he glimpsed the greyish blue of the morning sky. At last the footprints reached the edge of the sea.

Then he saw Inez. He saw, at least, her shining head surging and gliding over the clouded mirror of the sea. It appeared, so calm was the sea, that her head alone was floating in the air.

'Good God!' he cried.

He could imagine dazzled fish, attracted by her glowing hair, congregating around her as they did around the oil flares in the Gulf of Mexico. He could imagine the satisfaction of the sluggish water caressed by her flowing limbs, the sparkling bubbles released by her sweeping fingers. Perhaps, he thought suddenly, she'll get cramp and I'll have to rescue her.

But Inez showed no sign of getting into difficulties. She was now turning in a gentle arc and forging back towards the shore. Behind her stretched the vast, glinting tapestry of the dawn horizon.

As she swam in to the shore Boris found that a muscle in his right eyelid had begun a vigorous whirring motion like the wings of a bee preparing to take the air. He was obliged to squash the insect with a savage finger and then to pursue another muscle escaping down the side of his left cheek. The whirring started again, then another muscle in his temple. It was as if his whole face had suddenly decided to decompose into its separate parts. A few seconds elapsed while he put down these various insurrections and gained firm control once more.

Inez was now standing naked and motionless at the water's edge, with a serene half-smile on her lips as if at the recollection of some pleasant memory. Her slender right hand was raised to cover her breasts while the other trailed down absently over her sex. Her hair flowed down over her shoulders in golden waves. And there she stood, motionless, beside the sea.

As Boris stared at her over the rim of the sand-dune her expression changed. She scratched her thigh, smoothed back her hair and started off briskly towards the place where she had left her clothes. On her way she passed through a slight hollow in which a bank of coppery ground mist still lingered. The lower part of her body vanished into this shimmering vapour as she waded through it. When she emerged again it appeared that some of the golden mist had become adhesive and was clinging to the cleft of her thighs. Boris groaned. He had never seen a girl of such beauty.

He watched with respectful awe as she stropped her back vigorously with the orange towel, patted her armpits with it, polished up the glowing candy-floss on her mons veneris, dried her toes, and began to put on her clothes. In the meantime the magnificent morning sky had flooded back over his head towards the western horizon. Boris decided it was time to slink away before he was discovered.

We left Boris, that fateful evening of his first visit to this house, teetering on the cliff-edge of disaster. It is now my duty to push him over that cliff before the horrified eyes of the reader and, once pushed, to watch him as he plummets into darkness.

Well now. The French au pair (an expression that, amusingly enough, means 'as an equal'), dressed up in her maid's outfit, had just announced that dinner was served. The two old grannies somehow managed to have themselves ushered out of the room by old Dongeon and Maurice, leaving me to escort Flower who, at the period of which I speak, was then in her prime (or possibly a shade past it). I was later to learn, by the way, that her mother had died (very sensibly in my opinion) on giving birth to Maurice.

In spite of one or two remarks about his wife that Boris may have *laissé échapper* earlier in this work she was by no means unattractive as a young woman. Indeed, clad in a certain diaphanous black nightdress that happened to catch my attention one day while shopping in a Co-operative store, she still on occasions manages to rouse my enthusiasm.

On the heavy side, with dark hair, dark eyes and a dewy upper lip on warm days or when she is excited (on that particular evening her upper lip was perspiring freely as we marched in to dinner) she certainly has a genre, as they say. For some reason she reminded me of an early illustration of Carmen that used to stimulate me as a boy . . . perhaps it was the fact that her breasts rivalled the cheeks of her bottom in weight, size and roundness. When first introduced I had erroneously visualized her name as 'Flour', and murmured an urbane little compliment about 'farinaceous dishes being the most satisfying to the heart of man'. As I recall, the Carmen of the picture, like my wife, was what one might describe as *bien en chair* and was either dancing or about to dance on a table in a tavern surrounded by a ribald crowd of soldiers. While the soldiers flourished overflowing tankards above their heads and guffawed with laughter, Carmen held the foaming hems of her skirts and petticoats in both hands and displayed a segment of fleshy thigh, at the same time flashing fiery glances at young Boris who, for his part, was experiencing for the first time a prickly but agreeable sensation in his private parts.

In the early days of our relationship I once persuaded the reluctant Flower to dress up in some clothes I borrowed from a theatrical costumier. I even got her to stand on the dining-room table. Unfortunately, just as I was beginning to get in the mood old Dongeon (who I thought was taking a nap under a newspaper) came bursting into the room, and I had to pretend that getting a girl to dress up and stand on a table was a traditional European joke we always played on Bastille Day (by a fortunate chance it happened to be the Fourteenth of July). Somewhat alarmed at first old Dongeon laughed dutifully when he heard it was traditional and in his turn ordered the au pair girl up on the table (she seemed unsurprised by the tradition). However, by this time all the pleasure in it for Boris had evaporated. The following year I half-heartedly tried to revive the tradition in private but Flower accused me of being 'perverted'. This is another of her standard accusations, by the way, and has no more truth in it than her 'I picked you out of the gutter'. She doesn't really mean it, of course, and I think she realizes that she herself is naturally inhibited and that her approach to sex (which is roughly the same as her approach to vacuum-cleaning the carpets – a job she also 'performs' once a week) is not quite as red-blooded as perhaps it might be. But don't think I'm criticizing her. I'm not. If she prefers to ration herself as regards the deep, soul-stretching thrusts of Boris's love then that is strictly her business and hers alone. Personally, as concerns that sort of thing, if I'm not getting it, well, it doesn't worry me. I merely sublimate it into my work.

Yes then.
My wife. I did
love her, of course.
And I felt sorry for her
as she must have somehow felt
sorry for me. I remembered her there
in that gloomy seldom-used room that
smelled of furniture polish and fruit,
sitting motionless with downcast eyes
and an expression of vague distress
on her face. I can't remember
that she said anything but
I could see her doing
her best to modi-
fy that ex-
pression
to suit
the
ser-
pen-
tine
pro-
gress
of
our
conversation
while the men
chuckled and the
old ladies giggled
and I could see the
shadows of our flying
words gliding over her
features and vanishing
into a loneliness that
was perfectly unaware of
itself. 'I'm not much good
at talking,' she admitted to

me timidly a day or two later.
Yes, she was so defenceless and
shy, so bewildered by the world
and yet so eager to love someone.
She must have realized too
that I was lonely and
tired and almost
ready to give
up the preten-
ce that I wanted
to go on living.
It was somehow
as if the pities
that each had for
the other had snared
each other like grapp-
ling irons and that no-
thing then could have
dragged us apart. As
if she were saying with-
out having to speak that
there was no point in this
growing old alone in an echoing house with nothing but a
meaningless stream of household
duties to occupy her hungry
hands . . . that she knew
there was nothing
but darkness
and death
beyond
the
absurdly
regimented
walls of her
existence, though
she could never

have actually
had such a
thought . . .
Like
seaweed
that first
evening her lone-
liness choked the
propellers of my anguish
and I was strangely becalmed.
For the first time in my life I
began to feel not happy but calm in
a way . . . I felt that knowing her I
could perhaps grow old without coun-
ting the minutes. And the unbearable
knowledge of how everything must end,
that there was only one way in which
everything could end . . . and all the
other things I'd known, that people
are contemptible, that hope is a
lie, that life is a sordid
charade . . . all these things,
well, I didn't stop be-
lieving them, of
course, but
they became
somehow less
important simply
because there was
someone thinking about
me from time to time . . .
and though, of course, I
wasn't in love with her . . .
Yes, I did love her
then, in a way.
In a way . .

I'm sorry about that . . . Uh! Well, there it is. There it is. If we're to be realistic, of course, we must admit that Flower wasn't strictly speaking quite up to the standard to which I was accustomed. Nevertheless, there was little doubt on the evidence of the first evening that the poor girl represented a likely opportunity for the sex-starved Boris to get himself some exercise.

In the conversation over dinner (the forbidding but devoted servant-woman had made a mediocre stab at roasting a duck for the occasion) I happened to mention that if my London agent didn't do something quickly about selling up my Eastern European estates I'd find myself obliged to return to the Continent although . . . Here I paused to take a casual sip of white mine, savoured it and pronounced it excellent (though it was vile). However, the result was that I completely lost the thread of what I'd been saying the moment before and proceeded to make some interesting and daring remarks about the vintages of certain Californian wines.

'Although?' prompted old Dongeon, exchanging a rapid glance with Granny Marie-Thé. 'You'll find yourself obliged to return to the Continent although . . .?'

'Oh sorry, yes . . . What was I saying? Although I was very much looking forward to lingering for the summer or perhaps longer in this delightful town of yours.' I laughed pleasantly. 'You won't believe this but, do you know, I doubt if I have enough liquid cash at this very moment to buy myself a good steak!'

This sally was greeted with an appreciative roar of laughter and old Dongeon handed me an extremely dry cigar (I discovered a few weeks later while rummaging speculatively in a cupboard that they had been bought at Christmas and saved for an 'occasion').

While we were wandering back into the sitting-room for coffee Granny Marie-Thé drew old Dongeon aside and held a whispered conversation with him. Then they advanced on me, old Dongeon in the lead. At his shoulder Granny Marie-

Thé was nodding and winking encouragingly to me even before old Dongeon had cleared his throat and made his proposition. Would I like to occupy their spare room for the summer or at least for however long it took for my agent to clear up my business affairs? I would be most welcome. It was only a small room, of course, but it had a comfortable bed and there was a nice tree outside the window (he was referring to the neurotic sycamore I mentioned earlier in this narrative). It would be a pleasure to have me.

I'm easily moved by kindness and I'm sure there was a tear glistening in my eye as I thanked old Dongeon for his invitation. And, you know, when I thought how agreeable it would be to move out of my greenhouse and into a place with brick walls, my word, the idea didn't seem altogether unattractive to me. I pondered the matter for a few moments.

'Unfortunately, *mes chers amis*,' I said gravely, 'it is impossible for me to accept.'

'Impossible?'

'I'm afraid so. Because of the dog.'

'Because of the dog?' (For some reason the Dongeon family had taken to baying my own words back at me interrogatively as if we were taking part in some lunatic opera.)

I explained about Bonzo. A stray dog. I could hardly just leave him at the side of the road (I didn't mention that I'd already tried and failed). But, of course, my hosts would laugh at this Anglo-Polish habit of being sorry for animals but there it was . . . I was Anglo-Polish and I couldn't help it (I should mention that I'd decided to simplify my rather complex nationality for the evening) and as for Bonzo, he was so intelligent he could almost talk (I considered this to be a rather favourable view of Bonzo's cerebral processes but a pardonable exaggeration in the circumstances).

'But no!' chorused the Dongeon family. 'You mustn't think that *all* people of Huguenot extraction are so heartless where animals are concerned. Bonzo must come too.'

And so the matter was settled. It was agreed that I should

move in on the following day bringing Bonzo with me.

I later discovered that as soon as I had left the house the au pair girl was summoned and told that henceforth she would be sleeping on a camp-bed in the attic as the spare room was required for a visitor. In point of fact, this made little difference for Mélanie was an absent-minded girl and long after I'd taken up residence kept forgetting which bed she was supposed to be sleeping in.

When I got back to the greenhouse on that memorable evening I discovered that Bonzo had masticated our bedclothes in a fit of pique at being left alone for so long. Oddly enough, even as I slipped wearily between those damp, chewed sheets and thought back on the last few momentous hours, it still didn't occur to me that Fate by now had a firm strangle-hold on Boris. And yet . . . such was the case.

Fate, Boris was thinking bitterly. Fate. Why should I have to spend my unique life in this living graveyard by the sea? There are so many things to experience. People to know. Places to visit. And yet here I am . . . drifting slowly towards another heart attack in Maidenhair. Surely I deserved better.

Outside his window the sycamore was so motionless that it might have been made of steel. But its lack of movement didn't suggest tranquillity. On the contrary, it appeared to be the last moment of control before a violent fit of hysterics. Set me free! it pleaded silently. Destroy me or liberate me but don't let me go on suffering the violence of time and place like this! The torture of ageing and changing without the power to control my own destiny, this is too much to endure!

'I understand you!' shouted Boris suddenly, throwing up the window with a crash. 'I'll help you. Boris won't let you down!'

He was leaning passionately out of the window with his fist raised in the Communist salute when he noticed that old Dongeon and a couple of workmen were looking up at him from the garden with startled faces. No less surprised Boris stared back.

'Is everything all right, Boris?' asked old Dongeon in a worried tone.

'Perfectly,' muttered Boris. He withdrew his head and closed the window.

Later, walking in the sunlit garden, Boris said to Alessandro:

'I wonder if you've ever seen lizards eating moths? I remember watching them in Morocco. They used to come every night and wait on the wall of the terrace where a hanging bulb threw a pool of light . . . They'd wait there perfectly, yes, perfectly motionless in the pool of light, knowing that sooner or later their supper would come whizzing and bouncing and fluttering along towards the light bulb . . . Strange to think that that's my most vivid memory of what life was like in Morocco during the war.' (During *which* war? Alessandro might have been wondering as his eyes, black and shiny as olives, flickered over some roses, over a densely packed brigade of lavender and up the pink, glowing brick walls of Boscobel to the curtained window where Inez was still sleeping though the time was just past eleven.) 'It was perfectly inevitable. Moths are attracted to light. Lizards eat moths. A rapid lunge and then sometimes they'd hesitate, rock-still, with odd ends of dusty wings protruding from their mouths . .'

'Why d'you . . .?' Alessandro was beginning.

'Oh, no reason. I just happened to remember, that's all. The lizards and the moths. Some of them were very beautiful. After a while I used to stop switching on the light at night. I used to sit in the dark thinking of the lizards getting thinner. That was rather depressing too. It was either one or the other; the moths or the lizards. That's the essence of a tragedy, I suppose, if you happen to like them both. Everything, even something banal like switching on the light, everything becomes a responsibility once you start thinking about it. The whole thing became quite intolerable in the end. Out of proportion, as the doctor said. I had to leave the damn place just to get away from them. Not that that changed anything, of course. Mind you, I tried other things before I left – scraps of meat, vegetables, roast chicken – they wouldn't touch it. I even tried them with crumbs of madeira cake that I used to get sent up to me on the motor caravans crossing the Sahara. But you know what I found out?'

'What?'

'Lizards don't like madeira cake,' stated Boris gloomily. 'Actually, I don't blame them all that much . . '

Boris halted and moodily leant his shoulder against the wooden frame of the greenhouse, staring through the dirty glass at a tomato plant bound securely hand and foot to a bamboo stick and drooping one heavy red globe over the rich soil. With the index finger of his undamaged hand he punctured a blister of paint and watched it crumble into a miniature blizzard over the gleaming skin of his crocodile shoe.

Alessandro slid his hands into the pockets of his perfectly creased trousers and then withdrew them once more, watching Boris wordlessly, perhaps trying to visualize a caravan of lorries loaded with madeira cake being dive-bombed by Stukas as they crawled over the desert towards where Boris was waiting for them. Looking casually in the direction of the house where the curtains over the window might have opened a little he said suddenly: 'I must go and do some biology, Boris.'

'All right, old chap,' Boris said mildly. 'Don't let me keep you from your studies.'

He watched Alessandro move off towards the back door with stiff, careful strides, one hand placed rather than resting in the pocket of the grey casual-jacket of continental cut that he was wearing. This time he did look up at the window.

Boris scooped up a handful of gravel and sat down on the rotting wooden bench beside the ornamental pond. While he flicked tiny pebbles on to the lily-pads that armoured the pond's surface he noticed Flower on the far side of the thinned raspberry canes, approaching obliquely with a basket from which protruded a head of lettuce. She was not, as he had thought, coming towards him. She stopped at about where he judged the parsley to be.

'Can I help?' he called.

'No thanks, dear,' she said, and after a moment did come towards him, circling the pond and pulling off the stained gardening gloves she was wearing. 'It's such a lovely day,' she said. 'Almost like summer all over again.'

'Except for the leaves,' Boris said, 'falling all over the place.'

'The bees think so, anyway,' Flower said, watching a bee inspect the water-lilies. 'They're still hard at work.'

Standing behind him now, she rested a loose hand on his shoulder and then, leaning forward to stare at the water-lilies, placed her cheek against his. He shifted his head a fraction and Flower, mistaking his intention, withdrew her cheek and said vaguely: 'Oh well, I suppose I should be doing some hard work myself.' She sighed faintly. 'Would you mind taking the children for a swim? It's such a nice day.'

'Children?'

'Sandro and Inez. I expect they could go by themselves if you're busy, dear. It's just that with someone else's children one doesn't like to . . .'

'They're hardly children,' Boris said. 'I mean, good Lord, they're old enough . . . I wouldn't mind having a swim myself, though,' he added. 'Inez isn't a very early riser, is she?'

'I suppose the poor child was tired. At that age . . .'

'By the way, there's a tomato in the greenhouse you must have missed.'

'No, I saw it but I thought . . .' Flower raised a pink-tipped finger to her forehead, tracing the meandering course of a delicate blue vein. 'I thought I'd leave one for the plant.' She smiled faintly. 'But that's silly. It'll only go rotten. I'll go and pick it now.'

Alessandro had no swimming trunks. Though the boy had spent the entire summer at Maidenhair Bay he had never once been for a swim. Boris was surprised that he had never noticed this odd fact. While Inez was drinking coffee in the dining-room (she had announced with a vaguely sophisticated air that she could never manage to *eat* anything in the morning) Boris looked at Alessandro and wondered why he had never thought of asking the boy to come swimming with him. It seemed rather selfish, especially since Alessandro, staring at Boris with his fiery eyes clouded with amoebas, pseudopods, phagocytes and God knows what else, seemed enthusiastic about the idea. But he had no swimming trunks.

Boris scratched his head. It was a question of borrowing some. Maurice had gone away for the day to bathe elsewhere with one of his fat, sexy girls. Old Dongeon had not bathed since 1929 at

Biarritz. Flower, when consulted in the kitchen, suggested that Alessandro should borrow Boris's trunks since she was sure that Boris didn't particularly want a swim himself. Boris said he did. It was such a fine day (and he was looking forward to displaying his suntanned body). Rummaging in an airing-cupboard Flower unearthed a girl's swimming-costume (it had once been the property of Mélanie, the au pair girl, and thus caused Boris to experience a twinge of nostalgia when he saw it) and said that Alessandro could make do with that by tucking in the top half. Alessandro stared at the faded pink garment with horrified surprise, and when Inez came drifting into the kitchen with an empty coffee-cup, her blonde hair glowing like a multi-watt bulb, he blushed furiously. Boris, although he sympathized, couldn't help smiling.

'You'll look very beautiful, Sandro,' Inez teased him, putting a hand on his shoulder.

Alessandro seized the costume and left the room abruptly. Inez pursed her lips and raised her eyebrows in a look of interrogative concern aimed at Boris, who shrugged his shoulders. Flower went on calmly snipping pale-green feathers from the tops of carrots.

Alessandro was waiting for them in the garden, the pink bathing-costume tightly wrapped in a towel. Bonzo was waiting there too, his pale-blue eyes clouded with vague apprehension that Boris might not be coming. The dog was manifestly relieved to see him follow Inez out into the garden.

Inez was carrying a towel thrown over one soft, woollen shoulder but she appeared to have no bathing-costume. Could it be that she intended to bathe naked *again*? Boris wondered. He led the way recklessly across a flowerbed (ignoring a cloud of blue smoke that was rising from a deck-chair on the tennis-court) towards the gap in the hedge. While Inez was squeezing through it a few golden threads of her hair became entangled in a trailing bramble shoot. She waited, docile and smiling, on her knees for Boris to release her with trembling fingers. Then they continued on their way to the beach, Alessandro trudging behind in moody silence. Puberty, thought Boris, that's what the trouble is. That's what makes him so tense and awkward. And not surprisingly. It comes as something of a shock when an insignificant appendage which for years has seemed to be nothing but a water-tap suddenly wakes up and starts slapping you around.

Boris in the lead, they clambered down the rocky shelf and clinked across the pebbles towards an isolated patch of sand. The tide was halfway out. Not far away an immense, greenish rock lay dozing in the sea, lapped by small waves. The sky was blue and cloudless. The brilliant sunshine warmed his chest as he unfastened the buttons of his shirt. Inez kicked off her sandals, dragged open the zip of her slacks and slipped the palms of her delicate hands inside to ease them off. Alessandro looked darkly away towards a seagull gliding in the distance towards Maidenhair. Boris cleared his throat, afraid that he might groan. Her golden thighs were as soft as mink, as smooth as polythene. She was, however, wearing a bikini. This was a considerable relief.

Alessandro waited until Boris and Inez were splashing about in the water before retiring behind an outcrop of rock to change. With powerful, windmilling strokes Boris flailed his way into the sea for a few yards and then stood up, gasping for breath. Inez was surging with a calm and beatific breast-stroke towards the half-submerged rock and had possibly failed to notice his astonishing burst of speed. Furthermore, he had soaked the bandage protecting his wounded hand. He unwound it and let it drop into the water where it hovered a few inches below the surface, twitching and undulating slightly with the movement of the water like a giant tapeworm. Boris waded a couple of steps away from it but it followed him. Get a grip on yourself, he muttered angrily, grinning up at the blinding sun.

Alessandro had emerged from behind the outcrop and was hobbling towards the sea over the hard pebbles. His long legs were as white as ivory and the swimming-costume bulged incongruously where it was tucked in over his stomach. The expression on his face was set and determined. When the water had reached his waist he relaxed a little. Inez had now climbed out of the water and was sitting on the rock with her legs folded beneath her, perfectly still as if made of bronze. She turned her face towards Alessandro after a moment and smiled at him. Her teeth gleamed like the surf that boiled around the rock. Alessandro began to swim towards her with quick, breathless strokes, his head well clear of the water, mouth tightly closed against the slapping waves. Boris realized that the day had turned cold.

He was shivering uncontrollably. The water was freezing. The skin of his arms coarse with gooseflesh. Bonzo, with small freezing waves kissing his bloated stomach (an expanse of pink skin from which most of the greyish-yellow fur had been worn away), was staring at Boris with painful devotion, trying to nerve himself to swim out from the shore. Boris tried another violent burst of speed which exhausted him without making him feel any warmer. Alessandro was sitting on the rock beside Inez. Boris waded back to the beach with his teeth chattering. Bonzo began to jump up and down with excitement. Boris ignored the animal, dried himself and lay down on his towel. He was still shivering. Inez and Alessandro, sitting together on the rock surrounded by liquid green ice, seemed oblivious of the cold. The sun failed to warm his trembling limbs. He found himself obliged to get dressed. Clad in shirt and trousers he felt warmer. He lay down on the sand again and closed his eyes. I thought I'd leave one for the plant, Flower said.

Boris opened his eyes again. Though the sun was still shining the sky seemed dark and grey. Inez and Alessandro had left the rock and were splashing each other. Lying flat on the sand the waves appeared much bigger. Alessandro was standing with the water up to his chin, smiling tensely.

'Open your legs,' Inez was calling to him, 'and I'll swim between them.'

She ducked underwater and between Boris and the horizon there was nothing but Alessandro's head, looking faintly resigned like the decapitated John the Baptist. After a moment she reappeared, spluttering and laughing, her hair suddenly darker in colour and plastered against her head. She looked younger. A child, in fact, as Flower had said. Boris closed his eyes.

The heart's a muscle. That's all I know about the heart. Things change and die. It's natural, of course. There's a dimension of time as well as of space. By now, if she's still alive, she's a stout old party eating cream cakes under a flowered hat in Copenhagen. Well, there's no use arguing. That's the way it is. And God knows, who would want to spend eternity in Maidenhair? All misery is invented, my dear Boris. Happiness too, I dare say.

He could hear a distant violin now.

It's futile. I'd have committed suicide, of course, if I'd known. It would have been the least I could have done in the circumstances. It's futile to want to throw up a barrier against the tide of night.

And the days dwindle down, murmured Lash, the horse that could almost talk (though, even if he *could* talk, the chances of him saying anything interesting were remote). To a precious few.

The appalling sweetness of the madman's battered violin caused impersonal alkaline tears to ooze from beneath Boris's eyelids. He opened them, was surprised, really, to find himself almost warm, lying on the beach in the sunlight . . . though where he had expected to find himself he had no idea. The insane Robertson had stopped playing (if he ever had been playing).

Beside him a small lump of love with a body the shape and colour of a sandbag was staring at him with devoted blue eyes. Unnerved, Boris threw a stone at the animal but missed. Alessandro and Inez were splashing each other and laughing in the shallow, sand-clouded water. Flower, barefoot, was teetering painfully over the sharp stones carrying a basket.

'It was such a nice day,' she said, 'that I thought we'd have a picnic lunch for a change. Father has gone into Maidenhair to change the library books.'

Boris sighed. The muscles of his cheeks, he discovered, were aching as if he had been smiling continuously at people for the last forty years. Nevertheless, he made a token effort to revive, propped himself up on one elbow. The cold water had exhausted him.

Flower had put down her basket and stretched a rug on the narrow strip of grey sand. She began to unbutton the front of the cotton dress she was wearing. Boris watched without comment as the crack in the dress deepened, split open wide at the top allowing shoulders to bulge forth, revealed the straining cloth of her bikini. The dress slithered reluctantly over her solid hips and collapsed on the sand. Folds of dimpled skin gathered at the back of her thighs.

'You shouldn't wear a bikini. You don't look right.'

Without turning Flower said coolly: 'And how should one look? Like Inez, I suppose.'

They were running, skin gleaming with youth, sun and sea-water. Still laughing and panting, splattering drops of flashing water on the pebbles, they halted near by. Boris stared with dreadful fascination at the faint veins of sky-blue on the inside of Inez's thighs, at the skin as tight as ripe grapes. Alessandro's eyes were shining like stars. He murmured something and wandered off to get dressed. Inez picked up a towel and began to rub the gold back into her wet hair.

'Let's have lunch,' Flower said. 'You must be hungry after your swim.'

While they ate sandwiches the sun slowly dried the girl's hair. The golden glow intensified until Boris was obliged to put on his dark glasses against the glare. Alessandro had relapsed into silence and was moodily throwing stones at a tin can. Flower departed a few paces to bury some scraps in the sand.

'I used to have a lot myself,' Boris said with a cautious smile. 'Really thick, you know. Of course, it's receding a bit now.'

'Oh?' Inez said politely.

'Most girls only like men with lots of it. Funny thing. They say it only comes from having a lot of male hormones . . .' Boris sat up, hugging his knees. 'I suppose it's actually a sign of virility if you look at it that way.'

'Of course,' Inez said.

'I'm going to get Starlight,' Alessandro said suddenly. Getting to his feet he strode off without looking back.

'What's the matter with him?' Flower wanted to know coming back.

'He's gone to get his wretched horse,' Boris said. 'He can't leave the beast alone for five minutes.'

Inez had rolled over to lie on her stomach with her face buried in the crook of her elbow and her ultra-violet eyes (if they were open) warming the coarse grey sand. More probably she was asleep. Boris relaxed, somewhat encouraged by the sensible view the girl had appeared to take concerning the recession of his hair.

'I suppose it's all right to leave Granny Dongeon?' he said at random, thinking that Flower might find it necessary to return to the house. 'She won't set fire to the house or gas herself or something?'

Flower, eyes closed and fingers intertwined over her navel, merely grunted.

'Or fall downstairs and break her hip?' Boris added as an afterthought. But there was no reply. He sighed. A multitude of white rings wandered over the red glow of his closed eyelids. A distant drumming caused him to open them again. He sat up with a laboured contraction of his stomach muscles. Inez was lying with her chin cupped in her hands. Her arms, her legs, the curve of her naked back. Her body was covered with a delicate golden down. It was this ethereal mist of hair on her skin that caught the sun's reflection, made her skin glow as if lit up by some interior essence of beauty.

He yawned. He was old. He had passed his prime. He yawned again, agonizingly. Even in the sun he was cold. The drumming increased in volume. He could almost feel it reverberate in the sand. Or was it merely the wildness of his heart, that mere muscle?

His throat was gripped in the vice of another yawn and his protesting jaws forced open, filling his eyes with tears. A blear of gleaming white and fluid scarlet was flowing over the beach in a rhythmic movement of quite startling beauty. He blinked the tears away, washed the vision into focus.

It was Alessandro, of course, galloping Starlight over the ridge of hard sand. His charcoal head was buried in the long mane that flowed back like white seaweed in the wind. The scarlet cloak had become the wings of a giant bird gliding over the horse's streaming tail as they passed at full gallop. And then they were gone. The undulating muscles of Starlight's flank decreased into a blur of distance. Boris licked his lips.

Inez was sitting up now. She scratched her knee with an expression of wonder on her face.

'It looks easy,' Boris said, grasping a handful of sand and sprinkling it over his toes, 'but actually it isn't. Riding bareback like that takes a lot of practice, I can tell you.'

'I'm sure it does.'

'You have to hand it to him, that boy certainly knows how to ride.'

Alessandro had turned Starlight and was coming back towards them at a gentle canter. His face was transfigured. The moody expression had been replaced by one of grave calm. It was strange. He wasn't smiling. His lips were set. Yet it was somehow as if he were smiling with his body, with the hands which rested lightly on the horse's neck, with the knees clamped high on the horse's shoulder. Inez moved her eyes, blue as the dog's or bluer even, blue as the afternoon sky, from the horse's nodding head to the shining black eyes of the rider gazing down at her.

Boris cleared his throat dubiously.

The scarlet cloak had now exhaled the balloon of sea air and was draped with casual magnificence over Starlight's hindquarters. At Alessandro's throat a silver clasp pulsed in the sunshine like a distant planet. Inez appeared to have been hypnotized by it.

Boris groaned inadvertently. Or . . . perhaps not. Flower was snoring softly with her mouth open, her fingers rising and falling gently on her navel. She was naturally unaware of the danger. Boris himself, though alarmed as usual by the prospect of flashing hooves, willed himself to remain casually sprawled on the rails in front of the oncoming locomotive. He took the precaution, however, of drawing one foot up beneath him and tensing his thigh muscles in case a sudden spring out of danger was called for.

Inez continued to gaze at Alessandro as if in a trance.

'Alessandro!' she murmured at last. 'What a beautiful horse! I can hardly believe it . . .'

Alessandro smiled a trifle self-consciously and patted Starlight's shining brow. Inez had approached (rather rashly, Boris couldn't help thinking) to pat Starlight's head and mane. Starlight seemed to like it, however, and nuzzled the palm of her hand, bringing an indescribably sweet smile to the girl's face. For an instant, hearing a powerful humming sound, Boris thought that Starlight had started to purr like a giant white cat. A plane passed overhead, however.

'Watch this,' Alessandro said and whispered something into one of the big white ears. The horse whirled and reared up on its back legs (accidentally sending a cloud of sand into Boris's face as it did so). It waltzed back a few steps and then sank to the ground. Inez clapped her hands with excitement. Alessandro laughed.

Boris, spitting sand out of his mouth, murmured: 'Careful what you're doing with that animal . . .' but not loud enough for Alessandro to hear.

'Will you teach me to ride, Sandro?'

'Tomorrow. They have another horse we can have as well. I have to take him back now.'

And yet Ylva seemed to love me at the time, reflected Boris, staring at the numbing expanse of grey-green desert before him. She was even desperately in love with me. That surely is something. A period of someone's life entirely gobbled up by thoughts of Boris. That surely is not nothing. Even now, as she slowly inflates herself with cream cakes in Copenhagen a part of her (for nobody can disinherit his past) belongs to me, was formed by knowing and loving me. That surely, though admittedly not a lot, is at least something.

And yet . . . Boris groaned. He knew that he was groaning but lacked the incentive to stop himself. Once somebody has gone they have gone for ever. Memories, even the best documented of them, have no reality. They've even less reality than fantasies of future triumphs. There's something about the past tense that is perfectly crippling. There's no satisfaction at all in trying to furnish a room with memories and paper its walls with past triumphs. One has a roll of wallpaper, of course, but there's no wall to stretch it on. It may resist a passing glance. Otherwise you can poke your finger through it.

Ylva had once loved him (though he had now even begun to wonder about that). He had loved her. This was an indisputable success. All the same, Boris couldn't help feeling the sort of disbelief a butterfly might feel, remembering some triumph from the days when it was still a caterpillar.

All that remained, in fact (now that the girl herself had gone), was the loving, the distant ache, the stone in his kidneys.

He groaned.

Something was tickling the sole of his foot. He worked his toes and ground his teeth. The tickling stopped for a moment, began again. He opened his eyes. Inez was sitting crosslegged beside his feet, delicately working on them with the feather of a seagull. As he sat up she laughed. The clear notes of her laughter drifted slowly up into the blue void like a trail of silver bubbles. Bonzo, sprawled a few yards away, furrowed his brow anxiously. Boris was wondering whether he could trust himself to throw her playfully over his knee and spank her deliciously rounded bottom. But Alessandro was returning. He abandoned the idea with regret. Alessandro had removed his scarlet cloak and was normally dressed once more. The energy generated in Boris by the girl's laughter continued to prowl up and down behind his ribs looking for a way out.

'Let's see who's the strongest, Sandro,' he said suddenly, locking an arm round Alessandro's neck and dragging him backwards on to the sand. Alessandro was taken by surprise and struggled in vain to keep his balance. Boris quickly levered himself on to the boy's chest and pinned his arms back against the sand.

'Had enough?'

Alessandro's head was thumping in wild oscillations against the sand, his face flushed and determined. He began a bucking and rolling movement in an effort to dislodge Boris who found himself having to exert a lot of strength to stay on top.

'Had enough?' he repeated hopefully, breathing hard. Alessandro's only answer was a violent heave that toppled Boris on to his side. For a moment they grappled indecisively and then Alessandro began to get the upper hand. Boris in turn found himself pinned back on the sand. The boy was surprisingly strong.

'Good for you, Sandro!' cried Inez.

'Had enough?' demanded Alessandro of the feebly struggling Boris.

'Yes. Yes,' muttered Boris, trying to sound cheerful.

Alessandro released his grip and clambered off his chest. Boris sat up grinning sheepishly. To make matters worse he noticed that Flower was now awake and had been watching the incident. Inez was sweeping up a little pile of sand with her seagull feather and seemed to be treating the matter as of no importance.

A lethargic sense of humiliation stole over Boris. He was a piece of driftwood, inert, momentarily washed up there on the stony beach waiting (but not even waiting) for the tide *r* return and nurse him slowly and aimlessly out on to that undulating fusion of hydrogen and oxygen (or whatever it was). It was as if, in that brief and senseless struggle with Alessandro, the electric wires that ran between his will and his body had been wrenched out, disconnected. Even had Starlight suddenly reappeared flashing the whirring hatchets of his hooves Boris would have been incapable of movement to save himself. He was helpless.

Flower struggled to her feet and dusted the sand from the fleshy folds of her stomach before collecting up the scattered remains of their picnic and packing them in her basket.

The heart's a muscle.

Flower poked her head into the ring of blue cloth and her bare feet executed a faltering rumba as she struggled to pull it down over her shoulders and hips. When her head reappeared she shook the hair out of her eyes, forced the dress down over her thighs, smoothed it with her palms and buttoned it up. By the time she was ready to return to Boscobel with the basket Boris had been captured by sleep once more. But perhaps it was not quite sleep.

His eyes were closed, certainly. And he had no power to

dissolve the picture that hung in his mind, wavering slightly like the banner portrait of some totalitarian statesman in a procession. Flower's face, immense, wavering, now advancing and now receding but always with the same expression of sadness, the last expression that had appeared on her face before he had at last managed to close his eyes, to wind down the creaking, protesting metal hoods of his eyelids to shield himself.

Loneliness. Intimacy and understanding. A guest who stays for a while and while he stays . . . Love between lonely people. That love, Boris thought painfully, awake again but with the steel shutters still wound down over his eyes in case Flower should still be there, that love is slow and faltering like a tortoise, scarcely alive. Yes, he thought, it's like a tortoise that moves so slowly and so seldom that one would hardly know it's alive and when it dies, if it dies, one could hardly tell exactly, so tentative was its life, the precise hour of its death. Because, after all, there's no change in the shell of the tortoise though the creature inside it may well have been dead for months or years. Because, after all, one doesn't stop being lonely just because . . .

With an immense effort he contracted the muscles of his eyelids and exposed his eyes to the aching white world again. He was alone. Flower had gone. Inez was bathing. Alessandro, surprisingly enough, was not bathing but kicking with his heel at a large rock embedded in the shingle. Having dislodged it from its nest in the sand he heaved it up and staggered with it towards the sea, hurling it forward a few feet into an inch of water. As he did so a grey tongue of water sprang back and embraced the faultlessly creased right leg of his trousers. Retreating, Alessandro stared with irritation at the sea, then at his sodden trouser leg. Boris sat up wearily. The boy was slaving away furiously to rearrange a minute particle of the planet. All to no purpose.

'What are you doing?'

Alessandro lurched another rock towards the sea with a grimace of effort and then wiped his hands on his trousers, turning to Boris with a rather sullen expression.

'Oh, nothing,' Alessandro said removing his eyes from Boris's face to the ragged frontier of an expiring wave.

They stood in silence for a moment.

'Wasn't that a shout?' asked Boris. 'Wait a minute . . . Where's Inez?'

Then they heard it again, quite distinctly.

Alessandro was already sprinting towards the half-submerged rock with Boris galloping after him and muttering: 'Wait now. Easy does it. Watch your step there . . .'

Alessandro splashed straight through a shallow rock-pool, poised himself momentarily, leapt for the shoulder of rock and somehow managed to cling to it before scrambling up the slope and out of sight on the other side. Boris, who was apprehensive about the effect of salt-water on his crocodile shoes, hastened obliquely after him, jumping from stone to stone. As he slid down at last on the far side he saw Alessandro scanning the empty surface feverishly. Then it came, a curious echoing cry from somewhere beneath them. Boris unlaced his shoes and dragged them off, then began to struggle with the zip of his trousers.

Alessandro turned towards him for an instant, his face as pale as paper. He gave Boris a last, tragic look and plunged forward into the sea fully clothed.

'Hey now, wait a minute,' cried Boris at the foaming surface. He wrestled with the zip of his trousers but it had stuck. He teetered forward and almost overbalanced as he watched for Alessandro's surfacing head.

And then a head appeared. But it was Inez, not Alessandro. And she was smiling.

'Coming in for a swim?' she asked. 'I've found a cave with an echo.'

Before Boris could reply Alessandro's spluttering face appeared. He took a quick look at the serene smile on Inez's face, then struggled back to pull himself dripping on to the rock.

'But you've got all your clothes on, Sandro. Did you fall in?'

'Not exactly,' Boris said. 'You see, we heard you call and

thought . . .' His voice trailed off. He began to lace his shoes again. Alessandro said nothing.

'I think we'd better go home now,' Boris added without looking at Inez. 'You can follow when you're ready.'

He put an arm round Alessandro's shoulder and helped him towards the beach, splashing this time through the rock-pool without heeding the damage to his shoes.

'Why did you do it, Sandro?' he demanded fiercely. 'You could have drowned yourself, man. You might catch pneumonia! Why did you do it?'

Alessandro muttered something inaudibly.

'Damn that stupid girl!' cried Boris, tightening his grip on the boy's arm. 'The little fool. You could have been drowned!'

Boris was now shivering uncomfortably. They had reached the beach and were walking up the slope of shingle towards Boscobel. His head drooping he watched his sodden crocodile shoes playing erratic leap-frog one over the other in a wavering line. As each foot landed with a squelch the eyes through which the laces were threaded filled with tiny salt tears. And so on. He was feeling sick. The arm over Alessandro's shoulder, intended originally to support the boy back to the house, had now become the only thing which was keeping his wavering legs from folding beneath him. By the time they reached the house Alessandro had been obliged to grasp the wrist trailing around his neck and take care of the navigation. By some miracle they managed to slip into the house without being seen by Flower or old Dongeon (who had returned from the library and was engrossed in the memoirs of some minor aristocrat). Protesting feebly Boris allowed himself to be lowered on to the sofa in his room.

Boris lay on the sofa reading a glossy prospectus for Inez's finishing school which he had found lying on the hall table (together with an invitation to an exhibition of paintings by Maurice Dongeon and other young Maidenhairian artists).

'Our girls are given a thorough training to fit them to take their place in society as wives and mothers of the generations to come.' Jesus, thought Boris, the place is a stud farm. Whose idea was it to send the poor girl there?

There was a photograph of a cluster of girls, bored and promiscuous, gathered around a tweedy woman arranging flowers in a vase. This is all nonsense, they seemed to be saying. Show us the men . . . show us something in trousers. 'Deportment'. Ha! muttered Boris. Girls walking with glasses of water balanced on their foreheads, icily demure. Sitting in a long row with legs crossed like chorus girls. Enough of this nonsense, the girls were saying. Where are the blokes?

'Healthy exercise in the open air forms an integral part of our curriculum.'

There was, however, a picture of the school swimming-pool which was fairly rewarding. Over the page, 'Citizenship' and, more promising, 'Hygiene'.

'The School Matron, Miss A. R. Salmon, will give a course of instruction entitled "The Temple of the Body" to those girls whose parents request it.'

'Fees'. He threw the prospectus on to the floor and allowed

himself to doze off. He could hardly see this school doing much for Inez. She was already perfect. She was, in fact, finished.

The best that can be said for my marriage is that it was a gallant attempt. Did I ever really think that it would succeed? Perhaps I did – though I'm inclined to doubt it. But I was desperate, you see. I'd carried the luggage of my life just as far as I possibly could. My hands were blistered, my shoulders were aching. It just so happened that I reached the limit of my endurance in Maidenhair Bay, that it was here in this awful town that the leaden luggage of years finally forced open my numb fingers. After all, it could have happened somewhere more dashing, more suited to the kind of chap I was. And Flower, of course, sitting abandoned in that dreary house and perspiring an almost visible loneliness through her sensitive skin, oozing it from her armpits, her forehead gleaming with it, her upper lip beaded with it . . . Flower herself played a positive (or at least a negative) part in it. She sure did.

To put it another way. My life at that time was like the vast, empty page of a sketch-book. When one day I found that a little sketch of intimacy had been scrawled on it . . . well, could I be blamed for seizing the opportunity, for grabbing the fixative and spraying it on like a madman before anyone had a chance to erase it?

But even as I sprayed on the fixative, standing there at the altar clad in a morning suit last worn by old Dongeon at a memorial service for Lord Kitchener in whatever year it was (I'm too upset to document myself with the exact date), with the two grannies weeping so copiously behind me that it was a wonder that the aisle wasn't awash with their tears, weeping for their plump little Flower who was about to be skewered and barbecued over the flames of Boris's love, well, even then I must have known that it was nothing but a brave attempt. And it wasn't that the love vanished . . . that would have been easy to understand. It remained there between us, perfectly visible, but we were unable to use it. It was rather like a wedding present of expensive china destined to be kept in a

44

glass cabinet because it is too good to be used (indeed we had such a present donated by some insane relation of Flower's). We could see it. We knew it was there. But it was no earthly use to us . . . Well, perhaps that's not quite true. Knowing it was there may have given us a little confidence. There's nothing one can actually *do* with love once it has passed a certain stage. It's not an ointment one can rub on one's soul or a hallucinatory drug with which one can effect a semi-permanent transfiguration of one's life. One has to go on living in the ordinary way with only an occasional look at the china in the glass cabinet.

There was no honeymoon. The day after the wedding when old Dongeon took me aside and whipped out his wallet I thought for a moment that there might be. But he merely wanted to show me a letter from one of the Prime Minister's secretaries thanking him for his letter showing interest in something or other. When, on the following day at dinner, I was indulging in a little philological speculation and happened to let drop the interesting fact that the French used an identical expression (*lune de miel*) to designate a post-marital holiday he announced quite abruptly that we would do better to save our money (by which I suppose he meant his own). In any event, a fortnight in Jersey or three weeks in Dun Laoghaire would hardly have lifted our love to a satisfactory pitch of exaltation . . . so I let the matter drop.

I felt, not cheated exactly, but just slightly disillusioned. Oh, very slightly. Hardly at all. I felt as one feels when leaving a cinema where one has just seen a film in colour . . . that slight shock one experiences on finding that the streets and faces outside are just a little greyer than they should be. There's nobody to blame for it, of course. A small, transparent bubble of desperation forms in your brain as you look around and become accustomed to the greyness once more. Then the bubble floats away into nothingness and you forget about it as you walk away over the solid pavement. It probably bursts. In any case, you are too busy to think of it again.

In particular, I remember being slightly disappointed at the dutiful way in which Flower continued to perform the household chores after our marriage as if nothing had happened.

'Leave all that and come and have a siesta,' I told her sexily one afternoon while she was ironing shirts in the kitchen. No, sorry. What am I talking about . . . she *did* come that time. It was the following week that she said she had too much to do.

I was like a man who sees a breeze playing over a field of corn and is so inspired by its beauty that he buys it. Well, I bought the field but I couldn't buy the breeze. The breeze dropped.

Well, you say, that's all very well but there was no need to marry the girl. It's agreed that the luggage of your life had become too heavy, certainly, but all you needed was a rest. Why didn't you just drop your suitcases for a while and refresh yourself before staggering on a bit further? But it wasn't as easy as that. Once my suitcases had been opened and the contents spilled out by the rummaging fingers of the customs man I found (and it came as a shock) that I couldn't cram them all back. The contents of my jumbled soul had mysteriously swollen. They had spilled all over Maidenhair. It was out of the question to move on somewhere else and leave them.

Love is a moment here and there. It's moving and spontaneous. To bloom satisfactorily it needs intense concentration and great spiritual resources from both parties involved. It rapidly became apparent that in our union only one of us was tipping the scales at the right spiritual weight.

Oh, I'm not blaming Flower. She did her best. But the fact remains that she forestalled all my initiatives. On one occasion, for example, I came upon her in the tranquil twilight of the sitting-room engaged in tacking up the hem of a skirt. She looked so radiantly peaceful that I simply couldn't prevent myself from seizing her hungrily and pouring passionate kisses on her lips. How was I to know in that gloomy sitting-room that her mouth would be full of pins?

On another occasion she became upset because I put my hand up her skirt while she was washing the dishes at the kitchen sink. Unfortunately, we were surprised by the pseudo-fierce Scottish nanny who pursed her lips and reported the matter in vague but indignant terms to old Dongeon, giving him, incidentally, a totally wrong impression of what we had been doing by adding some completely irrelevant details (viz. the fact that I happened to be holding a cheese-grater in my other hand).

On yet another occasion (once again in the kitchen because that was apparently where she had decided to spend the greater part of her married life) Flower became quite hysterical because I deftly removed the brassiere casing from one of the ponderous breasts and wanted to see what it looked like when dusted with flour and lowered into a frying-pan (I was merely curious).

In this and similar ways Flower would put up barriers against the childish and charming lover's games that are the very life-blood of a vibrant romance. No sooner would I suggest some amusing little game than she would cram on the brakes and, skidding, clench her teeth desperately in case she should skid too far and crash into a spontaneous expression of passion. Unfortunately, it never came to that. Her brakes always had the better of me. And so she remained there, manacled to the kitchen sink by her inhibitions.

And yet, though I am not to blame, neither is Flower. I must have known what to expect the night before the wedding as I lay ruminating on my bed in that seedy private hotel behind the station (old Dongeon had slipped me a pound and suggested that for appearances' sake I should move out of Boscobel for the night). As I lay for the last time on a hard, chaste bachelor bed (that lowered itself from a large cupboard and hit the floor with a crash that shook the building), as I lay looking at the peeling wallpaper of that sordid room (the hotel was largely patronized, as far as I could see, by portly, retired cat-burglars and polite, dusky gentlemen cooking curries over small blue flames) I must have had some thought of flight and decided against it. Perhaps it's significant that old Dongeon was careful to give me no more than a pound. Not that it mattered very much, as it later transpired, because we'd only been married three or four weeks before Flower had her miscarriage . . . and as far as that goes, yes, I did love her then and I genuinely wanted her to be happy. I was very sorry indeed about that but it wasn't my fault and it's not right that I should be blamed for it. Not, of course, that anyone did blame me . . .

I loved her above all because she was so shy and lonely – she had given up hope that anyone would ever want her. She had accustomed herself to the idea and she wasn't even hoping any longer. She was lovable and pitiful at the same time. She was deeply pitiful. She reminded me of an anxious, lost dog on a crowded street at rush hour, dashing back and forth looking for its master vanished somewhere in the flood of hurrying strangers.

And not only had she given up hope. She had put up defences against it. And when I came along, well, even now my eyes fill with tears when I think of how pitifully lost she was then. She was terrified of hope. She had barricaded herself into her loneliness and bolted the door. She had pushed tables and chairs and bookcases against it. And when I came along and smashed in the door with one blow of my fist she was at one and the same time deeply frightened and supremely thankful . . .

In those first wonderful days she was completely disorientated. She would be laughing one moment and crying the next. She would suddenly burst into tears over nothing – over a romantic film on television, over a bird with a broken wing, over the baby hedgehog that used to come and lap up milk from a saucer at the back door . . . She would be watching the hedgehog as it stood there up to its diminutive ankles in milk and then she would suddenly burst into tears . . . but smiling at the same time.

She said: 'Anything at all will make me cry these days.'

'Wildflower saved from the mud by twelve men.'

An old gentleman was sitting on a wooden bench outside Maidenhair Central reading an evening newspaper under a street light. Boris, about to embark on the zebra crossing, found himself lingering in an attempt to focus on the words that sagged between twin congregations of hairy knuckles. It seemed incredible that there should have been twelve men. A symbolic number, in fact. A new band of apostles devoted to the rescue of one tiny spark of beauty from the chaos of the planet. It was most peculiar. A renegade jury, perhaps, tired of trying to disentangle right from wrong in a degenerate legal system.

Feigning indifference Boris circled the wooden bench for another glimpse of the newspaper. Ah, but it was all a mistake. He should have known. It was a 'wildfowler' that the twelve men had rescued. Sinking slowly. Up to his waist in mud. It had taken two hours' hard work to save him. It had taken, moreover, five firemen, four policemen, a chemist, a male model, and a man who described himself as a company director to drag the foundering wildfowler from the mud. I had plenty of cartridges, he had declared truculently. I wasn't scared. I could have gone on shooting them all night until someone came. My body, thought Boris, was returning to the earth from whence it came. Rather rapidly. But the soul was returning to God who gave it – or something like that. Something of the sort.

Boris realized that he was being surveyed with suspicion by

the old gentleman. He nodded and smiled politely. The old gentleman put down his newspaper and offered to call the police. Boris hastily moved on his way to the Railway Hotel Annexe where Maurice and his friends were holding their exhibition.

A smell of ashes and garbage hung in Empire Lane. Overflowing bins stood on the pavement outside shop windows. Crossing the street with his shoes ringing on cobbles as large as loaves he came upon a draper's warehouse and, a little further on, the faintly illuminated window of a butcher's shop, quite empty, a gleaming marble slab on which were arranged spotless white dishes, quite empty, that is, except for a few decorative sprigs of parsley and, in one of the dishes curled up and fast asleep, a tortoise-shell cat. Feeling that his new jeans (specially bought for the occasion) were uncomfortably tight about the crutch, Boris stopped outside a grimy building of ecclesiastical appearance, worked his fingers into his pockets and tried to free himself.

'. . . a great multitude of impotent folk, of blind, halt, withered, waiting for the moving of the water . . .'

The open door of the Railway Hotel Annexe was throwing a yellow oblong of light on to the cobbles not more than thirty yards away. From this door smoke was billowing in thin yellow clouds, only to be sliced off neatly by the slanting wedge of darkness.

'. . . For an angel went down at a certain season into the pool, and troubled the water: whosoever then first after the troubling of the water stepped in was made whole of whatever disease he had . . .'

Inez stood submissively beside Flower and rested an idle hand on a table of empty upturned glasses. Politely smiling she listened to a bald man who had just said something with great emphasis and with his cigarette was now chalking up visible support for it on the empty air between them. Nearer at hand Maurice was listening gravely to an elderly lady in a black evening dress, one ear lowered attentively to her working lips but with his eyes restlessly patrolling the room. In due course they came to rest on a pair of new jeans and a polo-necked sweater inside which Boris was standing. The trace of a frown added one or two small wrinkles to Maurice's smooth forehead. Then he came over.

'Boris, my dear fellow, how wonderful to see you here!' he declared with feeling. 'I was afraid you wouldn't be able to come. My dear chap, let me get you a drink. How nice! How very nice of you to come!'

Let's not get carried away, thought Boris, resisting the idea that Maurice was actually glad to see him.

'Wine cup. Quite potent.'

'Thanks.'

'I must act the host, I'm afraid, but you have a look round and tell me what you think of the paintings later. As you know, I value your opinion.'

Maurice retreated, leaving Boris to approach an orange canvas with vertical scarlet stripes. Nobody paid any attention to him. He drained his glass, looked round furtively for a refill, after a moment moved on to some pink and green concentric circles, more painful to the eye but nearer to the drink. They're ignoring me on purpose, he told himself. They're cutting me dead! He drew himself up to his full height and stared straight ahead with stony pride.

'Boris! Wherever did you get those awful trousers?' demanded Flower in an urgent, appalled whisper, encroaching mercifully on his view of the green and pink concentric circles.

'These are my blue jeans,' Boris replied with dignity. 'Nobody ever dresses up for a vernissage.'

'But everyone's in suits,' Flower said, taking an agonized look around the room. 'Why have you always got to . . .?' Her voice trailed away beneath the buzz of conversation.

'It's not my fault if people in Maidenhair don't know the form.'

'But you're much too old to wear jeans. And anyway they're much too tight. Oh, Boris, *really*! And why aren't you at work?'

'Oh, drop it, will you?' said Boris brusquely. He turned away and took three brisk strides to a brimming jug of wine cup beside which, like an angel in a dress of sparkling white lambswool, Inez happened to be standing.

She smiled at him as he approached and Alessandro, who had been standing near by, moved away a couple of paces and pretended to inspect a Head of Christ. Boris helped himself to a drink and choked on a floating lemon pip. Inez patted him on the back in a friendly way and as she did so the tears that Boris was coughing out of his eyes magnified the tiny pearls dancing on her breasts.

Purple in the face he at last managed to say:

'Well, what d'you think . . . of all this?'

'I quite like some of them,' Inez admitted cautiously, 'but then I don't really know much about it.'

'One or two of them,' Boris agreed, 'have a sort of superficial energy. But one could hardly say they were the real thing.'

He looked around for a painting he could be safely enthusiastic about. Behind the table stood a canvas of pure, silvery-white with a black metal frame. At one side the canvas was warped away a few inches but otherwise the silvery whiteness was unblemished.

'That one has a certain purity of expression,' he said.

Inez looked faintly surprised but said nothing.

At this point Maurice approached saying loudly: 'Inez darling, come and meet Henry, one of our best young painters.'

Deserted, Boris took Alessandro's arm in a friendly grip and, using him as a protection against conversation, drank his way twice round the paintings. Maurice and another man, he noticed uneasily, had dragged a projector mounted on a trolley into the middle of the room and were on their knees looking for a wall plug. Boris watched with mounting dismay as the projector was angled to point at the silvery-white painting he had recommended to Inez for its purity of expression. The lights were dimmed. Deeply mortified he seized a jug of wine cup and retired into the darkest shadows. The only place he could find to sit down was a wooden bench over which overcoats had been thrown. He burrowed into them until he had uncovered a patch of wood and sat down on it feeling, with the overcoats piled up around him, like some giant, wingless bird forced to remain in its nest by the evolutionary incompetence of its ancestors. From this nest he stared stonily down the room at a succession of coloured slides representing the work of Maidenhair's leading primitive painter (and sporting-goods dealer) who painted for preference on rock and stone in order to recapture (said Maurice who was commentating) the spontaneous creative inspiration of the first known human artists, the cave men. These paintings were called 'muralisms'.

I mustn't groan, he thought. If I groan it will be terrible. His mind wandered. He remembered a time when Maurice burned to become a great painter and not just a social success. At that time he had seen himself as working towards something, alone, detached from praise or blame. Even today there were times when a shadow crossed his face as if he were still haunted by some inner misgiving. Poor Maurice. He had a dream. His dream collapsed. Well, thought Boris sombrely, that happens to everyone sooner or later.

Inez and Alessandro had removed the empty glasses from a table against the right-hand wall and were sitting on it, Inez absently swinging bare legs no longer golden but dyed a bluish-red along the gleaming curve of the tibia by the reflection from the screen (on which was projected a muralism 'of great depth and savagery', said Maurice). Her kneecaps were glowing like sapphires. As Boris drank and watched her and drank again she turned her head from the screen and peered into the darkness behind the projector as if looking for someone.

'And all my fortunes at thy foot I'll lay . . .' she appeared to be thinking as her eyes travelled over the peopled gloom. But now she was examining the next muralism on the screen (in whose childlike symmetry Maurice, clearing his throat and ignoring a muffled whisper from the sporting-goods dealer to the effect that it was upside-down, was able to detect intimations of man's eternal quest for an answer, a higher truth). This muralism had instantly transformed the delicate diamonds of her kneecaps into flashing rubies. And then again she had turned her head and was looking for somebody in the darkness.

'. . . and follow thee my lord throughout the world.'

As Boris watched in drunken surprise she placed a hand on Alessandro's shoulder for support and slipped neatly off the table, extinguishing her legs. A moment later she was standing in front of him, advancing a groping hand and trying to see his face in the darker shadow that she herself was now casting over him. The blind hand she was extending struck him on the forehead, inflicting four tiny skin-wounds from her surprisingly sharp fingernails.

'Is that you, Boris?'

'Yes,' replied Boris huskily, grasping her arm and steering her against the bench on which he was sitting.

'I'm just looking for a handkerchief I left in my coat pocket . . . I don't suppose I'll ever find it in all this pile.'

' . . . As indeed we see', Maurice was saying, 'illustrated in the purified lust latent in the violently coupling blues and yellows of this next picture . . .'

'If it's a handkerchief you want . . .' Boris said to the sighing, burrowing girl beside him. But she paid no attention, merely went on turning up confused overcoats, pulling out strangled raincoats, dragging out scarves twisted like entrails and throwing them all back again until she had made a glorious spaghetti of cloth beside him in the darkness.

'Ah!' she murmured at last, wrenching a coat of soft red leather from the combined embraces of a fur wrap and an oily trench-coat. 'Here we are.'

She laid the coat flat on top of the pile and worked her hand into one of the pockets, drawing out first a paperbacked novel, then a handkerchief. With it she touched the end of her perfect little nose, sniffed, smiled briskly. Then tucked it into her sleeve. This done she bulldozed the coats ruthlessly on to the floor and sat down beside Boris.

'What's the book?' Boris wanted to know.

'It's in Swedish.' She fumbled in the darkness for a moment and then handed it to him. By angling its shiny cover against the light from the screen he was able to read: *Lady Chatterleys Älskare.*

'It's quite amusing,' Inez said in a sophisticated tone. 'Have you read it?'

'Some time ago,' Boris managed to say. A pure young girl like her! Encouraged by the darkness he had been on the point of quoting to her a poem he had composed during an idle moment of inspiration at The Groaning Board (of which the first line was: '*Il neige sur Inez comme il neige dans mon coer*'). He now thought better of it.

The exhibition had meanwhile come to an end. Everyone was milling around in the semi-darkness. Boris stood up to loosen the tourniquet grip of his jeans and as he did so bumped into a man standing in front of him. The man turned and gripped Boris by the shoulder, trying to see into his face. At that moment the lights were turned on at last and Boris found with a shock of recognition that the gaunt, grey face a few inches from his own was that of the ragged street-musician he had seen on the afternoon he had taken Alessandro to the cinema. Boris turned his head quickly but the man had recognized him.

'So we meet again,' the man said and his thin lips slid back from his discoloured teeth. It was a moment before Boris realized that the man was grinning at him. 'I know you. I've seen you before. I knew I knew you.'

Boris nodded with a fixed smile, looking for a way of escape. What was his name? He tried to remember. Yes. Robertson. He was no longer dressed in rags but in a clean white overall.

'But wait. Where are you going?' Robertson demanded without slackening his grip. 'You're an artist, I can see that. Truth. Beauty. You know what I'm talking about, don't you?'

Boris murmured something indistinct, trying desperately to catch Maurice's eye before the man became violent. Any moment now he would pick up a scarf from the floor and strangle him.

'Well, do you or don't you? Know what I'm talking about? Are you stupid or something? No sorry, I didn't mean that. Pleased to meet you. My name's Quinn. My father's name was Quinn too. What's that book? Let me see, damn you!' He snatched the book from Boris's fingers. Boris could see the muscles working in Robertson's jaw. The man was becoming dangerously excited.

'Lawrence,' Robertson said painfully. 'I knew him well. We were friends.' He was scratching his chest violently through the starched cloth of his overall with long, beautiful fingers. A trickle of saliva had escaped from the corner of his mouth.

'You're my friend,' he said to Boris in a voice choked with emotion. 'You know that, of course. It's as plain as a pikestaff. Lawrence, that was a man for you.'

'What was he like?' Boris asked soothingly.

'He was sunburned,' Robertson said in a voice full of despair. 'I met him in Paris. We were friends. He was leading the Arabs in some sexual revolution. There was a man for you!' Robertson's voice had dropped to a faint whisper, his eyes had filled with tears. 'We were friends,' he repeated in a broken voice. The wild light in his eyes had died. Boris half expected him to collapse at his feet. Instead he turned to Boris and said in a perfectly normal voice: 'I'm supposed to be washing glasses in the kitchen.' He nodded to Inez and made for the door, forging without concern through groups of talking people and scattering them in his path.

'What a peculiar man!' Inez said happily. 'I thought he was rather sweet.'

Boris wiped the sleeve of his sweater against his drenched forehead. The party was thinning out quickly. Someone had switched on a record-player that was making the floorboards quiver with a dull, insistent beat.

'Must you go so soon,' Maurice kept on saying in a ringing, jovial tone. 'There's still plenty to drink, you know. The party's only just beginning.'

Turning abruptly Boris saw that Alessandro was staring at him with a pained expression, but as soon as he caught the boy's eye he turned away. Boris closed his eyes for a moment and as the room vanished a surprising warmth stole through his body. Tightly gripping the jug and glass he made his way to the far end of the room and sat down on a wooden chair. Inez drifted after him but he was no longer thinking of her. He was isolated. He was looking down on the room from above. He saw the criss-cross threads of emotion with which, like mountaineers, the people in the room were trying to rope themselves together for the slow, dangerous ascent of their lives. The descent, I mean, from youth and strength. The descent from dreams. I know all about that, he thought, pulling with unsteady fingers at a loose thread of black cotton that hung irritatingly from the crutch of his blue jeans.

'Damn the thing,' he burst out in sudden fury as it slipped once more through his perspiring fingers. It was such a small thing. A small, black thread. He shuddered violently.

'Can I help?' Inez asked. She knelt down between his legs, gripped the offending thread between her sharp white teeth and with one sudden twist of her golden head bit it off. She stood up again smiling, removed the severed thread from her lips, held it up like a prize between finger and thumb and then let it drift to the floor. Boris gazed up at her in confusion.

'Come on. Let's dance,' Inez said moving backwards and already shaking to the rhythm of the music. She held out a small, imperious hand to the bewildered Boris. He got to his feet with an effort. Flower, he noticed, was already dancing in a stately fashion with the primitive, sporting-goods dealer.

Once on his feet Boris realized that he was immensely tall. A commanding figure. Warm oil was injected into the dry sockets of his limbs so that they flowed effortlessly with the corrugated current of music. I am young and everything is possible!

'Yo ho!' he cried, 'let's twist again . . . the way we did last summer . . .'

Then he fell gracefully. He landed with a crash in the record-player, quenched the music.

No, he wasn't hurt, he assured the faces that gathered round. In fact, he was feeling remarkably fit. At worst a shade winded. Nothing to worry about. As a matter of fact he hadn't felt in such splendid form for many a long day. He was glad to see, he went on, that no serious damage had been caused to the record-player. That would have been rather irritating. As it was, he had merely jolted the pick-up arm. So, he added, sketching the movement and rapping his knuckles unexpectedly against the leg of a chair. So. Thus was the arm of the beast jolted. But no permanent damage had been inflicted. This he could demonstrate by replacing the needle on the record. Well, anyway, the beast must somehow have unplugged itself in the general commotion but that, in any case, was the theory of the thing. That was the course of action to be pursued in the circumstances. But, he continued with sudden inspiration, why shouldn't we simply leave all this and all go for a midnight swim . . . the last bathe of the summer, the water still being perfectly warm, pack into cars and go screeching down to the beach on two wheels, sounding horns so that Maidenhair would for once know that someone was alive on the planet . . . and who knew? It might even start a chain reaction so that the impotent, withered folk of Maidenhair would throw off their miserable fetters and themselves crowd singing and laughing into the water so recently troubled by an angel. Why not? he cried. A midnight bathe was the thing. The only fitting end to the evening.

'He's going to be sick,' someone said.

'I most certainly am not going to be anything of the sort,' Boris replied with dignity.

'Come on, old chap,' Maurice said with a hint of authority lurking somewhere beneath the geniality of his tone. 'I'll give you a hand up.'

'I don't need . . .' Boris was beginning, but before he could finish or even recollect what it was that he had been about to say Maurice had seized him by one wrist and one armpit and hauled him to his feet. And once on his feet he found that he was moving again or, more exactly, being moved, carried almost, with vaguely bicycling legs, towards the door. It was a shade humiliating, he couldn't help thinking.

'You shouldn't have encouraged him, you know,' he could hear Flower saying to someone, perhaps to Inez, with unusual asperity. But by the time he had decided that it was certainly to Inez that his wife had been speaking, and decided furthermore that she should be rebuked for speaking in such a way to their guest, he was already out in the cool night air defying gravity with twenty-foot strides over the pavement in the direction of Maurice's Volkswagen. At the same time weakly resisting and feebly trying to help he found himself lowered into the front seat and strapped there with a safety belt. Conscious of the indignity he tried to unfasten the belt but he was unable to find the catch. After a moment he gave up the effort.

Maurice disappeared for a moment, shouted a few cheery remarks, waved and returned. He started the car and they drove off swiftly.

'The others are getting a lift,' he said. Boris, raising a hooked and heavy bunch of fingers to scratch his ear which was itching numbly, surprised himself by scratching his nose instead.

'Quite potent, eh? You can't say I didn't warn you, old chap, now can you?'

And yet, thought Boris, though I may have looked drunk, I wasn't. I remained perfectly aware of what was going on in spite of the momentary defection of my body. My mind was there watching the whole unfortunate episode, watching with a wry and experienced smile. It was as if my mind had remained there heroically on the bridge, standing stiffly to attention and saluting while my body slid under the waves.

A strong wind had arisen. A flurry of dead leaves against the windscreen. A glistening sheet of newspaper whirled up, hung for a moment turned inside out with the savage twist of a flamenco dancer and vanished again from the moving headlights.

'Still, I think it was a success. I think people enjoyed themselves once the ice was broken . . .'

'Oh, Maurice, you're so good to me,' Boris cried out suddenly, almost in tears. 'I keep making an idiot of myself . . . I don't know why . . . I don't know but somehow I just can't stop myself doing these stupid things. And you're so good to me. You put up with it all. How can I ever thank you!'

A flamenco dancer, Boris remembered with a pang of such acute agony that for a moment he wondered if he hadn't actually done himself some real physical injury, strapped into his seat though he was. A flamenco dancer in some remote village where their prehistoric bus had broken down. Was it Ylva he had been with or some other girl? The pain was intolerable. He must have been mad to drink so much. The silent streets, heavy with heat, so drastically black and white with shadow and sunlight. The man dancing with the savagely graceful revolutions of a newspaper caught by the wind. While outside on the glowing terrace the sun slowly bronzed their twin skins with eternal (or possibly temporary, depending on who the girl had been), with, say, eternal love. Yes. Or rather the sun had *branded* their skins. That was more like it.

'My dear old Boris, you don't have to thank me. I'm delighted to help you out and I'm sure you'd do as much for me if I was . . . you know, a bit inclined to go off the rails from time to time . . . Things haven't been easy for you, I realize that. Especially after that first spot of bother . . .'

A spot of bother, thought Boris wearily. That was certainly one way of describing the tiny, monkey-like creature with its hands over its face as if, somehow or other, it already knew what the world was like. Yes, that was certainly one way of describing that almost living creature with its face buried in its hands. A spot of bother. Maurice was so insensitive that he was almost perverted. But no, he corrected himself wretchedly, he was only being tactful. Only trying to help.

'There's nothing but love,' he said unhappily, 'and if that doesn't work . . .'

'There,' Maurice said, slowing the car for the turn off the coast road towards Boscobel. 'There I must beg to differ. As you well know, Boris, I have a great respect for your intelligence but I must take you up on that point. Love is valuable certainly. A valuable part of our experience. But it is far, very far, from being all there is. And that's where you make your big mistake, Boris . . .' He turned the car neatly into the drive, nursed it round the side of the house to the back door, stopped, pulled up the hand-brake, switched off the engine and, draping his right forearm over the steering-wheel, turned to Boris who, for his part, pinned securely back against his seat by the safety belt, abruptly felt as a circus girl in spangled tights might feel while awaiting with tightly bound limbs the arrival of an amateur knife-thrower . . .

'You give love too much importance in life. Love is like an hors d'oeuvre. You insist on treating it as if it were a main dish.'

'Well, there's nothing else for it. The children will have to sleep in the same room.'

It was Flower who had just mildly lobbed this conversational grenade into the middle of the breakfast table. Fingering one of the lateral shafts of her reading-glasses she returned her attention to the crumpled, crinkly letter she was reading.

'I'm sure they won't mind,' she added absently, 'but we couldn't very well ask Uncle Cecil to stay at a hotel.'

The grenade had exploded. The shock it caused, however, was curiously limited. Maurice and old Dongeon continued browsing peacefully on their toast and marmalade. Inez allowed only the most polite and enigmatic of smiles to appear on her face. As for Granny Dongeon, she was naturally well enough sandbagged with years to withstand any present disasters. She was shockproof.

In fact, the only apparent damage was to be seen in the two shattered faces of Boris and Alessandro. They looked at each other, horrified.

'But for Heaven's sake!' protested Boris. 'You can't do *that . . .*'

'Why ever not?' asked Flower innocently. 'You don't mind, do you, dear?' she added, turning to Inez.

'No, of course not,' replied Inez calmly.

Boris and Alessandro exchanged another horrified glance. The boy had turned as pale as the tablecloth.

'Here's one for you, Granny,' declared Maurice in ringing tones. '"Shropshire bride disembowelled by gypsy".'

'Serves him right,' muttered Granny Dongeon, 'the little fool.'

'"Police have been using dogs and helicopters to help them with their inquiries".'

'They didn't have helicopters when you were a girl, did they Granny?'

'People knew how to behave when I was a girl,' Granny Dongeon said crossly. 'Disembowelling a gypsy. I never heard of such a thing.'

'No, Granny,' Maurice explained patiently. 'It was the other way round. He did it to her.'

The woman must be mad, Boris thought gloomily. Throwing him into bed at his age with a girl who reads *Lady Chatterley's Lover* . . . whose sharp white teeth, he remembered, had come within an ace of clipping off his own private parts . . . God only knows what tricks she'll get up to in bed. Swedish exercises and all that sort of thing. He pictured Inez throwing icy water over herself and obliging Alessandro to beat her with saplings. The poor devil.

Inez had also received a letter. A letter with a Swedish stamp which she had propped unopened against the silver toast-rack in front of her. When she had finished her coffee and run the tip of her tiny pink tongue over her lips she picked it up, opened it and began to read. Boris watched her resentfully. No expression appeared on her face. She's a heartless creature all right, Boris thought.

'Was that from your parents, dear?' inquired Flower.

'It's about their divorce,' Inez replied blankly. To Boris's surprise her face had assumed an expression of unspeakable distress; her blue eyes had become shiny with tears.

'Never mind,' Flower said sympathetically. 'Things will turn out all right, you'll see.'

Though Inez had once more gained control of herself and though her face had resumed its habitual expression of angelic calm it was clear to Boris that she was suffering deeply. It was clearly indicated in the frequent blinking of her eyes and in the self-conscious way she was playing with her pearl necklace.

Flower must be mad, he thought with indignation. Hardly has the girl received a letter stuffed with sordid details about her parents, crammed with co-respondents, full of the facts of life and other things of which she is likely to have only the vaguest notion . . . hardly has she received this letter when Flower insists on tucking her into bed with a young man. It's well known that men reach their sexual peak during adolescence.

Somewhat uneasily he eyed his wife as she cleared the breakfast table, shook the tablecloth out of the window for a twittering squadron of sparrows and carried a tray of crockery into the kitchen. There he followed her.

'Now look here, Flower . . .' he said with authority.

'Oh, what is it *now*?' she demanded with unexpected vehemence, turning her still-bespectacled face towards him.

'What are you wearing glasses for?' he asked, disconcerted.

'What d'you think?'

'Now wait a *minute* . . . now just wait a *min*ute!'

'Oh, I'm sorry,' Flower said, reverting to a calmer tone, 'but you do get on my nerves the way you keep following me around and . . .'

'Oh, I do?' Boris said with icy dignity. 'I see.'

'Now don't get upset.'

'I'm not upset. I merely asked you what you were wearing glasses for. It seems a perfectly civil question to me.'

Flower sighed. 'I'm wearing them so that I can see things properly.'

'Well, they don't improve you.'

'I can't help *that*, Boris,' Flower said wearily. 'I'm tired of walking around in a haze. That may be all right for you but I'm tired of it. I want to see things properly.'

'What d'you mean "that may be all right for me"? My sight is perfect.'

'I'm sure it is, dear. But I'm going to wear glasses and that's the end of it. If you don't think they suit me then it's just too bad.'

'I never said you shouldn't wear them. I merely said . . .

Flower had turned back to the sink and was stacking the dishes noisily, perhaps to conceal tears. Boris hesitated for a moment, trying to make the bread-knife stick into the pale-blue Formica table. Without success. Typical. There was no point in bringing up the subject of Inez and Alessandro. He would just have to let events take their course.

Vanquished he retreated to his room and tried to review the situation. What could he do to prevent this dangerous, animal contiguity in the room below? He could offer his own room to Alessandro or Inez. But then where would *he* go? A tent in the garden, perhaps? But the nights were already too cold for that. If the girl had come in August . . . but she hadn't. Besides, Flower would certainly misinterpret in some sinister fashion his desire to separate 'the children'. She might conclude, for example, that he was jealous.

A nebulous desire for escape poured slowly out of a dark hole in his mind and advanced to the forefront of his consciousness. Escape from what? he was beginning to wonder. From somebody or something? It's nonsense. Forget it, he tried to tell himself, even as the idea wrapped itself around him in a flash of writhing coils. Escape! he gasped as the sudden, appalling pressure of the idea seized him and began to squeeze the resistance out of him as if he had been a tube of toothpaste. To travel again! To wander from place to place as free as the wind! It was as if . . . yes, as if he could actually feel his will, his self-control, being squeezed out of his mouth, his ears, his bulging eyes. Then, with the last cubic inch of breath that remained in his lungs before his ribs caved in, he managed to reassert himself. The serpent gave one final, spasmodic constriction before loosening its grasp and slithering in limp coils about his ankles. He stepped out of it and moved towards the window still grinding his teeth. But, of course, he reassured himself nervously, there was no need to make any drastic decisions. If he wanted to leave, all he had to do was to pack his bag and go. Nobody could stop him if that was what he decided to do.

It seemed at first glance as if the sycamore were relaxed and motionless, bathing itself, merely, in the ten o'clock sunlight. Looking at it carefully, however, Boris could see that the outline of the smaller twigs was blurred with an obviously pathological trembling, a trembling reminiscent of Parkinson's disease . . . as if the knotted, distended muscles that showed beneath the tree's bark had been so long tensed against the invisible menace of time and place that the wiring of nerves running along the branches had at last deteriorated, burnt out by the incessant warning of danger.

'Yes, yes. I'll help you if I can,' Boris muttered. 'But can't you see that I have troubles of my own.'

Sickened, he turned away.

Besides, he added, it's none of my business what happens to them. All I can do is observe with the proper scientific detachment.

Later in the morning, when he judged that there was nobody about, he slipped down to the garage and returned with a crowbar, a screwdriver and an electric drill (the property of Maurice) with which he promptly fused the lights. He hurriedly restored it to the garage and selected instead the largest gimlet he could find, pausing only long enough at the kitchen door to accuse Flower of having blown the fuse with her electric mixer before running upstairs once more and setting to work on the floorboards. They turned out to be tougher than he had expected, but after two hours' hard work he had created a hole the size of a small apple and enough wood shavings to fill a mattress.

Uncle Cecil (the younger brother of old Dongeon) arrived in a taxi in the early afternoon. There was a deafening and incoherent conversation with Granny Dongeon outside Boris's bedroom window about her steel shares, arthritis and the punitive nature of death duties. Then he went for a brief tour of the garden with old Dongeon in the course of which he delivered a violent attack on chemical fertilizers that started a dog barking at the farm down the road. Old Dongeon, impeded equally by his pipe and by his brother's eloquence, did his best to supply a contrapuntal harangue against coalmen who were, he said, these days as temperamental as ballerinas. A little education is a dangerous thing, he added darkly. On returning to the house Uncle Cecil produced a pack of cards, spread them out on the dining-room table and proceeded to play patience while old Dongeon covered his head with a newspaper and slept.

During this time Boris had made a lightning visit to the room below in order to remove the splinters of wood that had fallen from the pine ceiling. He was in little danger of being apprehended. Alessandro, after mooning about the house with his hands in his pockets for a while, had disappeared to ride Starlight. As for Inez, she had accepted an invitation from Maurice to pose for him in his room, obliging Boris to undertake an afternoon's vigil at his window in case Maurice's white plastic venetian blinds should suddenly blink out a message of disaster. But nothing happened. The afternoon wore slowly on. There was no motion from the venetian blinds. At half past three, when the sun had passed the corner of the house, the slats suddenly coagulated and the window was thrown open by a hairy forearm. Then silence and stillness returned.

Boris yawned agonizingly. He was tired. He was desperately tired. He sat watching the light as it slowly changed on the sycamore tree. There was no longer any point in sitting by the window but he could think of nothing else to do. And watching the interminable but remorseless decline of the light outside his window had drained him of all emotion. The whole thing was utterly futile. Nothing that Inez or Maurice or Alessandro could do would make the lightest difference to his own life. They were simply undergoing the same sort of evolution as the light on the sycamore tree, as the tree itself. Human beings all over the world at that moment were moving with steady inevitability through a cycle of impersonal change. Like vegetables, he thought with leaden distress. Just like vegetables. And of all their steaming passions no trace would remain. At most a trace of fall-out might collect, like strontium ninety in the milk, from the biggest explosions of passion . . . but bearing no relation to it, merely the debris, a sonnet here and there in a school textbook, or a scrawl of ink on yellowing paper bound with a dusty red ribbon, or the petal of a rose pressed to death between the pages of a volume of obsolete poetry. So why even pretend that it was important? It would be more courageous, more reasonable to look at the thing with the cold eye of logic, to admit to oneself that a hypothetical fertilization of Inez by Alessandro or by Maurice or by the postman was different in manner but similar in effect to the fertilization of one sycamore tree by another.

'So I'm not interested,' he said aloud to the gaunt, ephemeral face reflected in the window.

He got to his feet, stretched, yawned again and massaged his scalp vigorously. For some reason his damaged hand was throbbing once more. He must have re-opened the wound when he had dived into the record-player at Maurice's vernissage. It was painful, really very painful. But it made no difference. He was only a vegetable. He lowered himself on to the creaking sofa and stared unblinkingly at the ceiling which was of varnished pine planks running with distressing symmetry from one wall to the other. Without removing his eyes from the ceiling he groped around on the floor for Alessandro's biology book which he had borrowed on an impulse the day before

'All atoms, ions, and molecules, regardless of whether they are in a gas, a liquid, or a solid, vibrate constantly in random back-and-forth movements.'

Yes, he thought, well there you have it. Random back-and-forth movements. The situation in a word. Random.

Atoms, ions, molecules, pseudopods and phagocytes, amoebae and frogs and rabbits' digestive tracts, protozoa and dorsal columns and old Dongeon, Inez and Flower and Uncle Cecil and Maurice and himself and Granny Dongeon, they were all constantly vibrating in random back-and-forth movements. That was all there was to be said about them. And where did Love finish? Love finished nowhere.

It was already dark by the time Boris arrived at the hospital. He was met by a young and sympathetic house surgeon who told him that Dr Cohen was asleep and there was a chance that he might not wake up again before he died. It was unlikely that he would last out the night but one could never tell.

'I don't know whether you want to sit with him or not,' he added. 'I don't think there's much chance of him recognizing you if he does wake up.'

'Yes, I'd like to stay with him.'

The house surgeon nodded. 'All right then. I'll take you along to him. He seems to have been rather an extraordinary man. I'm sorry I didn't know him better.'

Boris was escorted along several corridors to a private ward. The room was in semi-darkness and as the house surgeon had said the doctor was asleep. His head looked very small and frail on the starched white pillow. But he appeared peaceful enough. Some of the grim lines that were normally gathered around the corners of his mouth had now relaxed, lending his features a curiously boyish expression. Boris remembered thinking before that the doctor must have been very handsome as a young man. He stood beside the bed staring down numbly for a long time at the old man's face. Then a nurse brought up a chair for him and he sat down. Time passed.

His mind wandered aimlessly about the shadows in the dimly

lit room. The nurse came and went a few times, moving silently about the room. It was very quiet and peaceful. From time to time there would be a muffled sound from some other part of the hospital, voices in the corridor or the closing of a door. The doctor was dying but Boris could find no sense of tragedy or grief in his death. The old man had merely reached the end of a natural cycle of birth, growth, maturity and death. Perhaps if the doctor had been in pain it might have been different. As it was, he could feel nothing except a distant sense of loss. A feeling that something that had been there up till now would be there no longer.

It must have been about an hour later that Boris realized that the old man was awake and smiling at him.

'What on earth are you doing here, Boris?' he asked. His voice was weak but otherwise normal.

'Your housekeeper told me you'd been taken to hospital. I came to see how you were.'

'She never could mind her own business.' He was silent for a moment. 'Well, Boris, I'm dying at last I'm happy to say.'

'Nonsense, Doctor,' protested Boris anxiously. 'You'll be out of here in no time . . .'

'I sincerely hope not,' the doctor replied feebly. 'And I forbid you to turn my departure into a sentimental tragedy, Boris. I know you too well. I had to send my housekeeper away because she insisted on weeping all over me in the most disgusting manner . . .'

Boris could think of no reply but smiled faintly. Also smiling the doctor closed his eyes and dropped off to sleep again. Time passed. The old man's breathing was inaudible. Boris wondered whether he might not have died and waited impatiently for the nurse to reappear. But a few minutes later the doctor opened his eyes again and said:

'I've nothing against dying, you know, except that it's so infernally boring . . .'

About an hour later again he murmured so softly that Boris could hardly hear what he was saying:

'It's true that there's something disgusting about living and dying in a place like this . . . I should really have stayed in Africa . . .'

The doctor died shortly before eleven o'clock without waking up again. Boris said goodbye to the house surgeon and left the hospital immediately. Outside the streets were dark and empty. He wandered about disconsolately for a while thinking about nothing in particular and then walked home towards Boscobel. He was very tired.

By the time he arrived back the house was in darkness except for one feebly glowing light on the stairs (an economy insisted upon by old Dongeon who kept a nervously tight rein on the potentially ruinous, wildly plunging horses supplied by the local Electricity Board). Everybody had long since retired to bed. He made his way mechanically through the sleeping house, reached the top of the stairs, switched off the only remaining electric light and felt his way with experienced fingertips towards the door of his room, flinching from habit away from Maurice's sharp and painful, metal incursion into the twentieth century.

In his room he was on the point of climbing into bed when he remembered the passionate hole he had dug in the floor earlier in the day. Moving aside the sofa he rolled back the rug and explored with his fingers in the darkness until he had found the hole. He applied his eye to it but could see nothing. Total blackness. A cold draught chilled his eyeball. The 'children' must have decided to keep their window open.

He was about to retire when he heard a violent creaking of springs accompanied by a sigh. He held his breath while his single eye strained into the blackness. Silence. Another sigh. Still holding his breath Boris stretched out on the cold floor and applied his ear to the draught of air, wiping away the tear that had formed in his eye.

'Sandro, are you awake?'

I remember the light on the pavements, the light on the shutters, the way the light was heaped like treasure on the floor by the window, the mildness of dawn and the slowly, the quickly rising heat that dampened our bodies and oiled our skins. And I remember thinking, in a rare moment of lucidity, pausing beside the open mouth of some stone lion and thinking that though everything around me was peaceful I was nevertheless in the midst of some wild and dangerous experience.

'I know you're awake. I can tell by your breathing.'

Staring then with a friendly smile between the granite jaws of the lion at the peaceful stalactites of sunlight that hung from the arched stone palate and bent forwards over the granite tongue and thinking how peaceful the lion and how well-ordered its universe I had at the same time a weird awareness of its insecurity. It was as if I were in an ancient car, as if I had my foot nailed to the accelerator in a speeded-up silent comedy, flashing in and out of the traffic, escaping death by inches, overturning apple-carts, careering on to pavements and driving through shop-windows, uprooting painters' ladders and scattering chickens in farmyards, zooming beneath the wheels of express trains and swerving through a long series of ever more miraculous escapes as I stood there safely with my feet firmly planted on the hard pavement and one careless hand resting on the grey stone curls of the lion's mane.

'Sandro, I'm thirsty. Get me a drink of water'

I remember the clock and its ticking, the heat of the afternoon and the dead echo of the ticking clock as the sounds trickled away like silver ballbearings on to the carpet of silence. I remember too the dampness of skin, the light in your eye, the light in my own. The slow movements of love that twisted the sheets, the fluid of love, the touch of your breasts and the scent of the fluid. The cheese and the milk and the sound of the traffic and wild strawberries and cream and time without end that inevitably ended.

'I'll switch on the light.'

The turn of a tap, the flowing of water, the fluid of love that drained away so slowly from that inevitably blocked hotel basin, so slowly that with a little help from the imagination one might have thought that it was perfectly blocked, not moving at all, not leaking away.

'Why not? You've got your pyjamas on.'

The imagination was there, no shortage of that. But imagination can only change things for a little while, preserve the illusion for the briefest of whiles, as a bull in a bull-ring with its wonderful muscles distracts the attention from the drops of its valuable blood on the sand, the drops becoming a scarlet river until, in the end, it wearily kneels and vomits the illusion by the bucketful on to the yellow-grey sand.

'You're terribly shy of girls, Sandro. Are you afraid I might attack you?'

Reality wins in the end. No doubt about that. And if it is destined to win in the end why bother to keep it at bay even for a while? Though sometimes, admittedly, it keeps itself at bay with a long winning streak of miracles . . . the dream swerves in and out of the traffic, ploughs through shop-windows and scatters the chickens, misses by inches the locomotive of reality and so on and so on until in the end it exhausts the patience of the law of averages. The law of averages picks it up by the ears and, smiling at its impertinence, breaks its neck, throws it into its hunting bag with all the other dead, furry, white dreams.

'Thank you, Sandro darling,' Inez was saying in an affected tone. 'You're such an absolute angel. I don't know what I'd do without you. I might even consent to marry you if you behave yourself . . .'

Boris, an ageing lover of beauty, was lying on the hard wooden floor, aware of his uncomfortably cooling limbs and the depth of his weariness, while a few hundred miles away the object of his love was slowly inflating herself with cream cakes under a flowered hat.

'Damn! I've spilled it over my nightdress . . . I'd take it off and sleep naked if you weren't such a baby, Alessandro. It'll be your fault if I catch pneumonia and die . . .'

Silence.

Ashen-faced, Boris got to his feet stiffly and crawled into his makeshift bed. He immediately fell into a deep sleep that crawled over his consciousness like a freezing acid. A sleep that was at the same time both dreamless and desperate.

'Boris must come too,' Inez said.

'But there are only two horses.'

'That doesn't matter. He can watch.' She took Boris's hand, smiling at him. 'I wouldn't feel safe if he wasn't there too,' she added silkily.

Alessandro shrugged and moved away a few paces to crush with his heel a mildewed tennis-ball that had lain abandoned on the lawn for weeks, months perhaps. What's she up to now? Boris wondered although, under the pressure of her soft, warm hand, he had already capitulated. What's her game?

'Now look here,' he said. 'I don't want to spoil your fun and what's more I wouldn't dream of trying to ride one of your horses. My riding days are over.' He somehow managed to resist an anecdote that at this moment came galloping into his mind (fully stocked with colourful detail about 'mettlesome steeds') to illustrate his former prowess on horseback. 'However,' he continued in response to the mute appeal from two large blue eyes and the increased pressure of a small brown hand, 'nowever, if you don't find my company a bit of a bore I'd be delighted to come along and watch you . . . but only if you're both sure you want me.'

'Of course, Boris darling . . . of course we want you,' cried Inez. 'It'll be so much more amusing . . . When I fall off and kill myself you'll be able to carry my lifeless body back to the house while Alessandro chants a funeral dirge or something.

It'll be wonderful fun.' She clapped her hands in excitement.

'I can't sing,' murmured Alessandro sombrely.

'All right then,' Inez said, ignoring him, 'that's settled. You go and get the horses, Sandro, and we'll meet you on the beach.'

Alessandro released the trapped ball from beneath his heel and watched it hop away a few inches. He said nothing.

'Well, go on, Sandro. What are you waiting for?' demanded Inez impatiently.

Alessandro aimed a sharp kick at the tennis-ball which sailed away to hit the trunk of a eucalyptus tree and glance off into a flowerbed. He shrugged again and walked off without a word in the direction of the farm.

'He's such a funny boy,' Inez said, taking Boris's arm and steering him towards the beach. 'He's so moody and young.'

'He's older than you are, isn't he?'

'Well, you know what I mean. He's so shy and awkward. Still,' she added in a rather superior tone, 'I expect it's just a phase he's going through.'

It had rained hard during the night and the ground over which they were walking was sodden with moisture. Crawling through the gap in the hedge Boris disturbed a bramble shoot and showered himself with fat raindrops. In the absence of sunshine the beach had taken on an appearance of desolation. Here and there pools of rainwater had collected on the rocks, reflecting the sky in sheets of dark shining metal. The sea itself looked as black as indian ink. Overhead the woolly black sky loomed towards them like a vast, knuckled fist, threatening to unloose another deluge of rain into the warm atmosphere.

'Unless he hurries you'll both be drenched before you even have time to get near a horse,' Boris said.

'We wasted so much time talking.'

Inez picked up a stone and hurled it into the sea with a hopelessly ineffectual, girlish throw which by its very awkwardness appeared to Boris to be appallingly attractive.

'I don't know why he was so sullen about you coming with us.'

'I suppose he wanted your company to himself.'

'I suppose so,' agreed Inez casually. 'I think he's probably got rather a crush on me.'

'What makes you think that?' inquired Boris uneasily.

'Oh, one can tell.'

Somewhere in the distance there was the dull rumble of thunder. A gust of warm air sliding in off the black waves struck them unexpectedly, stirring a heavy lock of Inez's hair and pinning it against her mouth and nose. Above them a magpie swooped out in a flash of black and white, hovered for a moment like a paper dart at the height of its trajectory, and then dived erratically inland on the freshening breeze.

'There he is!' shouted Inez and raised one slender arm to wave. Her movement lifted for a moment the hem of her sweater, revealing the swelling of her hips and a glimmer of smooth skin. Boris groaned.

Alessandro, mounted on Starlight and leading a superb black horse, was picking his way carefully towards them between two outcrops of rock. Alessandro's free hand secured his scarlet cloak to prevent it billowing out on the breeze in front of the black horse's eyes. He was talking to it soothingly as they approached.

Inez ran to meet Alessandro and the two horses leaving Boris to make a more circumspect approach.

'He's a lovely horse, Sandro!' cried Inez enthusiastically. 'What's his name?'

'Treacle.'

Inez raised a hand to pat the horse's shining coal-black brow but Treacle shifted his head nervously and danced back a couple of steps.

'Careful,' Alessandro said. 'He's rather uneasy today. The man at the stable says it may be because of the thunder.'

'He's magnificent. Boris, just look at him.'

Boris looked. In spite of the gleaming ebony flanks and the superbly sculpted neck and head there was something about the horse he didn't like. It had a wild look in its eye that reminded him strangely of Robertson. Beside this animal the normally terrifying Starlight looked like a spaniel.

Without letting go of Treacle's reins Alessandro slid to the ground and began to caress the horse's shining black head with an expert hand.

'It might be better if I ride him and you ride Starlight,' he told Inez.

'Nonsense. He'll behave himself.' Inez laid her fair cheek against the horse's neck. 'Won't you, Treacle?'

'I'm not sure . . . The trouble is we'd have to take the saddle off him and put it on Starlight.'

'I insist on riding Treacle,' declared Inez imperiously. 'He'll be perfectly safe. Besides, he's so nice and black. He'll make a beautiful contrast to my white sweater and trousers. Don't you think he's beautiful, Boris?'

'He certainly seems all right,' said Boris cautiously.

'Oh why didn't I remember to bring my camera? I simply *must* have a picture of me on Treacle. Boris, would you be a perfect angel and run back to the house for it? You'll find it on the dressing-table in my room.'

'Oh,' exclaimed Boris dubiously. 'D'you really think you need . . .?'

'*Please*, Boris.' Inez turned two large blue eyes pleadingly towards him, melting his resistance. While she was swinging herself gingerly into the saddle Boris retreated in the direction of the house. As he crossed the back yard random drops of rain were beginning to scatter dark circles on the concrete.

There was no sign of the camera on the dressing-table. With vague stimulation he rummaged in Inez's suitcase among some snowy underwear and unearthed a framed photograph of a moronic-looking blond boy clad only in bulging swimming-trunks. There was also a leather-bound diary which to his disappointment contained entries only in Swedish. Some letters also in Swedish. But there was no camera.

'Tell the children to come in or they'll get drenched,' Flower told him as he passed through the kitchen on his way out.

But the rain had slackened once more. He stood on the back doorstep and held his palm out to the sky. It was strange. The huge black cloud approaching from the sea had virtually swallowed the whole horizon. Only to the west was there a thin, diminishing patch of lighter grey. A whirlwind of dust and dry leaves sprang up in one corner of the yard, slid towards him in an erratic curve and then waltzed away again. Above him the sky was so dense and black that it seemed a miracle that it was not raining. But while he stood there a large drop of rain exploded in his open palm. He turned up the collar of his jacket and sprinted towards the beach.

Stumbling over the rocks and shingle the first thing he saw was Starlight standing calmly at the water's edge. All around him the rain was kicking up the sand like bullets. Then he saw Alessandro some seventy yards away with his hands on his hips and his scarlet cloak drifting inland on the wind. Beyond him Inez was riding Treacle along the beach.

'Sandro!' shouted Boris. 'Tell her to come back. There's going to be a storm.'

Alessandro waved and then shouted something to Inez who turned the horse's head back towards them. It was raining hard now but she was smiling serenely and leaning forward to pat the horse's neck. As she approached, Boris could see that the rain was streaming down her face, her hair clinging limply round her neck.

'We'd better take shelter,' he told her, 'until the storm's over. I'm afraid I couldn't find the camera.'

Alessandro said: 'I'll get Starlight. I won't be a moment.' He started to run back towards where Starlight was standing in the surf, motionless, looking out to sea in a bored fashion.

'You'd better get off that animal,' Boris told Inez but she didn't seem to hear. He pulled out a handkerchief and tried to dry his hair with it. There was no shelter on the beach. His jacket and trousers were already soaked. Inez had coaxed her horse a few yards down the beach towards Starlight.

Abruptly a vivid flash of lightning exploded. Boris sneezed at the same instant that the dark beach lit up, with the result that for a moment he considered the streak of light before his eyes to have been generated by the sneeze. But then he heard Treacle whinny, saw the black horse rear up violently, silhouetted against a second flash. Instantly it veered in a wild gallop through the surf, leaving a trail of glistening foam, and then back to the beach. Before Boris had time to move it was in full gallop away from Maidenhair towards the fringe of dark pines that came down almost to the water's edge. With Inez clinging on to its back the animal sped like a black arrow along the crescent of sand and vanished into the pine forest.

'Alessandro!' yelled Boris.

But the boy had already seen what had happened. He took three measured steps and vaulted on to Starlight's back. One moment Starlight was perfectly motionless, the next he was galloping towards the pines with the smooth and graceful power of a breaking wave. Another flash of lightning. A roll of thunder which rattled the stones on the beach. Boris found himself alone.

He ran back up the shelf of rock, squeezed through the hedge and pounded over the lawn, his shoes digging deep marks into the soft grass. Blinded by the rain he wrestled with the garage door until at last he succeeded in throwing it open. But the garage was empty. Maurice had taken the car out.

A bicycle. Yes. The bicycle, once the property of the pseudo-Scottish nanny, had been rusting away discreetly for some years against a wall decked with cobwebs. Boris seized it, saw that the tyres were flat, unhooked the pump and set to work. It seemed to him as his forearm shot back and forth like a piston that the air going into the tyres was being directly drained from his own lungs. He stood up dizzily, clambered on to the machine and sailed out into the rain. Flower hammered urgently on the kitchen window as he lurched past but he paid no attention. Heading towards the gate he wobbled into a flowerbed, capsized, picked himself up laboriously and set off once more in pursuit of the galloping horses.

His whizzing feet propelled him without further mishap as far as the coast road, but turning left he found himself faced with a steep slope that finally forced him to dismount and walk A couple of hundred yards further on there was a cart-track leading off into the pine forest. When he had reached it he remounted and pedalled slowly between the dripping ranks of trees.

It became very dark. The two white fists gripping the handlebars might have belonged to someone else. Water streamed from his legs as they pumped up and down as if in response to some rhythm of their own. He had forgotten Inez. Before his throbbing eyes Alessandro took three measured steps and vaulted on to a white horse, galloped away over the sand with effortless grace. A weak solution of blood and rainwater was dripping slowly on to his trousers from one of the handlebars, but while he laboured onwards through the driving rain with his breath whining hoarsely in his throat he could see nothing but that magnificent white horse speeding effortlessly away from him. On and on it swept.

And then he was in a silent land. The grey pines flitted past like cowled monks with invisibly moving feet. A hedge, a deserted hut, the blackened remains of a camp fire drifted by in the silence through the grey shrouds of rain. And somewhere in the distance ahead those two superb horses were sailing effortlessly over a sunlit meadow, their riders laughing with the gaiety of their indescribable youth, hair streaming on the warm summer breeze.

Silence. He was old, he thought. He was very old and monstrously tired. Youth was both ephemeral and eternal. It made no difference. There was nothing to be done about it. Nothing was expected of him. There was only the great and deepening silence into which he was plunging. It really made no difference. Silence and an impersonal peace.

Ahead of him the two magnificent horses galloped eternally away over the waving, sunlit grass.

For a moment he floated in the air. The front wheel of his bicycle had been stopped dead by a scarred and glistening pine trunk. He hung there, suspended in the air, savouring a sensation of great peace, enjoying the beauty of a frozen drop of resin momentarily glimpsed on the wounded white flesh of the pine. He hovered for a moment and then descended heavily into a rhododendron that grew out into the track. He hurt himself . . .

but only in distant, unreal fashion. He noted with detachment that the rhododendron had been harbouring on its waxed leaves a surprising amount of cold water. Nevertheless, he continued to lie there in the bush with heavy raindrops pattering on his closed eyelids. After a while he turned his head and vomited into some pine needles.

Some time later a large, dead sycamore leaf pirouetted twice before settling over his mouth like a clammy hand. He sat up wearily and peeled it from his face. The odd thing, he thought looking around, the curious thing was that there appeared to be no sycamore tree in sight. He stood up and began to shiver violently.

As he trudged home pushing the bicycle (he was trembling too much to risk mounting it) he thought no more of the horses galloping in the sunlight. His eyes remained fixed on the two white, rain-polished fists gripping the handlebars, from one of which a tincture of blood and rain water was incessantly dripping. He listened to the rattle of rain, to the steady ticking of the bicycle beside him.

Back at the house he stood in the kitchen with his eyes on the floor, watching a pool of water gather around his crocodile shoes while Flower listened with horror to what he had to say. Maurice was hurriedly summoned by telephone from a meeting in Maidenhair. Bonzo, who had been standing by anxiously, began to lap up some of the rain water leaking from his master on to the floor. Flower was walking up and down in agitation, asking Boris questions without waiting for the answers. He relapsed into silence, watching an escaping trickle make its way in a series of rectangular dashes along the grooves between the tiles towards the centre of the floor. It was as if he had been made of ice and was slowly melting away. After a few minutes Maurice arrived and took charge of the situation. Boris went upstairs and submerged himself in a hot bath, waiting for time to pass and for the affair to sort itself out.

At half past three Inez arrived. Boris got out of the bath, wrapped his lobster-pink body in a bath towel and went to the head of the stairs to hear what was going on. The girl had fallen off the horse as it jumped a hedge. Unhurt except for one or two insignificant and attractive scratches on her perfect cheeks she had made her way to the main road. A passing grocery van had seen her, picked her up and delivered her at Boscobel together with two packets of cornflakes, a stone of castor sugar and four ounces of yeast. Her criminal horse was still at large. The driver of the grocery van had a delivery to make at the farm, however, and had agreed to alert the animal's keepers. No, she hadn't seen Alessandro.

'You poor child,' exclaimed Maurice. 'You look like a drowned rat.'

Boris, peering over the banisters, agreed with this verdict. Inez's sophistication had been washed away by the downpour. Standing there in her sodden clothes, with her hair plastered over her face and mud on her limp sweater, she looked a pitiful sight. A little colour reappeared in her cheeks with the cup of hot soup that Flower made her drink. She appeared to be smiling, in fact. But no. All of a sudden she was crying. Tears were spilling down her cheeks.

'Into the bath with her quickly,' said Maurice.

Two hours later there was still no sign of Alessandro. The rain had ceased but the sky was still overcast and darkness was already falling. Maurice had organized a search-party with a police constable and two men from the farm.

'You need dogs,' declared old Dongeon authoritatively to the men grouped in the kitchen. 'That's what you need. It's the sense of smell, you know. Much sharper in dogs. They'll sniff out anything if you give them a chance.'

The men looked at each other dubiously but at length Maurice was dispatched to lift the sleeping and reluctant Bonzo from his basket and set him on the back doorstep. Bonzo sniffed at the cold, dark drizzle for a moment and then slunk back into the kitchen with his amputated tail between his legs. The men unanimously agreed to do the best they could without him and set off in the gathering dusk.

Inez had apparently regained her composure. While Uncle Cecil played his eternal patience at the mahogany table in the sitting-room and murmured a sotto voce commentary on the state of the game half to himself and half to Granny Dongeon, whose arthritic fingers were making erratic knitting motions (with knitting-needles but without wool) and who wasn't, in any case, listening to him, Inez sat by the fire with her eyes steadfastly on the book (which Boris believed to be *Lady Chatterleys Älskare*) which lay open on her shapely lap. But there was a certain tension in her concentration. Furthermore, she never turned a page. And at the least sound, a gust of rain against the window-pane, a creak of furniture, she would look up sharply. Boris himself moved restlessly from his room to the kitchen (where Flower was tragically kneading dough as if Alessandro's life depended on it) to the sitting-room and back again, but without speaking to anybody.

At eight o'clock the men returned, damp and dispirited. They had found Starlight, riderless, walking back along the beach towards the farm, but of Alessandro there had been no trace. At this news Inez turned very pale but said nothing, merely returning her eyes to her book.

The searchers were given food, flashlights were found for them and they set out once more. Boris resumed his patrol of the house with a heavy heart. Nobody had suggested that he should help with the search and he hadn't dared offer his services. At nine o'clock Flower helped Granny Dongeon up the stairs and put her to bed. At twenty-five past nine Boris noticed that Inez's blue eyes were glittering more brightly than usual in the firelight and at twenty to ten a solitary tear rolled down her cheek. Uncle Cecil, whose muttered commentary had increased in excitement and incoherence in expectation of his game of patience at last coming out, fortunately noticed nothing. Inez wiped away the tear with the sleeve of her pullover without removing her gaze from the page she was reading. Boris retired discreetly for another patrol of the silent house. At half past ten the searchers returned once more.

'There's nothing much we can do now until morning,' Maurice said in a worried tone, removing his tweed cap and running his fingers through his hair. 'As soon as it's light we'll stand a better chance. We may be able to pick up Starlight's hoofmarks in the forest.'

'Dogs are what you need,' old Dongeon said, appearing in a wine-coloured dressing-gown beneath which the shrunken legs of his pyjamas revealed shins of a startling and unnatural pallor. 'Trained dogs. Your trained dog can see things we can't.'

'We haven't *got* any dogs, Dad,' Maurice said with a touch of acerbity.

'I know you haven't. That's why I'm telling you. Animals have sharper senses than we humans. So have Negroes. It's the way they're brought up. In America they train dolphins to rescue people from drowning.'

'We don't have any dolphins either, if it comes to that, so we may as well stop thinking about it.'

Old Dongeon shrugged his shoulders and retired looking peeved.

There was a silence while everyone looked at the floor and listened to the ticking of the clock. Closing his eyes for a moment it seemed to Boris as if he were still in the forest himself, making his way through the nightmarish downpour with the bicycle gripped in his ivory fists and ticking away his youth as its twin wheel-tracks snaked in and out of the mud and pools of water and rotting leaves, converging and moving apart and converging again.

Maurice showed the searchers to the door and returned to the sitting-room.

'You'd better go to bed and get some sleep, old thing,' he said quite tenderly to Inez. 'You must be tired.'

'No,' she said sharply, 'I'm not going to bed until he comes back. It was all my fault in the first place,' she added softly.

'Don't be silly. Besides, we don't know whether or not he'll be back tonight.'

In the kitchen Boris found Flower weeping silently as she mopped the floor. She turned her face away from him but he had already seen that her eyes were red and swollen.

'What on earth are you doing this for?' he demanded. 'And at this time of night?'

'The floor wasn't very clean . . . I thought . . .'

'But you only mopped it this afternoon.'

'I can't go to bed, Boris,' she sobbed. 'Not while that poor boy is lying out there in the rain somewhere.'

Boris placed an awkward hand on her shoulder. 'Everything will be all right,' he said without confidence. 'I expect Sandro is sheltering somewhere.'

Flower nodded mutely and went on mopping the floor. She had almost finished. Boris was just wondering whether he should suggest taking the dishes out of the cupboard and washing them up for the second time when there was a loud rap on the back door.

It was the local scoutmaster clad in dripping oilskins. Behind him was Alessandro, supported by two muscular youths also clad in oilskins. A moment of silence. Then everybody began to talk at once.

Alessandro was helped into the kitchen and lowered on to a chair. His complexion was leaden and he had a large piece of sticking plaster over his right temple. Beneath it the cheekbone was swollen and bluish in clour. A patina of dark scratches ran down his neck. He smiled feebly at the exclamations of the Dongeon family but said nothing. He looked dazed.

The scoutmaster explained. The Eagle Forest Patrol had come across the boy lying unconscious in the forest. They had promptly concluded that Alessandro was in need of help. Having loosened his collar and applied artificial respiration without success (the boy was already breathing steadily) they had improvised a stretcher made of saplings and lanyards and transported him back to camp. There he had shown some signs of regaining consciousness but had evidently been suffering from concussion and had replied to questions in a foreign tongue, believed to be Italian. The scoutmaster had then taken the matter in hand, making an unsuccessful attempt to communicate with the boy in dog-Latin which he spoke fluently. After a brief consultation with the patrol leaders it had been decided to strike camp (the inclement weather had already rendered this move inevitable) and carry the boy to Seaford

Village where there was a doctor. The doctor had duly examined Alessandro, decided that the cut on his temple did not require stitching and ordered the boy to rest on the couch in his surgery for the rest of the afternoon while the scouts retired by special permission to the Seaford Youth Hostel to sing songs and fry eggs. The doctor had then been unexpectedly summoned to deliver a baby and had left the sleeping Alessandro in the care of his housekeeper. When the scoutmaster and two members of his troop had returned to recover Alessandro and return him to his home the housekeeper, a severe and punctilious lady, had refused to deliver the boy to them, insisting that she could not act without the instructions of the doctor. The birth had been difficult. The doctor had not returned until after ten o'clock. Alessandro, however, had been examined once more and pronounced 'as right as rain'. And here he was.

At this point Alessandro slumped forward in a faint, rapping his battered head sharply against the edge of the Formica table. Everybody, Boris included, froze with horror. Indeed, but for Inez, Alessandro might have gone further and smashed his skull with fatal impact against the damp tiles. He was already pitching sideways when she materialized from nowhere and slipped a soft hand beneath his descending head. One shod foot, wedged between the chair and the Formica table, poked stiffly into the air where the boy's head had been a moment before.

In the chaos of exclamations, advice, and jostling that ensued Boris slipped away to the sitting-room where Uncle Cecil was still unconcernedly playing patience.

'He's back,' he announced briefly.

'His back? Whose back?'

'He – is – back. Alessandro is back.'

'Oh?'

Boris and Uncle Cecil stared at each other uncomfortably for a moment. Then Boris retreated again. The scouts were being ushered out of the kitchen door by old Dongeon. Part of the noise had now transferred itself upstairs. Boris went up and poked his head through the open door of 'the children's' room. Alessandro was stretched on the bed protesting feebly that he felt perfectly all right while Inez bent over him, deftly unbuttoning his shirt. Beside her Maurice and Flower fumbled with the boy's muddy shoelaces.

'Leave this to me,' Inez said with sharp authority, almost with anger. 'I'll look after him. You go and boil some water and find another bandage.'

Maurice and Flower fell back uncertainly.

'Don't you think we'd better get the doctor again?'

'He needs rest. I'll look after him.'

Without ceremony she pushed Maurice and Flower into the corridor and closed the door.

'Well,' Maurice said admiringly, 'she's certainly a plucky little thing. Who'd have thought it?'

Boris hovered on the dark staircase for a while and then went on up the stairs to his room. Stretched on the floor he had an excellent view of what was going on. In the room below Alessandro was battling weakly to prevent Inez from removing his underclothes.

'I'm perfectly all right,' he kept repeating. 'I can manage fine . . .'

Inez paid no attention, however, and continued to denude him. Alessandro stopped protesting and sank back into a coma of embarrassment while Inez skilfully inserted his naked arms and legs into pyjamas. When she had finished and tucked the bedclothes around him she leaned over his inert body and planted a long, passionate kiss on his bruised lips.

Downstairs again Boris cleared his throat and said casually: 'You know, I still think that maybe they're a little old to be sleeping together in the same room. It's not important, mind you. Just a thought that crossed my mind . . .'

But nobody was paying any attention anyway.

One of the Urbino Sisters had fallen to her death!

This seemed to be the general opinion of the knot of anxious, excited people standing in the foyer of the Winter Gardens Theatre as Boris entered. She had been swinging backwards, hanging upside down by her slender calves, had launched herself in a graceful swoop towards a flickering bar which had somehow eluded her dainty, clutching fingers, sped across the theatre roof like a glittering arrow, cannoned into the ornamental side curtain dislodging a great cloud of dust that blazed fiercely in the spotlight, had hung there for a moment before plummeting into the orchestra pit and was quite obviously dead. Only a miracle could have saved her.

Boris had been hanging around on the deserted sea-front, waiting for the interval before taking his seat in order to avoid the trick cyclists and performing dogs. He had chosen his seat carefully, in the fifth row, near enough to see everything clearly without being dangerously exposed to the view of the performers (or, in case of emergency, of the lion). Just as the fire-curtain was being raised for the second half of the show he had planned to collapse neatly into his seat. But now something had gone wrong.

The centre of attention in the foyer was the commissionaire. One glance at the man and Boris's heart sank. It was Robertson. He was dressed in a commissionaire's uniform a few sizes too big for him, the sleeves of his jacket revealing only his fingers, the trousers piled up untidily on his shoes. Boris approached reluctantly, drawn by curiosity to know what was going on.

Or was it Robertson? The face was familiar, the thin face, the deep, sagging pockets under his eyes. But this man had a purple complexion and his movements were fumbling, lethargic. Moreover, while waiting on the sea-front a few minutes earlier Boris had heard the sound of a flute coming from somewhere in the direction of the hospital. The flute had been playing 'Smoke Gets In Your Eyes' with the same excruciating tenderness as the violin at their first encounter. Unless I was imagining it, Boris, wondered. But this man was almost certainly Robertson.

He was standing with his back to the window of the box-office ringed by a circle of women with short hair and heavy shoes who looked as if they might be bachelor schoolmistresses and were all talking at once in penetrating tones. Had someone sent for an ambulance? Why had there been no safety net? Was there a doctor in the house? Had he been called?

The commissionaire, who had been surveying his audience with a dazed and slightly bewildered expression, now began to speak, haltingly at first, then with increasing fluency. As he spoke his eyes flashed restlessly to and fro, the purple flush mounted on his sunken cheeks.

'An ambulance?' he demanded. 'What use is an ambulance? She was dead when they picked her up . . . The spark had gone out of her. Death was instantaneous. She fell with a terrible impact right into the orchestra pit . . .' The commissionaire licked his cracked lips.

'The safety net . . .'

'Ah! So you want to close the stable door . . . She was dead as mutton when they . . . But it wasn't the fall. She was transfixed by the metal shaft of a music stand. Clean through the breast. She fell on it with terrible force and it went through her clean as a whistle . . . Hardly left a mark on her body . . . One single drop of blood . . .'

Boris looked at the muscles working in the man's cheeks. He was clearly saying the first thing that came into his head. And anyway, how could he possibly know what had happened when he had been standing in the foyer?

'The show must go on!' he cried suddenly, looking around. His audience had melted away to a safe distance. 'Here, let me tell you something . . . He put a call through from this very telephone. The box-office . . . The manager . . . But not for a doctor. I recognized the number. For an undertaker. Buried? Not on your life. You can't bury them in consecrated ground. They have no souls. Cremate her. Cremate the bitch . . .'

The foyer bell had begun to ring and the commissionaire's eyes had suddenly filled with tears. One of the buttons of his frayed blue tunic was open revealing not a shirt but a patch of yellow woollen vest.

'Though our hearts are breaking the show . . . But wait. Wait . . .' People were leaving the foyer to return to their seats. 'D'you think it's the girl I care about? Not on your life. They can die. Let them die. I don't give a damn. It's the musicians that break your heart. The poor musicians sitting down there in the dark, stinking orchestra pit. Sitting there like rabbits being bombarded by these bloody girls who don't know their job . . . I tell you one thing . . .'

The foyer was almost empty. Afraid of being recognized by Robertson (he no longer had any doubts about his identity) Boris went into the theatre. He was just in time to hear an announcement to the effect that the Urbino Sister who had fallen had merely broken an ankle and collected a few bruises. The lights dimmed. The theatre was almost empty. There was nobody at all sitting in the first five rows. He would be sitting there alone.

The curtain went up and the show started. Lash appeared and was asked some coy questions. The act dragged on interminably. At last the curtain came down once more. A comedian pushed his way through to tell some jokes while Boris ground his teeth nervously. He ran his finger along the rim of his collar which had inexplicably tightened. The comedian's face dissolved into Robertson's tensely working features . . . They asked me how I knew . . . The eggs on the ceiling! Whatever made me do such a crazy thing? Flower was perfectly right when she said it was such a waste of good eggs   But she didn't say that. I did. I said . . . My hand, though. I hurt my hand. The pain needed an outlet. Ignoring the pain in my hand (it still throbbed all last night, still throbs now) the pain nevertheless expressed itself in smashed eggs drooping from the ceiling.

These few precious days . . . I spend with .

Sweating profusely in the warm theatre he now found himself looking at an iron cage around which a lion was wandering, apparently in search of a comfortable place to sit down. There was no sign of Lady Jane. The lion collapsed wearily in a corner and prepared to doze off.

'Ladies and gentlemen!' cried a man in a shiny suit of electric blue. 'I have the great honour and pleasure . . .'

There she was, staring sulkily at Boris and tapping the haft of her whip against her black boots. Boris, hypnotized by the size of her breasts, stared back. She was a big girl with broad shoulders and an ample waist girdled with a studded leather belt. Above the belt her diaphragm had piled up in a sloping wedge. Her thighs, though, were curiously slender in the tight white trousers she was wearing, making her look top-heavy. She said nothing, removed a small revolver from the holster that drooped against her broad hip, spun the chamber, slipped it back and moved towards the cage. The lion gave a shuddering yawn and licked a paw. The girl's bottom was enormous and flat, straining the white trousers into three horizontal ridges between the base of her spine and the cleft of her buttocks. At the gate of the cage she cracked her whip sharply. The lion got to its feet with an effort and prowled around dangerously. Lady Jane opened the door of the cage and slipped inside to a roll of drums. But before she had even entered the cage Boris knew he was going to be disappointed.

Snarling, the lion was prodded into a corner by the legs of a wooden stool that Lady Jane held with one muscular arm. She put the stool down and the lion climbed on to it. There was a burst of applause. Then another roll of drums. The lion allowed its mouth to be prodded open with the whip. Its teeth were large and yellow as egg-yolks drooping from the ceiling. There was a hush as Lady Jane bent forward and stuck her head between the two rows of teeth. The lion's eyes opened very wide as if it were about to gag, then closed completely. The bloody beast is going to fall asleep, thought Boris bitterly. I might have known. He stared resentfully into the cage at the enormous white bottom facing the audience. Lady Jane might have been looking for something in a deep wardrobe. He groaned and the lion opened its eyes again. More applause as Lady Jane withdrew her head, left the cage and bowed to the audience.

The poor devil will lose his job, Boris muttered, looking at the lion but meaning Robertson. There's no doubt about it. The manager must have heard what he was saying. But there again, perhaps he's always like that and they don't mind. And if he's new to the job perhaps they'll make allowances. The poor chap must be insane, frightening all those women with his wild words. Transfixed with the shaft of a music stand. Christ, he should be locked up! There must be places for people like him. These precious days . . . But it was *me* he was talking to . . . I know that much. That much I knew from the start, from the very beginning . . . He knew me all right. He recognized me.

A volunteer is needed to fall to his death!

The girl cannoned into the curtain, hung there for a moment and then fell like a stone into the orchestra pit. A cloud of dust, dislodged from the curtain, blazed fiercely in the spotlight. Blinded by the blazing dust her dainty fingers clutched and missed. The girl has flown her last. May she rest in peace.

A volunteer?

I love life, Boris may have said. Did she realize, the girl, as she hung there for a moment, that this was the end? That her days had dwindled down? And all through August and the first days of September she had watched the people leaving, the dying echoes of laughter, seen the leaves grow dusty, the bright petals lose their glow, too many people on the beach and then too few, the summer's collapse, the empty streets, closed cafés and yellow leaves. Oh Lord, I'm much too tired for all this!

His bandaged hand was throbbing so painfully that he held it up in front of his face in despair looking for a place to put it. But there was nowhere. It was attached to his arm. There was nowhere he could put it. It had become a giant ear through which he heard the boom of a drum that hammered on and on relentlessly.

He can read your mind!

Someone was speaking to him. Yes, there was no doubt about it. A man with a black mask was speaking directly to Boris from the stage. Leaning over the footlights. Below the mask his lips were smiling. Above it his eyes were cold. Boris tried to sink lower into his seat but there was no avoiding the man's eyes. There was a roar of laughter from behind him.

'There's no need to be shy. We only need one more volunteer and then we . . .'

The lion had disappeared. The man turned and made a sign to a girl in a silver bathing-costume with a large green plume sticking out from the base of her spine.

'I'm sending reinforcements,' he said, winking over Boris's head into the darkness. Laughter rolled back towards him over the empty seats. The girl in the silver bathing-costume came tripping down the steps at the side of the stage and approached Boris. Boris watched her with alarm. Without hesitation she grasped his bandaged hand firmly and led him trembling up the steps to the stage. Three other men were standing there uneasily, grinning at the lights with their gleaming faces. To his right a man in overalls was standing in the wings talking to a girl wearing a striped tiger costume and holding a tiger's head in her hands while she scratched her collar-bone. Neither of them appeared interested in what was happening on the stage.

The Mysterious Eggs, said the man in the blue suit, will now read some minds. There was a long roll of drums. The Mysterious X approached. He stopped in front of Boris, whose eyes were on the ground examining a long streak of moisture that curled in front of his feet like the crescent of an Arab dagger. Could it be lion-saliva? Boris was asking himself as two shiny black shoes came to rest in front of him. I mustn't look up, he thought desperately. But his eyes disobediently began to travel upwards, up the sharp creases in the trousers, over a crimson cummerbund, up a long row of pearl buttons set in a frilled white shirt, a black bow tie, a jaw of bluish-white marble, thin lips, twin needles of black moustache, a black mask and . . . there was a vivid blue flash, a clash of steel. The Mysterious X had vanished.

Boris licked his lips. Just for an instant he had experienced an appalling vibration as two pale drills sank deep into his soul. The Mysterious X, staggering slightly, was moving towards the front of the stage with one of the other hostages who was wearing a green tie on which a pink flash of lightning had been depicted. He beckoned the girl. She went over to him, the green plume of her tail oscillating wildly. The Mysterious X whispered something to her. She hurried into the wings and reappeared with a glass of water. This she handed to The Mysterious X, who raised his mask an inch or two and took a deep gulp. The compere had taken the microphone again and was saying:

'Ladies and gentlemen, unfortunately one of our volunteers isn't feeling too well so we'll have to excuse him. Let's all wish him a speedy recovery!'

He began to clap politely, looking towards Boris whose bandaged hand was once more grasped by the girl with the green tail. He was towed off the stage and back into the gloom of the auditorium. There the girl pushed him firmly into a seat and left him. He immediately fell into a deep and thunderous sleep.

Enormous pink spheres sped like planets through the green darkness and burst around him. Then he was clad in spangled tights, balancing on a tiny spotlight perch way up in the darkness under the theatre roof, launching himself in a graceful swoop to the other side of the theatre. Robertson, also clad in spangled tights, snatched him out of the air and swung him back to where The Mysterious X was hovering with a green-plumed tail beating the air, but he hardly had time to meet the terrible pale eyes over the mask before he was swinging back once more and this time he knew he was swinging too far and too fast. He flashed past Robertson's desperately clutching fingers, cannoned into the ornamental side curtain, hung there for a moment and fell with terrible impact into the orchestra pit while a cloud of dust dislodged from the curtain blazed fiercely in the white spotlight.

He stood up sharply and sat down again. His face was running with sweat. The house lights were on, the stage was empty and the audience had gone home. At the back of the theatre cleaners moved slowly between the ranks of seats as if reaping corn. Nobody was taking any interest in him.

A very small man with a large head was sweeping the stage. Boris made his way unsteadily towards the steps and climbed them.

'Where are the dressing-rooms?'

The man looked up with a smile on his face but no sign of comprehension.

'The dressing-rooms,' Boris repeated. The man smiled vaguely once more and went on sweeping, dragging his broom through the sawdust and lion-saliva and horse-droppings. Boris tried digging his fingernails into the palm of his undamaged hand, hoping that the pain would help both himself and the man with the broom to take a firmer grasp on reality. After a few moments the man stopped sweeping and looked up at Boris with a peaceful smile on his wizened face. Then he touched his ears and lips and winked.

Boris said: 'So sorry, old chap. I didn't know. You look perfectly . . . I mean, one would never . . .'

He wandered into the wings. A man in overalls told him where to find the dressing-rooms. He climbed some worn wooden stairs and found himself in a feebly illuminated corridor. Some demolished scenery was propped against the walls. A faint smell of sweat hung in the air. He advanced cautiously.

A few paces further on he came to a half-open door on which

a yellow paper star had been fixed with a brown drawing-pin. The points of the star had curled inwards with age to give the impression of a dying sunflower.

Lady Jane was sitting at a dressing-table plucking her eyebrows. Boris cleared his throat and advanced a few steps into the room. He was on the point of speaking when he froze abruptly. The lion was lying on the floor at her side.

Lady Jane turned and looked at him. She was clad only in a pair of embroidered pink pants. As she turned, a huge naked breast peered round her shoulder at him like a bulging, featureless face.

'Oh, it's you,' she said. 'I suppose you've come to apologize.'

'Apologize?' murmured Boris, all his attention concentrated on the lion which was regarding him sleepily.

'For not clapping . . . but don't think I care whether you clap or not. It's all the same to me. I get paid just the same.' She turned back to the mirror and studied her face carefully. 'There was no need to groan though. It wasn't that bad.'

'Groan?'

'Yes. It upsets the lion. He's very sensitive, you know. They all are. He gets depressed and refuses to open his mouth.'

'Is he safe there?' Boris managed to ask.

'Still, it was nice of you to come and apologize,' she went on, ignoring his question. 'We appreciate it.'

The lion had lost interest in Boris and had begun to lick one of Lady Jane's naked legs with a languid movement of its massive head.

'Stop that,' she said sharply. 'It hurts.' She clipped the animal on the nose and it dropped its head to the floor, looking up at her dubiously. 'He likes the taste of the skin-cream I use,' she added for Boris's benefit. 'But his tongue is like sandpaper. Still, I suppose it saves me having to shave my legs.'

'Actually,' Boris said. 'I was wondering if you could tell me where I could find The Mysterious X.'

'Next door. He's in the shower.'

'Thanks,' Boris said, edging away with his eye on the lion.

'He doesn't give autographs, though, if that's what you're

after. He's afraid someone may analyse his handwriting.'

The neighbouring door was closed. Boris could hear the sound of running water. He knocked loudly. A voice shouted for him to come in and he pushed open the door. The Mysterious X was standing in front of a shower curtain completely naked except for his mask. His body was still running with water.

'Oh, it's you,' he said tonelessly. 'I was afraid you'd come. What d'you want?' He picked a white towel from the back of a chair and began to rub his head vigorously.

Boris had steeled himself for another painful blue flash when he looked at the man's eyes but this time nothing happened. The eyes that had seemed so terrible on the stage were now dead and glassy, somewhat bleary from the shower. He wondered why The Mysterious X should wear a mask in the shower.

'Because it's waterproof, that's why,' The Mysterious X said petulantly, reading his mind. 'Don't ask stupid questions.' He put one foot on the chair and began to dry his private parts with tender care.

'I want to know what you saw in my mind.'

'Oh, Lord help us,' The Mysterious X said. 'I didn't see a bloody thing in your mind.' He was now examining his toes with exaggerated attention, drying them one by one.

'And why shouldn't I dry my toes?' he demanded. 'I suppose you want me to get athlete's foot!'

'You saw something. I know you did.'

'I saw nothing!' cried The Mysterious X. 'Don't you understand? Can't you get that through your thick skull? Nothing!'

'You're lying. I know you saw something.'

The Mysterious X slowly stopped drying his toes. His body drooped wearily. When he turned Boris saw that his pale eyes had filled with tears.

'Why can't you just leave me alone?'

He slumped down on the chair and buried his masked face in his hands.

'You've got to tell me,' Boris said sharply.

'You must believe me,' muttered The Mysterious X. 'I saw nothing at all. Just pain, maybe . . . You'd hurt your hand. Pain and . . . darkness. Just darkness . . . Nothing.'

Boris stared at him coldly without speaking.

After a moment The Mysterious X said slowly: 'You see, I was mistaken at first. You'd hurt your hand but I didn't realize that straight away. At first I was mistaken. It was the way the lights were shining on you. I saw my own reflection in your eyes . . you know the way one does sometimes . . . I saw . . .' He hesitated.

'Go on!'

'I made a mistake. I thought I saw myself . . .'

'You saw mortality and the death of love!'

The Mysterious X grasped the white towel and dried his armpits mechanically. Tears were flooding from his eyes now and rimming the black mask.

'But I made a mistake, you see. I saw that the heart was a muscle. I saw . . . You moved your head and the light changed . . . and then I saw nothing but darkness.'

'And then?' Boris cried suddenly. 'Did you see an immortal soul? Did you see one of those?'

'I'm not sure,' The Mysterious X said miserably. 'I don't think I'd know one if I saw one.'

'For God's sake, man,' shouted Boris wildly. 'You must have seen something. Look at me now.'

The Mysterious X turned his eyes towards him but they were blinded by tears.

'I don't think I'd know one,' he repeated wretchedly. 'Not even if it were staring me in the face.' He began to sob convulsively.

The door burst open. It was Lady Jane. She looked from Boris to The Mysterious X who was now howling bitterly.

'What have you been up to now?' she demanded angrily. 'You've gone and upset X again. It'll take us ages to calm him down now.' She took the towel from The Mysterious X's limp fingers and dried his eyes tenderly, murmuring soothing words to him. Turning to Boris she said: 'Well, what are you waiting for? Don't you think you've caused enough trouble?'

'I just wanted to ask him . . .' Boris said contritely.

'That's what they all say. Are you blind? Can't you see he's sensitive?'

Boris sighed and turned to the door. The lion was peering in anxiously but moved aside to let him pass. He wandered down the corridor with a heavy heart. And yet, as he emerged from the theatre into the grey light of evening, he experienced a sensation of bitter resignation that gradually became, to his surprise, a feeling of calm that was quite new to him.

'Treat them rough, that's my advice.' Boris had just delivered this remark in a confident, slightly disabused tone that blended to perfection with the heavy perfume of lavender that hung in the autumnal air at a certain point along the perimeter of the lily-armoured pond. Alessandro scowled at his fingernails, nodded, but said nothing. Perhaps he was simply waiting for Boris to continue with his advice before asking a question. But Boris found himself inexplicably at a loss, could think of nothing more to say. Meanwhile, though moving at a slow stroll, they had completed an entire lap of the circular pond and were assailed once more by the smell of lavender in which Boris's words still seemed curiously to hang, though their confidence was now somewhat faded.

'Well, anyway,' he went on with an effort. 'Don't let them get the upper hand. Polite but firm. That's been my experience. Don't let her see you're too interested, that's the best advice I can give you.'

'But Inez . . .' began Alessandro.

'Is different? Nonsense. They're all the same, you can take it from me.'

In strained silence they completed another revolution of the pond. This time the lavender air had become a cobweb on which his words hung like dead flies, ironic question marks now floated aimlessly in the red heaven of his momentarily closed eyelids

'I hope you don't mind me bringing this up,' he concluded hastily, anxious to drop the subject. 'It's none of my business, of course, but I just thought you might need . . . you know . . .' His voice trailed away.

'Well, thanks a lot, Boris,' Alessandro said with a trace of relief. 'It's very kind of you.' Just for a moment it had seemed as if the boy might be on the point of unburdening himself of the great weight of tender confidences that Boris supposed him to be carrying round the pond. But the moment was gone. Furthermore, the failure of nerve, Boris realized, had been his own. He had at last crossed the final bridge separating youth from age. Now there was nothing more for him to do but watch and remember.

Remember. The agony of the time before their (in itself agonizing enough) status quo had been reached. The time before the time had been bad enough.

'Let's stop walking round this bloody pond.' But where on earth could they walk where they hadn't already walked a million times? The predictability of all possible movement abruptly paralysed him. He stood with his hands in his pockets looking around unhappily for a point of the compass that he had so far failed to notice, the three hundred and sixty-first degree. 'By the way, how did you come to fall off that wretched horse?'

'An overhanging branch knocked me off, I think,' Alessandro said, leading the way towards the kitchen garden in the wake of a cabbage white that was fluttering erratically by. 'I don't really remember. I know something hit me.'

'The unexpected,' Boris said with animation. 'That's what always trips us up. That's what tripped *me* up. Now, Sandro, I know what you're thinking,' he continued, putting a hand on Alessandro's shoulder. 'You're thinking that I'm brutal with women. I know, I know. In a way it's natural that you should think that . . .'

'But . . .' Alessandro began, as if to protest that nothing had been further from his mind.

'You can be frank,' Boris cut in. 'I'm not afraid of the truth. But if I was brutal then it was an accidental brutality, an unexpected brutality over which I had no control. It tripped me up when I was least expecting it.'

'I see.' Alessandro frowned once more at his fingernails.

'All I said was: "I can't stand pregnant women. They always look so self-satisfied." It was a joke. Nothing more. I didn't know what was going to happen the next day . . . or was it the day after. I forget. I had no way of knowing. In any case, it wasn't meant to be taken seriously. Then, after what was going to happen *did* happen I found myself in an impossible position. I was hunted, Sandro, hunted through the house by accusing glances as if I'd been a criminal . . . and at the same time nobody would look at me. They'd become absorbed in newspapers or books or knitting whenever I came into a room. And Flower would lie there day after day as pale as a sheet not speaking to anyone, scarcely eating, not listening to what I said. Simply from time to time her eyes would fill with tears and I knew she was thinking about the beautiful shining egg of love I'd brought into the loneliness of that unspeakable house . . . and how it had hatched out into a reptile. But it's not my fault! I wanted to shout at her. It was just an accident. We can try again. I wasn't to blame. Not of course that she did ever blame me except once when I got my hand inside her nightdress in an attempt to comfort her and she said: "Don't you think you've already done enough damage?"''

'Actually, Boris,' Alessandro said, lifting his wrist to look at his watch. He stared past it, however, at the white butterfly which had now settled on the flesh-coloured brick of a partly demolished wall. It flexed its wings a couple of times and folded them neatly. 'I'm afraid I'll have to go and do some biology . . .'

'Of course, of course, biology,' Boris cried excitedly, leaning forward to examine the yellowish-white wings on the pink brick. 'That's it exactly. That's what I tried to tell her. It's all a question of your internal biology. It's got nothing to do with feelings. But try and explain that to *her* . . . and even Maurice, who isn't a bad chap in his way, though perhaps not too quick with the wits, even Maurice though he tried to be polite to me...

Anyway, then Christmas came and you can imagine what that was like . . .'

'See you later, Boris,' Alessandro murmured and set off rapidly towards the house.

'A week beforehand Flower threw back the bedclothes and got out of bed with bones sticking out all over the place, grim and determined and pale as death. "I'm all right," she kept saying. "I can't stay in bed for the rest of my life." So Christmas came and of course there was holly and mistletoe all over the house and a Christmas tree with coloured lights and little parcels wrapped in festive paper with labels saying: "For Boris with love and best wishes for a Merry Christmas from Flower" and other parcels saying: "For Boris with lots of love from Flower" until, well, I couldn't stand it any more . . . It was too much. And I just stood there with a fixed grin on my face unwrapping bottles of after-shave lotion and ties and socks and cigarettes thinking that my heart would burst with misery. And everywhere I went during those grey festivities there seemed to be little tickets of love from Flower tied round bottlenecks and hairbrush handles and lying in wait for me in boxes of cufflinks and packets of nougat. "Here," said Maurice, handing me a festively wrapped parcel and avoiding my eye, "you might give that to Flower and say it's from you . . . I just thought, well, that you might have forgotten to get anything for her . . ." And I think that was the worst moment of all because I had, in fact, got something for her (some "modern" pyjamas that had happened to catch my eye on a curiously life-like tailor's dummy in the window of the Maidenhair Boutique) and a book too, oh not much, but I'd been a little short of cash and so . . . anyway, it made no difference . . . Flower thanked me for the presents but didn't open them. She left them on her dressing-table where they collected a fine grey film of dust until Easter (which was irritating because I rather wanted to read the book myself), or possibly until after Easter, I just forget. But Christmas.

'I can still see us all sitting around the table in paper hats, gloomy with drink, while old Dongeon hacked away with a carving-knife at the dead grey turkey on the table, and hardly anyone could think of anything to say so that when on pulling a rebellious cracker with a vindictive spasm of strength I accidentally dragged Granny Dongeon's wiry arm against the sauce boat, upsetting it, frankly it was almost a relief to let oneself sink into all the commotion that that caused. And those endless infernal carols on the radio, endlessly repeated good wishes of people totally unconscious of your separate existence. It was all rather hard to take, if you want to know the truth . . . This too will pass away, I thought as I attacked a superbly indigestible lump of Christmas pudding prepared (according to one of those rapid "traditions" that grow up so readily in such households) by the pseudo-Scottish nanny (naturally, this tradition was summarily strangled the following year or possibly, for all I know, transplanted to the home of the *nouveau-riche* manufacturer of patent glucose drinks). This too will pass. And it did pass.

'It passed into an even more peculiar situation. I don't quite know how to explain it. The whole family with the exception of Uncle Cecil (who had been invited for Christmas and subsequently stayed until the following May) took to shaking their heads over me with a mixture of disapproval and . . . well, pity. Rather like a child who has been discovered with a packet of contraceptives. Guilty but not wholly responsible for my actions. As far as I can judge, the start of this new situation coincided with the arrival shortly after Christmas of a letter (which I wasn't shown but which I happened to come across in my wife's writing-case) from the mother of some faceless girl cousin called Dilys or Penny or some such name who had been staying, altogether unnoticed by me I might add, in Boscobel during November. This letter hysterically conveyed the news that Dilys (or Penny) was pregnant and had apparently become so during her stay with the Dongeons. I couldn't really see what all the fuss was about, myself. I should have thought that the mother of this mousy creature ought to have been delighted at some chap taking an interest in her daughter. According to the letter, she wasn't.

'Incredible as this may seem, Sandro, the entire Dongeon

family appeared to have been seized by the insane notion that while the drama of my wife's miscarriage was taking place on the stage I had somehow been busy fertilizing Dilys in the wings. Nobody actually accused me of it, however. Dilys herself, with remarkable presence of mind for such a timid and sexually inexperienced young girl, had sworn that she would rather die than reveal the name of her lover. So nobody actually accused me.

'In one way this was unfortunate because they obviously thought I was responsible. I couldn't deny the charge, however, without being accused. I couldn't even refer to the incident, word it deftly into the conversation in my usual discreet and tactful manner, without revealing that I had been perusing my wife's letters uninvited. So there was nothing I could do but suffer in silence.

'"Whatever are we going to do with him?" I overheard Granny Marie-Thé sighing one day. "One feels that it really isn't his fault. He just can't control his impulses."

'"Who can't?" I barked, coming into the room.

'"Oh, nobody," murmured Granny Marie-Thé in alarm as if she thought I might suddenly rip off her clothes and rape her.

'This too will pass, I tried to reassure myself. It didn't. At best one might say that it changed its nature a little. The vapour of guilt and pity in the atmosphere clung to our relationships and hardened like varnish. My own candidate, by the way, for the role of seducer would be Maurice who showed the girl his paintings, I now remember, on one or two occasions. This may seem an unlikely choice given the extensive array of contraceptive equipment I once happened to come across in Maurice's bedside drawer (apart from the conventional devices and some extraordinarily luxurious French letters made of leopard-skin there were also a number of syringes, tubes, nozzles and foaming agents, to say nothing of other magnificently baroque objects, including what appeared to be a mink Dutch cap, whose manner of employment even my exceptional inventiveness was unable to fathom) but then *il peut arriver des accidents*. Or so I'm led to believe.

'Anyway, all I'm trying to say is that though it may have *appeared* brutal . . . Well, put yourself in my position . . .

'One evening I left the house and stalked about the streets of Maidenhair until after midnight snatching drinks in pubs and coffees in cafés. And the next night I did the same. And the next night. And then, it was most curious, I could no longer stay in the house. Every evening I'd say to myself: Boris, this time you're going to stay in and talk to Flower and show her how much she means to you. But then an irresistible force would seize me and throw me outside, in the rain, in the snow, it made no difference. You must believe me, I wanted to stay but I couldn't. Every evening. It was like a drug. Every single evening . . . You know, Sandro, I sometimes feel that I'm made up of a whole series of antechambers with interconnecting doors leading by stages towards my real self. You deal with almost everyone you meet in the first antechamber, the people you know well in the second or third antechamber and so on . . . But something has gone wrong. I've never been able to find the person who can unlock those final doors and enter the room where I really am . . . the real *me*, sitting and waiting in utter silence for someone to get to know me at last after all these futile years of my life . . . It's strange. It's most peculiar, don't you think? Or could it be, I sometimes wonder, that it's up to *me* to unlock those final doors? Because to be frank I don't see how I can . . . Without the key, I mean.'

The yellowish-white butterfly had now vanished from the rose-coloured brick of the partially demolished wall separating, for no apparent reason, a row of cabbages from a row of spinach. The butterfly had vanished. And so, oddly enough, had Alessandro.

The newspapers had not arrived until late in the morning on account of some minor railway strike which had been engineered, according to Uncle Cecil (who claimed to have inside knowledge from high places, much to the admiration and envy of old Dongeon), direct from Peking. Precise instructions written in Chinese, he said, had been found on half a dozen porters and ticket-collectors in key railway junctions. The result was that the 'keeping interested' of Granny Dongeon had to be postponed from breakfast to lunch. So this meant that the conversation at lunch was largely dominated by the account of how a man in East Sheen had been buried alive in quick-drying cement the day before, interspersed with random speculation as to whether or not Granny Dongeon might be well advised to move out of steel and concentrate more on electronics . . . 'an expanding field' pronounced Uncle Cecil with numbing authority.

On his way upstairs it occurred to Boris that he knew how the man in East Sheen must have felt. Still, he reflected, things are better than they were. Alessandro has made an impression on Inez. She looks at him and smiles. She touches him often, leaves her hand on his shoulder and teases him by ruffling his hair. She grasps his sleeve when she wants to ask him a question. Sometimes grasps his sleeve first and then tries to think of a question murmuring: 'Oh now what was it I wanted to ask you . . . ?' In the presence of adults she is as silent as he is, but tries to catch his eye from time to time, asks him in private about the girls he has known and whether they all thought him as handsome as she does, teases him about his enormous dark eyes and the softness of his skin. Alessandro, meanwhile, has become less tense, talks more, even smiles occasionally in the most dazzling way, tells her to do things and not to do things and she obeys him. He has even started smoking and makes Inez get out of bed to look for the matches or an ashtray. When he goes riding by himself she moons about the house listlessly or whiles away the time watching Maurice paint in his room or plays games with Bonzo, who detests equally both games and Inez and even went so far as to bite her shapely ankle on one occasion. All in all, Boris thought with some comfort, things aren't as bad as they might be. It may be true that I'm no longer young. All right. But so what? At least youth still exists. At least love exists and beauty. That surely is something. That surely is not nothing.

But outside the window the sycamore tree, pessimistic to the last, was invisibly drowning in quick-drying cement beneath the soft, autumn sun.

Boris stared at it for a while without sympathy. The theory of vegetablism, he reflected, on which he had been planning to write a treatise, had been rendered obsolete by the love of the children in the room below. It was nonsense to say that because there was no way of recording emotion in particular cases it ceased to exist. It existed in the room below as surely as it had once existed in the tender kisses exchanged between the young, ardent Boris and the plump lady in Copenhagen, as surely as it would again exist between future young men and girls. It was the flame of a torch that was never extinguished, handed directly from one couple to another through the centuries. Like an athlete with a torch. This would be the theory he expounded. In search of inspiration he rolled back the carpet and applied his eye to the hole in the floor.

'Well, go on. Tell me,' Alessandro was saying.

'Mind your own business.'

'And you still haven't told me why you're crawling round the floor.'

'Mind your own business about that too.'

Boris could see perfectly into the room below. At first he thought Inez was saying her prayers. She was on her hands and knees with her head beneath the hanging counterpane of the bed on which Alessandro was lying. She appeared to be looking for something.

'Damn!' she said and slid further under the bed so that only her white woollen bottom and slender legs were visible to Boris.

'Go on. Tell me.'

'Tell you what?' came Inez's muffled voice from under the bed.

'You know very well. This thing that happens every month.'

'I thought I told you to mind your own business. Besides, I don't want to shock you. You're such a baby about girls. I don't know how it got so dusty under this bed. My dress will be filthy.'

Alessandro was lying flat on his back, his eyes absent-mindedly roaming the ceiling. For a moment he seemed to be staring straight at Boris, as if he had discovered the single eye embedded in the varnished pine ceiling. But then his gaze wandered away again.

'If you don't tell me I'll ask Mrs Slattery what the cotton-wool was for.'

'You wouldn't dare.'

'What d'you bet me?'

'I still say you wouldn't dare . . . Damn all this dust! If you want, Sandro, I'll tell you in Swedish or in Portuguese.'

'Tell me in English.'

Inez slowly wriggled back from under the bed, her face pink from her exertions, feathery balls of fluff clinging to her long tresses of hair and the front of her woollen dress. She leaned against the edge of the bed and placed one hand in Alessandro's. The other she kept in a tightly closed fist in her lap.

'If I tell you will you sweep up the dust under the bed?'

'I'll think about it.'

'No. You must promise.'

'All right then. I promise.'

Inez smiled mysteriously. 'Every month something happens to me.'

'What happens?'

'A pearl drops into my womb. That's what the cotton-wool is for . . . to catch it when it falls out.'

'I don't believe you,' muttered Boris and Alessandro in unison.

Inez continued to smile mysteriously. As she raised her glorious golden head to look up at Alessandro it really seemed to Boris that there was something divine about her.

'Look, if you don't believe me.' She slowly raised her closed fist and opened her fingers. In the hollow of her soft, pink palm lay a single, gleaming pearl. There was a breathless hush as three astonished eyes looked from the pearl to the radiant countenance of the girl on the floor. Her face became sad for a moment.

'I sometimes wish I were the same as ordinary girls,' she said wistfully.

And then she smiled once more, stood up and began to dust the fluff from her dress.

'Don't forget you promised to sweep the floor if I told you,' she added briskly.

Flower had ordained that Inez should change into her school uniform on the last afternoon of her stay at Boscobel so that her other clothes could be packed. Boris had expected her to demur at this indignity but she shed her sophistication without apparent regret and on this last afternoon wandered around the sunlit garden clad in a navy-blue-and-white sailor costume and straw boater that filled Boris (who was observing 'the children' from the lavatory window) with nostalgic recollections of his own youth. With Alessandro, who was to leave on the day after Inez, Flower was unsuccessful. He refused to put on the regulation navy-blue blazer and grey flannels until the last possible instant. There was a brief clash of wills. Flower sighed and wondered aloud what the school matron would think . . but finally gave in.

The sun falls towards the horizon. In the gathering dusk the air seems to become heavy with romantic foreboding. The feeling that life will never be the same again invades the tranquil evening, hangs in the heavy scent of roses and lavender, glimmers in the long shafts of dying sunlight that filter through the hedges. Somehow it is felt most strongly in the long, blue shadows of the trees and the radiant blue of the sky in which a thin streak of cloud slowly flares into a blood-red wound.

In the intimate gloom a white skirt drifts from flower to flower on a leisurely tour of the garden like some evening moth taking advantage of its last hours of life Together 'the children' wander into a dying patch of sunlight, linger there a moment dappled with blue and gold, hesitate, move on. The blue stencilled square of a sailor's collar is eclipsed in a bluer shadow. Now a slim white hand glimmers towards a folded rose-bud, caresses it for an instant and fades once more. The boy and girl have become merely dark silhouettes against the foliage but still the soft murmur of their voices can be heard against the hush of evening. Clear voices, notes of laughter like drops of crystal in the stillness.

Someone tried the lavatory door, muttered incoherently and stumped away down the corridor. Regretfully Boris left the window, flushed the lavatory and went to his room to dress for work. As he knotted his tie he felt almost sick with the sudden acceleration of time's passing, the dull excitement of romantic parting, the swelling of imminent loneliness inside the youthful breasts of the children in the garden. Even now, on their last stroll through the garden he could hear them saying: We'll write, of course. Nothing can stop us from meeting again. After all, we're free. We'll write to each other. I'll write to you on the train. Yes. I'll post it when we change trains at the frontier.

What frontier could she have possibly meant? Boris now wondered uneasily for the first time in twenty-odd years. The French frontier? In a train leaving from *Atocha*?

When he had finished dressing and gone downstairs he found that they had come in from the garden and were standing in the kitchen. Flower was preparing supper. Inez was stirring something at the stove, her long lashes thoughtfully lowered to the bubbling pot, wearing a pinafore to protect her sailor uniform like some obedient child. Alessandro was fingering a carving-fork uneasily. When he saw Boris he dropped his eyes to the table and with a sudden, oddly convulsive stab of the fork tried to gouge a hole in the Formica.

'Don't do that, Sandro dear,' Flower said absently. 'It's bad for the fork.'

'I'll be off then,' Boris said.

'Perhaps you'd better say goodbye to Inez now. Her train leaves early tomorrow morning.'

'Oh, I'll be up to see her off,' Boris said cheerfully. 'By the way, I think these two should go for a walk on the beach after supper. It's a lovely night. The water might even be warm enough for a swim after today's sun.'

A faint glimmer of hope lit up Alessandro's gloomy face.

'No,' said Inez succinctly.

Once more Alessandro jabbed convulsively at the table-top. But the Formica remained hideously invulnerable. Inez hadn't removed her eyes from the liquid bubbling sullenly under her delicate fingers. Alessandro threw an anguished glance after Boris's retreating form. Disconcerted, Boris closed the back door gently behind him and set off in the direction of The Groaning Board. Well, I understand in a way, he told himself, that she wants to make the parting as painless as possible.

In the restaurant the evening dragged slowly by, heavy with its sweet burden of romantic pain. Better just to go away and leave the station. There's no point in waiting. How can I *not* wait when I know you're still in . . .

'No time for dreaming, Boris. There's still plenty to be done.'

There's nothing to be done. Nothing at all.

You may go now, Boris. From ten o'clock when silence once more closed over the restaurant in the wake of the last departing clients Boris kept a weary but hopeful eye on the smoky, scarlet lips of his employee, waiting for her to remove the spell from him and set him free. Jean Arthur had decided for the fifth consecutive night to forgo her evening with the television set in her private quarters. For the fifth consecutive night Boris had been prevented from retiring to his palm refuge. Instead he leaned, silent and lax, against the wall beside the kitchen door, waiting for something to happen, occasionally making a round of the tables, changing the position of a salt-cellar or flicking away a non-existent crumb before returning to his berth against the wall. Jean Arthur sat at the furthest removed of the tables with a cup of rank coffee and an ashtray that Boris automatically emptied every ten minutes. Spread out on the table before her was the book of accounts which for the fifth consecutive night she was studying with intense curiosity. From time to time she would give an order without looking up. At twenty to twelve, with the air of someone performing an act of exceptional charity, she said: 'You may go now, Boris. I don't think we'll have anyone else tonight.'

Without a word Boris lurched away from the wall and headed for the kitchen.

'Just see that all the food has been put away and that the stove has been properly cleaned before you go. And make sure that the empty milk bottles have been washed and put outside. Good night.'

Outside he was surprised to find that it was almost light. An enormous, reddish moon was rising ponderously through the trees, making the calm surface of the sea glow with a weird phosphorescence. Above his head glittered a vast field of stars. And the night seemed to have grown warmer, damply aromatic with rotting leaves and a scent of seaweed.

Enticed by the warmth and the moonlight Boris turned towards the water and strolled along the glimmering beach. The tide had receded, leaving a bank of untouched, virgin sand beside the water in which a wandering red moon was now visible. It might have been a ripe pomegranate. Any moment the old dry skin would split open and release its shower of lustrous red seeds. The athlete and the torch.

The heart is more than a muscle, the doctor said. I was mistaken.

At the far end of the beach, where the weird moon-shadows from the pine forest were already beginning to recede from the shore as the moon climbed the sky, he came upon footprints in the virgin sand. Footprints. Two pairs leading into the sea. Two pairs leading out. Twenty yards away where the pine shadows were beginning to ebb. So Inez had changed her mind.

A great feeling of relief took hold of Boris. Everything had turned out all right in the end. The summer had reached its fruition after all. And throughout the long winter ahead, frozen up in Boscobel in the freezing tundra of banality, snowed up with the corpse of poor old Granny Dongeon, there would remain an afterglow of warmth from the summer.

The footsteps wandered ahead of him up the beach, along the curving edge of shadow as if seeking concealment among the pines. They faltered now and then, hesitated, turned towards each other as if for a kiss, continued again hand in hand.

As the footprints neared the dark mass of overhanging rock Boris came upon two small pieces of pink cloth discarded on the sand. He stooped and picked them up. The twin halves of a bikini. Boris examined them reverently in the moonlight. This strip of pink cloth, he thought, once restrained the girl's superlative milky breasts. And this, he thought, once housed her magnificent cleft.

It was as if she had vanished, melted away with the passing of summer, leaving only her clothes in a little heap on the sand. As if, in a way, she had never really existed except in his own thoughts.

And she had indeed melted away. Her footprints ended with the empty bikini. Beyond, there continued merely one lonely track of footprints pressed deeply into the sand.

The poor boy, he thought with sympathy. Just as Ylva vanished in a puff of steam at Atocha all those years ago, so has Inez vanished now. I should have realized that it was inevitable. Standing there in his white tie and tails Boris pondered the sweet melancholy of love, the passing of love, the passing of the year. A scent of pines drifted to him on the damp air, the perfume of youth. It seemed to him that he could hear the drumming hoofbeats of two superb horses galloping over the moonlit meadows. Galloping away over the softly stirring grass.

It was late. Regretfully he dropped the bikini on to the sand and followed the lonely track of footprints back up the beach towards the dark, gluey shadow of the rock. Ten yards away he heard a deep, shuddering sigh which he at first took to be some strange echo from the sea, a midnight movement of the water. He stopped short, trying to penetrate the thick gloom. He saw nothing, heard nothing. He advanced a couple of paces and stopped again. Protruding from the dense black shadow were four feet and a discarded sandal. Boris peered at them in astonishment. The two middle feet had large and horny soles, yellowish in the moonlight and tapering into clumsy toes embedded in the sand, Enclosing them like round brackets in some obscene equation were two small, shapely feet. Boris recognized them. He also recognized, first Maurice's sandal, then his disgusting feet.

He stood there for a moment, immobilized by shock. Then he began to run home through the hideous moonlight.

He watched her departure from his window. At half past seven Flower had knocked on his door and told him to hurry up if he wanted to say goodbye to Inez. He had made no reply.

After a few minutes he heard Maurice backing his car out of the garage and slowly got out of bed. It was chilly. The weather had changed again.

A little group had formed under his window. On the back doorstep in his wine-coloured dressing-gown old Dongeon had struck a seigneurial pose of valediction with one palm raised and a commanding expression on his face. In front of him stood Flower with her hands tightly clasped and the cold morning wind tugging at her apron. Maurice had just finished stowing Inez's baggage on the back seat and was getting in behind the wheel. Alessandro stood a little apart, his head bowed, scratching at the ground with the toe of one shoe.

Inez was dressed in a grey school overcoat. She approached old Dongeon who had to abandon his seigneurial pose for a moment to shake hands with her. He resumed it, however, while she hugged Flower briefly and approached Alessandro, kissing him on the cheek and patting his shoulder. Alessandro turned away, looking agonized.

Before getting into the car she paused for a moment and looked up at Boris's window, exactly as she had done on her arrival. Boris didn't move away. He simply looked down at her blankly as their eyes met. She started to smile at him in a friendly way but his features remained rigid. After an instant, still smiling, she ducked into the car beside Maurice. The car moved slowly away and disappeared around the corner of the house. Boris retired to bed.

The following day he told Maurice that he would like to take Alessandro to the station.

'That's all right, old chap. I don't mind doing it.'

'No. I mean I *want* to take him to the station.'

'All right then. Take the car. Sure you can manage it all right?'

'Perfectly sure.'

Boris sat grimly behind the wheel on the following afternoon while Alessandro said his goodbyes. Flower kissed him with great tenderness and told him to be sure to write as soon as he arrived and to tell her if he needed anything. She waved with tears in her eyes as he got into the car.

Boris started the car, put it in gear and released the clutch, accelerating sharply. They sped back into the darkness of the garage. A moment later they emerged again, Boris looking grimmer than ever. Maurice tapped on the window and said affably:

'Wrong gear, old man. You had it in reverse.'

'I realize that,' said Boris sharply.

As they drove into Maidenhair Alessandro looked pale and rather dazed. He said nothing but cleared his throat from time to time, peering out of the window with desperate intensity at the fleeting grey countryside.

The station was almost deserted. Alessandro insisted on carrying both his suitcases. Boris stalked jerkily into the station behind him, looking around with sightless eyes. They halted beside a pile of cardboard boxes and looked at each other.

'I've got my ticket,' Alessandro said. 'Don't bother to wait.'

'I'll get a platform ticket.'

He approached an automatic ticket machine. It was about his own height, squarely built, clad in metal plates painted grey. Standing in front of it he found that a flaking oval mirror screwed on to the metal plates exactly reflected his own haggard features. For an instant he seemed to be looking at his double, a person constructed of grey metal plates from which stared a human face, ruined and mad. He put a penny in the machine but there was no response. He punched it savagely in the stomach and watched its grey features decompose.

'I think you need three pennies, Boris,' Alessandro said, leaving his suitcases and hurrying over. He put two pennies in the slot and this time the machine yielded a ticket without argument. Boris looked at his skinned, bluish-white knuckles from which a few pricks of scarlet blood were beginning to spring. I still bleed, he thought with wonder. As he left the machine he saw it resume a blank grey mask from some distant reflection, from the sky perhaps.

He asked a man in a station-master's uniform which platform Alessandro's train left from. The man stared at him suspiciously.

'I saw you assault my machine,' he may have said. 'I know you did. In a boat-house at lunchtime. I know you did. I saw you.'

Boris stared at him with hostility.

'Number two. Due in any minute. Front half of the train. Number two. Due in any minute.'

'Why didn't you say so in the first place?' demanded Boris belligerently. Alessandro gave him a suitcase to carry and took his arm, ushering him on to the platform. There they waited in silence for three minutes.

The train arrived. A number of passengers got out of a compartment opposite them leaving the door open. Boris helped Alessandro to put his suitcases on the luggage rack and then they both climbed down to the platform once more. Neither spoke. When the guard blew his whistle they shook hands stiffly and said goodbye. Alessandro climbed back into the compartment and closed the door.

The train began to move out slowly. Boris looked up at Alessandro's pale, handsome face and experienced a feeling of immense sadness. The boy was trying to shout something but with the noise of the locomotive Boris couldn't hear him. Alessandro feverishly tried to open the window but it had stuck fast. Boris was running beside the train now. Alessandro was still wrestling with the window-catch.

The train gathered speed and disappeared in a puff of steam.

Boris had stopped groaning and retired into himself. Although he was perfectly polite he hardly said a word during the next few days. On two occasions, however, he accosted the postman in the drive and asked for his letters. The postman replied that there weren't any letters for him. At this Boris angrily accused him of having them and not handing them over. He seized the postman by the lapels of his blue uniform and shook him violently. But no letters fell out of his pockets. Three days later he again ambushed the terrified postman and once more accused him of not handing over his letters . . . but this time with less conviction. After that he no longer bothered him.

Two other slightly odd incidents occurred, both attributed by the Dongeon family to Boris. The first was the disappearance of a potted yellow chrysanthemum (given to Flower by Inez as a farewell present) from the sideboard in the dining-room where it had been smiling its mysterious golden smile into the surrounding gloom. It was later discovered on the beach, the pot smashed and the flowers trampled. The second incident was still more peculiar, even rather alarming. One morning the Dongeon family awoke to notice a subtle change in their environment. At first they could not quite put their finger on what was different. Somehow everything seemed lighter. Then they realized. The sycamore tree had vanished!

It was, in fact, lying in the shrubbery. Only a stump remained upright. Now they began to remember a strange crash during the night. They looked at each other in alarm. Where would it all end? The sheer physical strength involved in sawing through the trunk of such a large tree was prodigious. It hardly seemed possible that Boris should have accomplished it unaided and with so little noise. It was uncanny. And why had he done it?

It was thought best not to bring the matter up with Boris. He had become so silent and withdrawn during the last few days. And perhaps, after all, he had merely wanted more light in his room. Besides, the tree was already down. There seemed no particular reason to revive Boris's memory of it. Nobody voiced the fear that mentioning the sycamore to him might inspire him to take an axe to the furniture and the banisters, if not to the Dongeons themselves. Old Dongeon and Uncle Cecil went together to the public library to consult some psychiatry textbooks and see if there existed a mental disturbance called a 'gardening syndrome' that Uncle Cecil claimed to have heard of vaguely. They returned without precise information but deeply disturbed by all they had read.

However, apart from his silence and the fact that he had stopped groaning (the Dongeons would have given a lot to hear him utter a good, healthy groan once more) Boris continued to behave normally. The general alarm slowly subsided. Only Flower remaining anxious.

One evening she found him sitting alone in the dark sitting-room staring out of the window at nothing.

'Are you all right, dear?' she asked.

'Yes,' he said. 'I'm fine.'

There was a long silence. Boris continued to stare at the empty black window-pane without any sign of animation.

'Are you still thinking about that girl?' Flower dared ask.

'I was rather fond of the child,' Boris said bleakly. 'But I wasn't actually thinking about her.'

There was another long silence. Flower was about to tiptoe away when Boris suddenly said:

'You know, life is really rather sad when you come to think of it. You can try everything to give it some colour. You can try everything and it still makes no difference. It rather reminds me of an alcoholic friend I once had . . . I did everything I possibly could for him. I took him to doctors. I bought him medicine. I tried to interest him in other things. I went on and on trying to persuade him and suffering for him and trying again . . . but nothing worked so that in the end I found myself saying: All right then – die, you bastard . . . and see if I care.'

Flower said: 'I don't think I quite . . .'

'Oh, nothing,' Boris said. 'Nothing.'

Jennifer Johnston

'Jennifer Johnston has the most original talent of any Irish writer to have appeared in the past decade.'

Irish Independent

'An honest and shrewd writer. Funny too.'

Sunday Telegraph

'Her ability to convey the deft and deep drama of relationships is matched only by the fine economy of her graphic, expressive, well-pointed prose.'

Scotsman

The Old Jest *(winner of the 1979 Whitbread Award)* £1.00

How Many Miles to Babylon? £1.25

The Captains and the Kings (September 1982)

The Christmas Tree (October 1982)

FONTANA PAPERBACKS

Beryl Bainbridge

TWICE WINNER OF THE WHITBREAD AWARD

'A brilliantly talented writer.' *The Times*.
'It is a joy to find writers with the skill and observation of
Miss Bainbridge.' *Daily Mirror*.
'Alarming humour . . . a powerful talent.'
Sunday Telegraph

A Quiet Life   £1·50

The Dressmaker   £1·25

The Bottle Factory Outing   £1·25

Harriet Said . . .   £1·25

Injury Time   £1·50

Young Adolf   £1·25

Another Part of the Wood   £1·25

Winter Garden   £1·50

Fontana Paperbacks

Fontana Paperbacks

Fontana is a leading paperback publisher of fiction and non-fiction, with authors ranging from Alistair MacLean, Agatha Christie and Desmond Bagley to Solzhenitsyn and Pasternak, from Gerald Durrell and Joy Adamson to the famous Modern Masters series.

In addition to a wide-ranging collection of internationally popular writers of fiction, Fontana also has an outstanding reputation for history, natural history, military history, psychology, psychiatry, politics, economics, religion and the social sciences.

All Fontana books are available at your bookshop or newsagent; or can be ordered direct. Just fill in the form and list the titles you want.

FONTANA BOOKS, Cash Sales Department, G.P.O. Box 29, Douglas, Isle of Man, British Isles. Please send purchase price, plus 8p per book. Customers outside the U.K. send purchase price, plus 10p per book. Cheque, postal or money order. No currency.

NAME (Block letters) _____

ADDRESS _____

_____

_____

While every effort is made to keep prices low, it is sometimes necessary to increase prices on short notice. Fontana Books reserve the right to show new retail prices on covers which may differ from those previously advertised in the text or elsewhere.